Call It What You Want

ALISSA DEROGATIS

sourcebooks landmark

Copyright © 2024 by Alissa DeRogatis
Cover and internal design © 2024 by Sourcebooks
Cover art and design by Hailey Moore
Inside cover art by Blinx/Shutterstock
Internal design by Laura Boren/Sourcebooks

Published by Sourcebooks Landmark, an imprint of Sourcebooks
P.O. Box 4410, Naperville, Illinois 60567-4410
(630) 961-3900
sourcebooks.com

Originally self-published in 2023 by Alissa DeRogatis.

Cataloging-in-Publication Data is on file with the Library of Congress.

Printed and bound in Canada.
MBP 10 9 8 7 6 5 4 3 2 1

For a younger version of myself.

PROLOGUE

•————————•

Sloane

December 2018

The sun pours through the small window in my bedroom as I roll over and snooze the 6 a.m. alarm. Most New Yorkers are already wide-awake, grabbing their oat milk lattes and avocado toast, while my head is pounding from a few too many glasses of wine and three hours of sleep. In an instant, the memories of last night's events flood back, and I feel the agony coursing through my veins all over again.

The pain still lingers. I remember how much it hurt just to look at him. Ethan had always been the one to make me feel safe, but last night was different. It was as though he'd taken a knife and repeatedly plunged it into my chest. Each time I looked at him, the wound was reopened, the pain as fresh and raw as the first time. It was like death by a thousand cuts.

He cut me off midsentence. "I can't do this anymore, Sloane. I think this needs to end."

I was holding a glass of my favorite cabernet, and within seconds, it was out of my hand and on the floor. Instinctually, I quickly bent down to pick up the pieces. I hate messes, and I would rather have focused on anything but this conversation right now. I looked down at my hands to see that my right palm was gushing blood. *Why can't I feel it? Why can't I feel anything?* I watched as he pulled out his phone to call us an Uber. He was moving so quickly, but in my world, it was like time had stopped.

I stared at him as he frantically moved around my kitchen, grabbing anything we might need for the emergency room, and I wondered where the guy I met in college went—the guy in the worn-out Yankees T-shirt with a soft smile and trusting eyes. I never would have thought I could have hated him, and yet I couldn't even look at him. I never wanted to see him again, but at the same time, I didn't want him to leave. Ever. I'd loved him for over two years. How could he have ended two years with four words?

I can't do this.

The words were on replay in my head as if they're a new Taylor Swift album that I was trying to memorize every chorus of. I think the worst part was realizing that somewhere deep down, I knew it the entire time. I knew he wouldn't be able to get where I wanted him to. I just hoped that I was wrong.

No, we never dated. He's not an ex-boyfriend. He's an ex-almost. Maybe that's all we'd ever be—an incomplete sentence or a book that someone put down halfway through and never picked back up, finished without an ending.

PART 1

THEN

1

Sloane

August 2016

Just like that, the first day of my senior year of college arrived. I woke up with a flutter of excitement in my chest and eager anticipation for what the year would bring. I splashed water on my face, swiped on some mascara, and brushed through my naturally straight auburn hair. I didn't typically wear much makeup, and for class, I always preferred the bare minimum. I threw on a large fraternity T-shirt, athletic shorts, and tennis shoes before grabbing my backpack and heading out of my room.

The apartment was quiet. My two roommates—braver souls than I—opted for 8 a.m. classes and had already left to start their day. I, however, was more of a 9:30 girl. I scanned the kitchen for a travel coffee mug and brewed myself a quick cup, checking my phone and tapping my foot as the Keurig took its precious time.

After finally getting out the door, I ran to the shuttle bus stop, my heart skipping a beat when I noticed the doors gliding shut. I hated being late to anything, and imagining myself walking into a lecture alone and tardy made my palms sweat.

"Hold the doors!" a voice yelled from behind me.

I turned to see a tall and (from what I could tell) attractive guy running toward the bus. He passed by me with a smile, charming enough to convince the driver to reopen the shuttle doors.

"After you," he said from the step of the bus entrance, motioning for me to get on board.

Tall, dark, and handsome hardly did him justice. His wavy dark-brown hair framed a chiseled face with a strong jawline. His deep brown eyes held a certain charm that was impossible to ignore. He had an effortlessly cool and confident aura that made my heart race.

I brushed past him while my eyes quickly browsed the selection of seats until they landed on a small set of two in the back row. I knew exactly who I'd be sharing it with. I slid into the window seat and watched him walk the aisle purposefully. I tried not to stare until I noticed his T-shirt.

"Mind if I sit?" He approached the end of my row.

"It feels like the least I can do after you ensured the bus didn't leave without us." There's an undertone of nervousness in my voice. "Are you from New York?"

He seemed surprised by the question.

"Your shirt." I pointed to his worn-out gray T-shirt with the New York Yankees logo plastered across the front. Even though it looked like it had been through one too many loads of laundry, it still clung to his body in a flattering way.

"Oh, this." He looked down to see what he was wearing. "No. My dad's a fan. Are you?"

"A fan or from New York?"

"Either? Both?" He laughed.

"Neither. I've wanted to move there for as long as I could remember though."

As he squeezed into the seat, his leg rested on mine, and my entire body lit up. How was it that I felt so attracted to someone whose name I didn't know?

He introduced himself like he could read my mind. "I'm Ethan, by the way. Ethan Brady."

"Sloane Hart."

"Is this your first year living in Ascent?" he asked. "We just moved into one of the buildings near the pool."

"My roommates and I live back there too! Apartment 3221. It's our second year. We love it. We tried to get a house in Wrightsville but didn't have much luck. Apparently, they get snatched up quickly," I said.

His eyes widened. "I guess we're neighbors—I live in the unit above you. Better not call the cops if our parties get too loud."

"We'd never. Unless you don't invite us…"

"Noted." Ethan nodded. "What's your major?"

As I answered, I couldn't help but steal a sideways glance, noticing how his eyes crinkled when he smiled and the easy confidence in his posture. "Communications. I would've chosen journalism, but Wilmington College doesn't offer it, so I had to settle for a minor instead. Let me guess…yours is finance or business?" I raised an eyebrow.

"Don't stereotype me like that, Hart." The name rolled off his tongue like he'd been waiting his entire life to say it. "I'm a comm major too. I got kicked out of the business school after I failed precalc twice."

"You don't know how many times I've heard that. I'm horrible at math, so I couldn't even imagine taking precalc once, let alone twice. I barely passed statistics." I felt myself easily opening up to him.

"What class are you headed to now?" I liked how he asked a lot of questions. It made me feel important.

"Advanced Creative Writing. How about you?"

"Intro to Public Speaking." He managed to get the words out without laughing.

"Isn't that a freshman course?"

"I've been putting it off. I hate public speaking. Now I really wish I had just gotten it over with four years ago."

"Look at it this way: you'll probably be speaking to a room full of eighteen-year-olds who are way more intimidated by you than you are of them."

"Good looking out, Hart."

There it was again. The name that made my heart skip two beats.

The shuttle screeched to a stop on the north side of campus. We waited for everyone else to get off the bus until we were the only ones left. Ethan led the way, and I followed suit, knowing we were headed to the same building, where most communications classes were held.

"Well, this is me." I had to crane my neck to look up at him as we continued to walk. He had to be at least a few inches over six feet tall.

"Do you have class after this, or are you headed back to Ascent?"

"I have another class, and then a meeting,"

"Guess I'll be riding home alone. See you around, Hart?" He asked a question he already knew the answer to.

• • •

I got back to Ascent a little after 3 o'clock, and as I walked up the stairs to our apartment, I could hear my roommates blasting Drake. I wanted to slow time down. As excited as I was for the year ahead, I didn't want college to end.

I met Lauren Ellis and Jordan Coleman by the luck of the draw when the university randomly assigned us to the *worst* freshman dorm, Moore Hall. It was the only high-rise on campus that hadn't been torn down and rebuilt yet, and we were among the lucky few to live in it during its final year. I'd like to think the experience that we liked to call Moore Hell made us closer.

Lauren is my best friend. She's strikingly beautiful, with long platinum-blond hair and the sweetest smile. Whenever something bad (or good) happens, Lauren is the first person I tell. She's the kind of person who never lets you down. As an education major, Lauren has a passion for shaping young minds. She's honest but gentle, always able to deliver tough truths with care. Lauren really is the most genuine person I've ever known. Jordan is the source of light and laughter in our group. She's the most free-spirited and selfless of us all. Her go-with-the-flow attitude matches her dirty-blond beach waves and tan skin; just by looking at her, you can tell she's a Wrightsville Beach native. The three of us are so different yet fit together so perfectly.

"Oh my god, finally, you're home!" Lauren's dramatics were one of my favorite things about her.

"Has she already started drinking?" I turned to Jordan.

"Not yet, but soon." Jordan laughed.

"Very funny, very funny," Lauren mocked us. "Can't a girl just be excited? We just finished our second-to-last first day of class! It's monumental. Also sad. But let's try not to think about that. I don't want anything to ruin our first night out of senior year!"

"Is it weird to go to Jerry's on a Wednesday? I'm surprised the frats aren't doing FDOC parties," Jordan said.

"Guys." Lauren threw herself onto the couch. "Seniors never go to the FDOC parties; they're only for the underclassmen. We're all finally twenty-one! That's why Jerry's is the move tonight. Get a grip."

"That makes so much sense," I replied while Jordan nodded in unison.

"We have about three hours until we need to start getting ready. What do you guys wanna do for dinner? I know we have a ton of groceries from our parents moving us in. Frozen pizza?" Lauren was definitely the planner of the group.

"Yeah, a frozen pizza is perfect," Jordan agreed.

"Wait," I interrupted. "I have to tell you about the guy I met on the Ascent shuttle."

"Hold up. You've been home for an entire five minutes and have been keeping this from us?! Spill!" Lauren was giddy. She loves love and knows how hard it is for me to find it.

I moved around a lot growing up. My mom's a surgeon; at the beginning of her career, she transferred hospitals every few years. That made it extremely hard for me to make friends, let alone find a boyfriend. The closest I'd gotten was Carter.

Carter was, in many ways, a breath of fresh air. Our dates were spontaneous, every night with him fueled by adrenaline as I could only guess what would come next—being with him made me excited and nervous at the same time. Even though our relationship was on the more casual side of things, he asked me to senior prom. He showed up at my house with his mom and a corsage that didn't match my dress, but of course, I wore it anyway. We took pictures and piled into a limo with my friends, passing around wine coolers and mini bottles. I lost my virginity that night. I thought it would be so much different. I was expecting this grand romantic gesture, and instead, it was just a few minutes in a spare bedroom at my friend's house that resulted in a broken condom.

A few weeks after high school graduation, my parents sat me down and told me they were getting a divorce. I was blindsided. Twenty years of marriage ended in the blink of an eye. Had I missed the warning signs? Sure, they bickered like any other married couple, but I didn't think they'd ever take back their vows. As if the divorce wasn't enough, the timing was less than convenient for me. I was months away from going to college, a few hours away from home, and now I didn't feel like I knew what home was. My parents were so focused on dividing assets and selling the house that they didn't have the time to support me during a transitional time when I really needed them to.

For the rest of the summer, I had sex with Carter whenever I could—while our parents were at work, in cars in parking lots, at parties, after parties—I was willing to do it whenever and wherever because I thought it would make him love me. I was desperate not to be alone. *Spoiler alert: sex never makes someone love you.* Even though we weren't "together," I would still see Carter when I'd go home on breaks, mainly to avoid being around my parents, who were already dating other people. I spent my freshman year of college hoping we'd become more than just a hookup, and the year after trying to find something that compared to the exhilarating feeling he gave me. Eventually, junior year rolled around, and I took a break from my love conquest. I chalked it up to the idea that the love of my life wasn't in Wilmington. Maybe he was in a big city or on another coast. I'd find out one day. For the remaining two years of college, I was determined to focus on school and finding my dream postgrad job to get out of North Carolina. Life got so much better when I stopped looking for love in every guy I met.

"Well, thanks to our Keurig, I was running a few minutes behind. I swear it takes ten minutes to brew just one cup. We really should look into getting a new one." I could sense myself rambling.

"Get on with it!" Jordan interjected.

I hurried to get to the heart of the story; the excitement bubbled up within me. "Anyway, I was walking toward the shuttle, and the doors started to close. I was sure I was going to miss it and be late for class until this guy ran up from behind me and got the driver to open the doors. There were two seats left next to each other, so we took them and talked the entire way to campus. He's a senior, a communications major like me, and the best part is he lives directly above us."

"No way." Lauren's eyes widened as she took in every word.

"I hope his roommates are hot!" Jordan chimed in.

"When I tell you he might be the most attractive guy I've ever laid my eyes on…" I gushed. "I'm not kidding. He has fluffy brown hair and a great smile, and I can just tell he works out at least five days a week."

"Okay, so just like every other frat douche on campus." Lauren rolled her eyes.

But Jordan was already sold on the fantasy, "He sounds hot to me!"

"Did you ask bus boy if he's going to Jerry's tonight?" Lauren asked.

"No. Shit, I should've!" I grabbed a throw pillow sitting next to me on the couch and shoved my face into it.

"I'm sure he'll be there!" Jordan was always the optimistic one. "According to Laur, all seniors will be."

"That's right, and we need to look hot. So stop pouting. Let's get ready!"

I followed Lauren's lead as we went into our respective bedrooms and blasted our getting-ready playlists. I found myself smiling at the idea of running into Ethan twice in one day. *Here's to hoping.*

2

Ethan

August 2016

After I got to class, all I could think about was Sloane. She was quiet yet seemed like she'd tell you anything if you asked. She was beautiful but not in the way most girls on campus were. I could tell she didn't try too hard or take herself too seriously; she didn't have to. I'd never been attracted to redheads before, but something about her was different. I tried to snap out of it. I'm not that kind of guy—I don't fall for girls. Especially not ones that I respect. I know how that sounds, but it's true. I'm fucked up in a lot of different ways, but the biggest is that I wouldn't know a healthy relationship if it slapped me in the face. You can thank my parents for that.

Sloane was right; my public speaking class consisted of all freshmen. I could tell by the way everyone bought the textbook. You couldn't catch me wasting my money on textbooks. That's what fraternity brothers and cute girls who sat next to you in class were for. I listened to the professor as she rambled on about the six speeches we'd give over the course of the semester: informative, persuasive, entertaining, demonstrative, motivational, and impromptu. God, I really hated myself for pushing this class off for so long.

Our professor ended class well before the hour and fifteen-minute mark, leaving me a lot of time to kill before the next, so I headed to the library. I wasn't sure if anyone would be there on the first day of class, but the third floor was where Greek life usually hung out during the day.

"Brady!" someone shouted from across the quad. I turned my baseball cap so that it was backward and I could get a better view of whoever I was about to run into. It was my roommates, Graham and Jake.

"What're you two doing on campus this early? Specifically, you." I nodded my head in Jake's direction.

"You act like it's eight a.m." Jake scoffed.

"Let's get something to eat. Chick still serves breakfast if we get there in the next few minutes." Graham redirected us.

Graham was like a brother to me. I'd lived with his family since I was in eighth grade, so it felt right to room with him in college too. Out of the three of us, Graham was the smartest. He came from a family of good genes, and it also didn't hurt that they were loaded. Graham and I were opposites in almost every way, yet he's the only person I've ever let get close. We met Jake freshman year when we all pledged Pi Kappa Alpha—the memories sometimes send shivers down my spine. Needless to say, we bonded in a way most people don't. Jake is the type of guy who hunts and fishes, while Graham and I are likelier to spend our time tossing a football or ripping some waves.

"Thank fuck, the line isn't long," Jake said as we walked through the doors of the student center. "I could devour ten chicken minis right now."

As we waited in line for our breakfast, my interaction with Sloane from earlier started to creep back into my mind. How had I never seen her at any of our parties or out at a bar before? Surely, I would remember her. A small part of me hoped she'd be at Jerry's tonight, or even better, our pregame at the Pike house.

3

Sloane

August 2016

Uber's here!" I yelled over the music.

Our apartment was more packed than usual. Even though we dropped our sorority halfway into sophomore year, we stayed close with many girls in our pledge class. Taylor and Hailey also lived in Ascent but toward the front of the complex. I could always count on the five of us to pregame together before any event—even if that pregame was for another pregame.

"Alright, ladies, let's pack it up." Lauren disconnected her phone from the speaker and placed a few empty cups in the sink. "Sloane, you got an XL, right?"

"Yep, we can fit five and not have to lap up!" I assured her.

I led the girls down the stairs and to the parking lot, where the minivan awaited us.

"No one has any roadies with them, right? My Uber rating can't survive another one-star review after I threw up on the way home from the White Trash Bash freshman year." I shuddered at the sheer thought of that memory.

"Oh god, don't remind me." Taylor pretended to gag. Everyone else shook their heads and then piled into the car one by one. I took the front seat, and the driver offered me an aux cord.

"Any requests?" I asked, twirling it around in my fingers.

"That new Chainsmokers song!" Jordan pleaded. "I'm obsessed!"

"'Closer'! Yes!" Lauren reiterated.

"'From your roommate back in Boulder, we ain't ever getting older!'" we screamed at the top of our lungs. These were the moments I didn't want to forget.

It was about a fifteen-minute drive from Ascent to the bar, and we played "Closer" on repeat the entire way. I'm sure our driver hated us, but we didn't care. The song was catchy, and we were trying to live up to our expectations of the first night of senior year. He couldn't fault us for that.

We strategically arrived at Jerry's twenty minutes early so we wouldn't have to wait in line. I was pleased with our decision. The bouncers barely looked at our IDs, even though this was one of the first times we'd been here and been of age. It was more crowded than I'd expected.

Just before the entrance, there was an outdoor patio that I usually loved to hang out on, but not on a humid August night. Jerry's was just like any other hole-in-the-wall college bar. At night, they cleared out the high-top tables and barstools so there was plenty of room for dancing. Flat-screen TVs and neon signs with beer logos were plastered on the walls, and they didn't serve drinks over $10. Every time I stepped inside, a wave of nostalgia washed over me. I couldn't believe we only had a year left in this town. Of all the places I've lived, Wilmington had grown to be my favorite.

"Let's get in line!" Lauren's voice echoed over the music. She intertwined her hand with mine while I took Jordan's and we beelined it to the bar.

"Can we get two vodka sodas and one Mich Ultra?" Lauren slid the bartender her debit card and turned to us. "I still don't get how you drink these things."

"It's dollar beer night!" I argued. "And they go down easy."

"Since Sloane's drink is basically free, I've got the next round," Jordan said.

Out of the corner of my eye, I saw Hailey and Taylor talking to a few of our guy friends. After four years of mixers, parties, formals, and spring breaks, the Sigma Chi boys had basically become our brothers too. Except for the ones we'd slept with anyway.

"Let's mingle!" Lauren led us over to where the rest of the girls were.

"There they are!" Hailey greeted us.

"How are we?" One of the guys came up and put his arms around Lauren and me.

"Oh my gosh!" Lauren squealed. "It's been months! How was your study abroad?"

As conversations of summer trips, senior schedules, and postgrad plans ensued around me, I excused myself to the bathroom and then found my way back to the bar for another drink. Jerry's was filling up fast but there was no sign of Ethan. Maybe Lauren was wrong. Maybe not *all* seniors hit the beach bars to celebrate FDOC. Before I could give it much more thought, someone squeezed my shoulder.

"Can I buy you a drink?" Six words every twenty-one-year-old wants to hear.

I spun around and was face-to-face with the only guy I wanted to see tonight.

"How am I supposed to say no to that?" I asked, already knowing the answer.

Ethan's response was laced with confident charm. "I'm pretty hard to say no to." He smirked. His gaze swept over the crowded space as he added, "Damn, it's packed in here."

"Yeah, the line for the bar hasn't budged." I sighed, the wait was starting to dim my spirits.

"Follow me." Without hesitation he grabbed my hand and led me to the very end of the bar. In seconds one of the bartenders looked in his direction and made her way toward us.

"Ethan, what can I get you, hun?" She asked, batting her eyelashes.

Hun? Of course, he knew the bartender. *I wonder if he's slept with her.* I took in every detail from her fake blond hair to the way her breasts were practically spilling out of her crop top. *Is this the kind of girl he's attracted to? If so, I'm wasting my time.* For a minute I debated skipping the drink and finding my friends…until he used that name again.

"So, Hart," Ethan started. "Do you like beer, or are you just drinking it because it's a dollar? Do you want a vodka cran? Vodka soda?"

"Honestly, I don't mind beer. Liquor and I don't have the best relationship. I want to at least remember the first night of senior year you know?"

"Two Mich Ultras it is."

The hum of conversation swirled around us, a symphony of flirty banter and catching up with old friends. A roar of excitement erupted from a group in the corner, and as I looked over to see what they were shouting about, I noticed two guys on their knees chugging Smirnoff Ices. I didn't even know Jerry's sold them. I took note of that so I could ice Lauren later in the night, it was a tradition of ours—usually on birthdays and special occasions.

"Cheers," Ethan said as he handed me a beer.

"Thanks for this." I smiled as I lifted the bottle to my lips and took a small sip.

"Where are your friends?" he asked.

"Last I saw they were near the windows, but I'm not sure now. I can't see through all of these people."

"Well, let's go find them." He held his hand out again and I took it without question as he led me back through the crowd. Even though I had known Ethan for less than twenty-four hours, something about him made me feel safe. It was a calming sensation I hadn't felt around a guy before.

"There they are!" I tugged on Ethan's shirt and pointed to Lauren. "The blond in the blue top is my roommate. Thanks for helping me."

"You're not getting rid of me that easily. I should at least meet my other neighbors, right?"

My stomach fluttered at his reminder. Was this a good idea? Having a crush on my neighbor? It's not like he was someone I could dodge like my usual one-night stands. There was no escaping Ethan Brady.

"There you are!" Lauren exclaimed. "We thought you'd left."

"Leave? Why would I leave?" I responded, confused.

"Come on, Sloane." Jordan jumped in with a teasing jab. "You're famous for the Irish exit."

"Who's this?" Lauren, the social butterfly, introduced herself to Ethan. "I'm Lauren."

"Ethan. My roommates and I live above you guys." His introduction was simple.

"Oh, so you're bus boy! I'm Jordan."

Ethan's head swiveled in my direction for an explanation. "Bus boy?" he questioned with a playful frown. "What a terrible nickname."

"Blame Lauren; she came up with it." I could feel my face growing red, so I took a gulp of my beer, seeking some extra liquid courage.

The conversation shifted as Lauren asked, "Where are your roommates?"

"Are they hot?" Jordan's curiosity was more direct.

"Guys!" If my face wasn't red before, it definitely was now. *Thank god for the dim lighting.*

Ethan stood tall above the crowd, his height giving him an easy vantage point. "They're around here somewhere," he said, his eyes scanning the room. He offered a casual "Be right back," before weaving through the crowd.

I watched as he walked away, hoping he meant what he said and that the girls hadn't scared him off. It was refreshing to have a crush again. Since Carter, I'd tried to keep my dating life casual and not get attached to any hookups. It was easier that way, since most college guys weren't looking for anything serious. I'd made that mistake before, and I swore to never let myself again. But something about Ethan made me feel different, like I'd be willing to put my heart on the line just to see if or what we could be.

Within minutes Ethan returned with two similarly attractive guys.

"Graham and Jake, this is Sloane, Lauren, and Jordan, our upstairs neighbors." Ethan began the introductions. Graham—with his shaggy blond hair, blue eyes, and golden tan that probably lasted year-round—looked like he was plucked out of a Billabong campaign. I could just tell he grew up at the beach and had no intention of ever leaving. Jake, however, was the opposite—dark complexion, buzz cut, and a small scattering of facial hair.

Over the course of the night, our separate groups of friends eventually merged into one. I watched as Lauren and Graham hit it off, effectively cutting anyone else out of their conversations. It was like they were the only two in the bar. Jordan didn't seem interested in Jake, so the four of us danced and talked until the lights cut on.

Lauren begged us to not let the night end, and the guys agreed. So we decided on drinking games at our place. Though I'm not usually one for postgames, it wasn't hard to convince me to spend more time with Ethan.

"What does everyone want to drink?" Lauren asked, her eyes darting between us, already playing hostess as we stumbled into our unlit apartment.

"I'll run upstairs and get our case of Miller. I don't want us to drink all of your alcohol," Graham offered, but before Lauren could say no, he was out the door.

"Should we play Circle of Death or Ride the Bus?" I asked.

"Ride the Bus," Jake and Ethan said in unison.

"Ride the Bus it is."

Graham got back with the beer in record time, and we all managed to squeeze onto our sectional couch while Jordan reminded us how to play. Nothing said college like a room full of drunk twenty-one-year-olds arguing about which set of rules to use. Toward the end of the last round, I excused myself to use the bathroom. Lauren was riding the bus, which she always had the worst luck with, so I knew I had plenty of time until a new game would start.

I closed and locked the bathroom door behind me. It wasn't until I sat on the toilet that I realized how tipsy I was. My face was warm, my body was tingly, and my eyes were starting to get heavy. Even though I was enjoying flirting with Ethan, I wasn't sure how much longer I would make it. When I opened my bathroom door, I found Ethan standing in my bedroom. He was staring at the picture frames I had lined up on my dresser, picking them up and examining them one by one.

"Hey," I announced myself.

"These your parents?" he asked without looking up from the photo.

"That would be them." I walked over to where he was standing so I could get a better look.

In the sunflower picture frame was our last photo ever taken as a family of three. I was standing between my mom and dad, a smile plastered on my face even though I was wearing red (my least favorite color) and a graduation cap that kept sliding off my head. I remember exactly how I felt that day: excited to finally be in control of my future. A few weeks after that picture was taken, my parents told me they were getting a divorce. My dad had lost his job, had fallen into a depression, and hadn't put any effort into finding another place to work. After almost two years of trying to help him, my mom said she had had enough. I didn't blame her, but I did feel sorry for my dad.

Ethan set the frame back down on my dresser and turned to face me. It felt like his big brown eyes could see right through me. My heart rate was increasing by the second, and with a newfound drunk confidence, I closed the bedroom door. Taking the hint, he made his way closer to me and placed one hand on my lower back and the other on my face. Gently, his thumb stroked my cheek, and I could feel the rest of his hand grasp the back of my neck. Goose bumps.

When our lips finally touched, it was like they had met before.

• • •

First kisses can be two things: terrible or incredible. There is no in-between. My actual first kiss was of the terrible variety. I was fifteen and it was New Year's Eve. I remember tasting toothpaste on his tongue and thinking he'd brushed his teeth to be courteous. It turns out he was wasted and had been throwing up in the bathroom right before the ball dropped.

Then, there was my first *good* kiss. It was like a scene out of any coming-of-age movie or book made in the past ten years. One Saturday night during the spring of senior year, I stayed out past curfew. "Crazy Rap" by Afroman was playing on the Bluetooth speaker while we passed around whiskey and a bottle of Dr Pepper as a chaser. I knew it was wrong to let Carter drive me home after he drank, but I was seventeen and didn't always make the best decisions. He parked his car at the top of my driveway; then he kissed me. I can still remember the way my entire body lit up like I had been going through life on autopilot until that very moment.

That's not what this first kiss with Ethan felt like. Kissing him felt familiar, like our lips were puzzle pieces that fit together just right. He didn't make me nervous in the way Carter used to. He made me feel comfortable. He made me feel at home.

4

Sloane

September 2016

Lauren started dating Graham Clark three weeks into the semester—which was a lot sooner than I had ever anticipated. We'd gone to only a few Pike parties over the years, mostly their iconic LDOC parties each semester, but other than that, it wasn't a house we frequented. With Lauren's new girlfriend title though, we started getting invited to everything—pregames, parties, mixers, date functions, you name it.

Every Friday after our morning classes, Lauren, Jordan, and I would meet on the quad so we could walk to the food hall together for lunch. Most seniors didn't eat on campus unless it was a grab-and-go situation, but we started that tradition freshman year, so of course we had to see it through. Plus, I'd never turn down Chick-fil-A.

"I still think it's criminal that we have Friday classes. So many colleges don't have them, or if they do they're few and far between. Why couldn't the orientation leaders warn us?" Lauren asked.

"We did go a little too hard last night," I replied with a soft grin.

"Don't remind me," she groaned.

"And that's exactly why they should serve chicken minis until at least noon—especially on the weekends," Jordan added.

"J, that might've been the best idea you've ever had. Maybe you should DM them that suggestion on Twitter. Whenever they get my order wrong, I send it to them, and they give me a gift card," I said.

"Oh my god, Sloane! You're the worst." Lauren playfully shoved me while Jordan laughed. "I'm glad we have a night to recover. What jersey are you guys wearing tomorrow?"

"Basketball jersey and Converse," Jordan replied.

"Me too," I chimed in.

"Easy enough." Lauren laughed. "I feel like we haven't been to a jersey party in years."

"I think the last one we went to was Pike's. What was that—sophomore year?" Jordan recounted.

Lauren thought for a second. "That sounds about right."

"Do you guys think Ethan will be there?" I asked.

"Well, considering he's not only a Pike but also Graham's roommate and best friend, my money's on yes. How serious is this crush anyway?" Lauren's eyes lit up.

"I don't know that I would call it a crush…" I backpedaled. "It was one kiss."

Jordan leaned forward, intrigued. "Do you want there to be more?"

"I don't know. I think so?" I admitted, fiddling with the hem of my T-shirt. "I just wish I knew how he felt. I don't want to waste my time if he's not interested."

"Laur, now that you and Graham are official, I think you need to do a better job of wingmanning our girl Sloane."

I approved "I like that idea, J.".

"Alright, alright." Lauren shrugged. "I know I haven't been the most present roommate the past few weeks; things with Graham just went from zero to a hundred."

Jordan rolled her eyes. "We know. You haven't slept in your own bed since you met the guy!"

"Be nice." I nudged Jordan.

Lauren stood up, stretching. "I'll try to nonchalantly bring it up to Graham after the party tonight. Maybe he can give us some insight on Ethan's love life, or better yet, how he feels about you."

"That would be amazing," I said, feeling a wave of relief.

"Consider it done," Lauren said with a confident nod. "Now, let's focus on more important things. What are we pregaming with?"

• • •

Graham invited us to pregame the jersey party at his apartment, and then pledges would sober-drive us to the house. I was scanning the room for any sign of Ethan, when out of the corner of my eye I saw him duck out onto the balcony. I hugged Graham as Jake handed us each a cup of PJ—better known as party juice—a concoction of vodka, rum, tequila, and fruit punch.

"You're a Celtics fan?" a voice asked from behind me.

I turned around and was greeted by a very smiley, likely high Ethan.

"Believe it or not, I found this jersey at Goodwill a few years ago, hours before a Pike party." I took a sip of PJ.

"Damn, quite the snag. I'm surprised to hear you were at a Pike party though. I thought you only fucked with Sigma Chis back then."

"Yo, Brady." Graham interrupted us. "Pledges are pulling up; you're in our car." We followed him to the parking lot where a line of cars was waiting.

"Lap up!" Jake instructed us as he took the front seat. Jordan sandwiched herself in the middle, and Lauren took her place on Graham's lap, which was when I realized I'd have to do the same.

"Watch your head," Ethan cautioned, his voice feeling slightly low and intimate in the close space.

I ducked, a shiver shooting down my spine, not from the cool September air but from the anticipation of proximity to Ethan. As I swung my legs over his, the brush of his skin against mine sent a wave of electricity through me.

Ethan's hand came to rest on my thigh, a simple gesture that felt weighted with unspoken attraction. His other hand found a place around my hip, gripping me with a gentle pressure that made the butterflies in my stomach multiply. He pulled the door closed, and I watched the muscles in his forearm contract, the same way my heart seemed to any time I was around him. He'd kissed me only once and barely laid his hands on me, but somehow, I'd already melted into a puddle at his feet.

When we walked into the party together, it felt like we were *together*.

The house was exactly what you'd expect. Beer cans and empty liquor bottles were scattered on the floor, which was already coated in a layer of stickiness from the last party. Ethan led me to a keg on the back porch, introducing me to every person we passed. I felt important, and I never wanted the night to end.

"Thanks for the drink." I smiled. "I need to go find the girls."

"I'll come. I'm gonna see if Graham wants to run the pong table with me."

We made our way back through the party and into the kitchen where we found Lauren and Graham already playing beer pong.

"We've got next game," he bent down and whispered in my ear.

"I feel like I should warn you that I kind of suck. Flip cup is more my thing."

"Well then, I want you on my team for that too."

"Let's gooooo!" Graham held up his cup and chugged it to let everyone in the room know that he won—again. "Brady, you up next?"

Ethan guided me to the other side of the table by taking my hand. He rearranged the cups while I filled them with keg beer.

"Be right back," he mouthed. Shortly, he returned with two fresh drinks. "Alright, let's do this."

To no one's surprise, we lost.

"Told you I was terrible," I said, hanging my head.

"We'll get 'em next time," Ethan assured me.

I weaved in and out of the sweaty crowd until I located the line for the bathroom, where I was hoping to find Jordan.

"What's taking so long?" A girl in the front of the line banged on the door. "Some of us out here actually have to pee!"

Not even a few seconds later, a guy opened the door hand in hand with a girl. That girl was Jordan.

"Sloane!" She wrapped me in a hug as I watched the girls around me roll their eyes. I was too sober and too embarrassed to be here right now. "We're going home. Will you be good?"

I looked past her and gave the guy from the bathroom a full up-down. Before I could ask any questions, Graham came up from behind him and they dapped each other up.

"Leaving so soon, Jordan?" He winked.

"Yep," she declared. "With your good pal Pat here."

"Don't worry, Pat's a good guy," Graham assured me. "There's another bathroom upstairs if you want to come with me."

I followed Graham up the wooden staircase, past all of the fraternity composites that dated back to the '90s. I wondered where the rest were, but before I could ask, a group of guys emerged from one of the bedrooms with a beer bong that was at least twenty feet long.

"'Sup, Graham, you guys headed to the bathroom?" a tall blondish guy asked.

"Yeah, didn't want her to have to wait in that line downstairs," Graham explained.

"Don't blame you, but when she's done, you've both gotta do this." He held up the beer bong.

"Dude, stop making people pay to use the bathroom.," another guy said. "You guys can use mine."

"Thanks, Reese," Graham said as he motioned for me to follow him. "Reese, this is Sloane by the way. She's my girlfriend's roommate."

"*Roommates* make us sound like we met on Facebook or something. Lauren's my best friend," I interjected.

"Nice to meet you Lauren's best friend and roommate, Sloane." Reese stuck his hand out and I followed suit. "I'll leave you guys to it. See you down there."

"You go ahead. I'll wait in the hall. Don't need you to get peer pressured by the beer bong on your way out."

As he closed the door behind him, I made my way through what seemed to be the master bedroom. It was unusually neat for a college guy. He had a bed frame, box spring, four pillows, and curtains that matched his bedding. Once I located the bathroom, I turned the lock on the knob so that no one accidentally barged in. The bathroom mimicked the same cleanliness as the bedroom, which was refreshing for a frat party. Before I rejoined Graham in the hall, I fixed my hair and reapplied a quick layer of lip gloss.

As Graham and I made our descent down the stairs, a group of guys at the top were funneling the beer to the guys at the bottom. I couldn't imagine what kind of sticky mess they'd wake up to in the morning.

"There you are!" Lauren greeted us in the foyer. "I just beer-bonged a whole Twisted Tea!"

"That's my girl! Now let's go get you some water." Watching Graham and Lauren together made me happy. Lauren's last boyfriend was the worst. If you looked up *cheater, liar, manipulator,* or *gaslighter* in the dictionary, his picture would be next to all of them. She met him in high school, and he followed her to Wilmington for college (as the most toxic of people do). He cheated on her for the entirety of our freshman year, but she didn't find out until the girl he was sleeping with messaged Lauren directly. It was a whole thing. Luckily though, she grew a lot from it and is finally with someone who couldn't be kinder.

I walked out onto the front porch, where a few people sat on the stoop, passing around a joint. I pulled my phone out to call an Uber when a familiar voice called out from behind me.

"Leaving already?" Ethan asked.

"Yeah, thinking about it. Jordan left, and I really don't want to spend the night following those two lovebirds around," I explained, only half joking.

"Why don't we go back to my place? I have some weed, and I bet there's leftover PJ. I'll call us a pledge; that way you don't have to spend money on a ride."

"Are you sure? You don't have to leave with me."

"I know I don't have to. I want to." In one swift motion, he put his arm around me, locked my phone, and with the other hand dialed a ride on his.

• • •

Ethan and I stumbled up the staircase, and our tipsy laughter immediately faded when we opened the door to his apartment. The sight that greeted us was more than unpleasant—empty beer cans and plastic cups littered every surface, like an art installation gone incredibly wrong. The freshly painted walls had a few mysterious stains and smudges, while the lingering scent of spilled drinks and weed filled the living room.

"Where are your trash bags?" I asked as I stepped into the kitchen, nose scrunched.

"Don't worry about it. The guys and I can clean up in the morning," Ethan replied.

"How can you sleep knowing all of this"—I motioned to the mess around us—"is right outside of your bedroom door?"

"If you insist on cleaning this up with me, the trash bags are under the sink, along with Clorox. Will you set a bag out for me while I grab a charger for the speaker? I can't clean in silence." He walked away while I got to work dumping half-empty beers, stacking cups, and throwing them all in the trash bag I hung on a cabinet.

"How does a 2000s hip-hop playlist sound?" Ethan emerged from his room.

"Lauren loves this playlist!" I said. "Can you start with 'No Scrubs'? That's my favorite pregame song."

"That would be your favorite pregame song." Ethan rolled his eyes but scrolled to find it anyway. "That song isn't even on the playlist."

I frowned. "You probably don't have the right playlist up."

"This is the top-ranked on Spotify." Ethan held out his phone so I could see for myself.

"Lauren must've made her own then. Let me look up her profile." I took it from his hands and within seconds had our go-to playlist on the screen.

"Hart, this is not the best of 2000s hip-hop." He scanned through every song. "Usher, Fergie, TLC. Who the hell is JoJo?"

"An icon. Just play it. This is the best of 2000s hip-hop according to us," I insisted.

After thirty minutes of cleaning and Ethan begging me to let him change the playlist, the apartment was finally spotless—besides the four trash bags and broken-down beer cases we left near the front door. Ethan poured us each a cup of PJ and led me onto the balcony, where two lone folding chairs sat overlooking the pool.

"After you." He motioned to a chair.

"I love what you've done with the place." I laugh and settle into my seat.

"We're three college dudes; what do you expect?" He scooted his chair closer to mine before sitting down.

We sat in silence for a few minutes while the light in the pool changed colors. Our apartment had the same view, just one floor lower, and I don't think I'd stepped on the balcony once.

"Want a hit?" Ethan picked up a bong off the ground and held it out to me.

"No, thanks," I replied. "I don't smoke."

"Have you ever?" He seemed surprised.

"Never. I'm a pretty anxious person, and I think smoking would make it even worse," I explained.

"What makes you anxious?" Ethan asked as he packed the bowl and reached into his pocket for a lighter.

"A lot of things." I thought for a second. "Change is a big one. New schedules, new classes, new professors. It's kind of ironic though. I grew up moving around a lot because of my mom's job, so I never got to really settle in anywhere. You'd think I'd be used to the idea of change by now."

I took a sip of my PJ and watched as he inhaled. The bubbling water in the bong produced a soothing sound that filled our silence.

He exhaled before replying. "Was that hard for you? I've only ever lived in Wilmington my entire life. It's lame, huh?"

"That doesn't sound lame to me. I've always wondered what it would be like to live in the same place for more than a few years. I wonder how different my life would be if that had been the case."

That conversation was deeper than I ever expected to get with Ethan. Even though it wasn't much, I could tell he was getting comfortable opening up to me—well, at least when he wasn't sober.

"So if you don't smoke, how do you relax? Like to calm your anxiety?" His tone was genuine.

"Hm." I thought for a second. "Besides surrounding myself with friends, I like to watch a comfort TV show or write."

"Write?"

I could feel my face turning red. *Should I have mentioned that?* I can never understand the line between sharing just enough and sharing a little too much.

I swallowed. "It's just something I've always done since I was younger. When I have a lot of overwhelming feelings that I don't know how to process, I write them down. I also started freelancing for a few publications last year to make some extra money. What about you? Do you have any hobbies?"

"Sports," he replied instantly. "I played football my entire life and had always dreamed of playing in college, but it just didn't work out. Now I just watch a lot of sports and coach kids part-time at the YMCA."

"Do you coach football?"

"In the fall, yeah, but in the spring, I also do soccer and baseball. It's easy since they're all under twelve years old."

"Do you have younger siblings?"

"I'm an only child." He took another hit from the bong.

"Me too. I wish I had siblings though, like a big family. Have you ever watched *Shameless*? They're the least functional TV family, but there's never a dull moment. I feel like that'd be more fun than the loneliness I felt growing up." I knew I was past tipsy by the way I couldn't keep my mouth shut.

"I get that. I've known Graham since first grade. We got really close, so he and his brother became like family to me." He fell silent for a second. "*Shameless*, should we watch?"

My heart was pounding in my chest as Ethan led me through the apartment and into his room. I was in Ethan Brady's bedroom—the room he slept in, the room that knew all his deepest darkest secrets—I was standing in the middle of it. For a split second, I wondered how many girls he'd brought back here before. Surely I couldn't have been the first. I tried to drown out the thought.

His bed was placed in the same spot as mine, in the corner against the wall. He had a gray comforter with navy blue sheets, and a New England Patriots flag hung above the headboard.

I took a seat on the edge of his bed and unlaced my high-top sneakers as he flicked through Netflix to find the show. He sat upright so that his back was flush with the headboard and patted the mattress as if he wanted me to sit next to him.

"You like this show?" he asked a few minutes into the first episode when someone's bare butt came across the screen.

"We can shut it off." I laughed awkwardly. "I forgot there was some nudity."

"Nudity. So formal."

The show continued to play while he turned to face me. I did the same. We stared at each other as I took in every detail of him. His long eyelashes, the freckles on his nose, the way he licked his lips when he was nervous. Then he leaned in to kiss me. Our mouths became one, and I felt more at home than I'd ever been. My tongue followed his motions as his hand made its way to my back and up my shirt. We didn't go any further, even though every ounce of me wanted to. I liked that we were taking it slow.

"You wanna know something, Hart?" He parted his lips from mine.

"Sure." I backed up so that our faces were more than just a few inches apart.

"I don't really talk to people the way we talked outside earlier," he admitted.

"You mean to girls?"

"To anyone. Not even Graham."

"What makes me different?" Curiosity piqued my interest.

"I trust you." He pulled me toward him so that my body was flush with his, and then he kissed me again. I wondered if he meant what he said or if he was just drunk or high. Either way, I fell asleep in his arms and hoped that it wouldn't be the last time.

• • •

The next morning, I woke up fully clothed on top of Ethan's comforter—basketball jersey and all. His arm was draped over my stomach, and the sound of light snoring filled the room. I quietly wiggled my way out from under him and grabbed my shoes before sneaking out of his apartment. I didn't want to risk a sober run-in with Graham or Jake, because the thought of holding a conversation with anyone right now made my head throb.

The alarm clock on my nightstand read 7:45 a.m., so I changed into pajamas and climbed back into my bed to make up for the hours of sleep I lost the night before. As I drifted off, I replayed everything over and over again.

I was falling for Ethan Brady, and I couldn't stop myself. I didn't want to stop myself. I couldn't remember the last time I felt this alive.

5

Ethan

September 2016

I opened my eyes to an empty bed, expecting to find Sloane next to me. Hoping to wake up to her freckled nose and hazel eyes, I was disappointed to realize she snuck out on me. After a few groggy minutes, I picked up my phone to check the time. It was barely 10 a.m., which meant I had at least another two hours before the guys would drag my ass to the gym. I ripped off my shirt, threw it on the ground, and got under the sheets. I hated sleeping with clothes on.

"Dude, get up." Graham burst through the door.

"Knock much?" I groan.

"We have to be at the house by eleven for the tourney, remember?" He was gone before I could even argue. Reluctantly, I got out of bed, but before I made my way into the shower, I shot Sloane a quick text.

10:06 a.m.

Me: Where'd you sneak off to this morning?

10:08 a.m.

Sloane Hart: I needed a few hours of sleep in my own bed. Lauren's dragging me to the volleyball tournament today.

Shit. She was going to be there? Usually each year I looked forward to the tournament, but knowing I'd be playing in front of Sloane on less than six hours of sleep made me sweat a little.

10:08 a.m.

Me: To cheer for me, right? 😊

10:11 a.m.

Sloane Hart: I'll be cheering for Graham's team, so if you're on that one, then I guess I have no choice. 😑

• • •

The sun beat down on the sand as I stood with Graham, Jake, and a few other pledge brothers waiting for our turn. We hadn't won the tournament in years past, but now that we were seniors, we were determined to. It'd be embarrassing if we didn't.

Sports have been a part of my life for as long as I can remember. When my dad wasn't at work, he would toss a football with me in the front yard until the sun went down. Graham and I played on the same recreational soccer team until middle school when I signed up for football. I could've gone to college to play; I almost did. I got a few offers from out-of-state schools, but the tuition was insane, and they weren't full rides. Instead, I chose to end my football career, stay close to home, and attend Wilmington College alongside Graham.

As we took our positions on the court, I couldn't help but scan the crowd for Sloane. My heart raced with anticipation as I spotted her and Lauren walking into the backyard, the sunlight catching the lighter streaks of red in her hair. She was wearing a T-shirt dress, sneakers, and a baseball cap; you couldn't even tell that she'd barely slept the night before. Of course, I knew.

The game began, and I was doing my best to focus on the match, but my eyes kept finding Sloane. She was engrossed in conversation with one of our brothers, Reese, and watching the way he made her laugh caused a ping of jealousy to rush through me. I couldn't tear my gaze away, even as the volleyball sailed over the net, untouched by my distracted hands.

"Come on, Ethan, stay in the game!" Jake shouted, snapping me back to reality.

I shook my head and refocused. We were down a point, and I needed to make amends. The next serve came rocketing towards me, and I dove for it, sending it soaring over the net with a powerful spike. The crowd cheered, and I allowed myself a quick glance in Sloane's direction, hoping she had noticed my play, but she was still wrapped up in conversation.

We battled on, point by point, but my mind kept drifting back to Sloane. Whether she was sharing a joke with one of my fraternity brothers or just sitting there, her presence was a constant distraction. Our team made it to the third round, but we were losing ground fast.

With the score tied at 13–13, it was do or die. The other team served the ball, and it came hurtling towards me. I knew I had to make this play count, but as I jumped to spike it, my thoughts strayed to Sloane once again. My spike sailed wide, hitting the grass just outside the court.

We had one more chance to come back from that embarrassing play. They served the ball, and unknowingly Graham and I dove for it at the same time. Just as luck would have it, we collided, causing the ball to land in the sand between us.

"Match point," the ref called, and my heart sank. I had let my team down, distracted by my infatuation for Sloane. Why couldn't I get her out of my mind?

"Brady, what was that?" Graham stood up and slapped his hand onto my shoulder. "You played horrible, man."

I looked over to Sloane, who was now seated in the grass with only Lauren. I was glad that Reese was nowhere to be found. Graham must've followed my line of vision because it only took him a second to put two and two together.

"Is Sloane the reason you left the party early last night?" He kept his tone low. "And the reason we're the losing senior team?"

"I dunno," I huffed. "I need a drink. Is there any beer here? Or just mimosas?"

"Grab me whatever you find. I'm gonna go chat with our girls." Graham winked and then jogged over to where Lauren and Sloane were before I even had a chance to rebut.

I dragged my feet up the stairs of the deck and into the house. The back door led right into the kitchen, where a bunch of brothers seemed to be concocting Bloody Marys.

"Lemme get two of those."

"Anything for our MVP," one of the younger guys said. "You're the reason we actually have a chance of winning this year. Thanks, Brady."

"Fuck off." I rolled my eyes.

"I'd say better luck next year, but you won't be here," another chimed in.

"Go easy on him." Reese emerged from the hall. Great. He was the last guy I wanted to see. I stood in silence hoping to avoid further conversation with him while the pledges finished making our drinks.

"Tough loss," Reese said.

So much for that.

"I'm blaming it on the jersey party. Didn't get much sleep last night." I kept my sentences short.

"Oh yeah, Brady, that redhead I drove you home with is hot. Good for you, man," one of the pledges cut in.

I didn't even have to make eye contact with Reese to know that he knew exactly who the pledge was referring to.

"For that comment, you're on sober-driving duty for the rest of the month." And with that, I grabbed the two Solo cups off the counter and slammed the back door behind me.

From the top of the deck, I could see Graham, Lauren, and Sloane right where I'd left them. I thought about turning back around to get the girls fresh drinks, but I really didn't want to know what was being said in the kitchen after I'd left. It was clear Reese was into Sloane. I wasn't exactly sure how I felt about her yet, but I knew enough to know that I wasn't going to let him have her.

As I approached the group, a smile immediately appeared across Sloane's face.

"Sorry about your loss. You played well though!" she offered.

"You clearly know nothing about volleyball." I laughed and sat next to her in the grass. "I sucked. But thank you."

"Is that drink for me?" Graham interrupted us and reached over to grab his Bloody Mary. "Brady, this really isn't your weekend. First beer pong then volleyball. Maybe you're losing your touch?"

"Yeah, where'd you disappear to last night, Ethan?" Lauren asked before turning to Sloane. "You both must have left around the same time. You should've shared a ride. I hate when you Uber alone!"

Out of the corner of my eye, I saw a smirk appear on Sloane's face. God, she's even cuter when she's uncomfortable. Her cheeks turned a shade of pink I'd never seen before, and she couldn't stop the corners of her mouth from turning upward, unveiling a big toothy grin.

"Oh, they did." Graham smirked.

"What!" Lauren choked back her drink.

"Don't act like you didn't already debrief this morning. I was the last one to find out," he added.

"Sloane, why didn't you tell me?!" Lauren exclaimed.

"You guys wanna grab some food at Jerry's?" I cut in to save Sloane from having to answer.

"Let's make moves; I'm starving," Graham stood up and reached out for Lauren's hand to help her up. As if it were instinct, I did the same for Sloane. We piled into Graham's Jeep. Lauren took shotgun, but I wasn't complaining because I got to sit next to Sloane.

"So why'd you really run off this morning?" I lowered my voice.

"I, um, just thought it would be less awkward that way," she explained nervously. "Plus, sleeping on top of your comforter in my clothes from last night wasn't exactly comfortable."

"You could've gotten under them." I placed my hand on her leg. She shot me a look that said *What the fuck are you doing?* and then removed my hand. I could tell she liked it though.

Since the day that I met her, I thought about kissing Sloane every time that I saw her. That moment was no different. I stared at her mouth and swallowed heavily. My eyes shifted from her mouth to her eyes. I knew that she knew exactly what I wanted.

6

Sloane

October 2016

I sat on the edge of my desk in the dimly lit classroom, the anticipation gnawing at my insides as I waited for the professor to pass out our exams. My last two assignments had been nothing short of creative misfires, each marked with a disappointing score that rattled my confidence. Doubt started to creep in. If I struggled with a college-level writing course, how could I ever hope to land at a major media publication after graduation? The future I had dreamt of—full of ideation, writing, and publishing—felt so uncertain. I fixated on the clock above the door, its second hand ticking away like a time bomb, while the professor slowly made his way around the room. As he approached my row, the blue book slightly trembling in his hand, I could feel my throat constricting, a lump forming as anxiety held me in its grip.

After what felt like an eternity, the exam ended, and I handed mine in with a mix of relief and dread. The weight on my shoulders seemed to dissipate, if only temporarily. Stepping out of the classroom, I plugged my earbuds into my phone and shuffled top hits. "Love Yourself" by Justin Bieber played as I made my way through campus to the parking lot where the bus waited. Just as I started to hum along, my phone vibrated in my pocket and Ethan's name was on the screen. I thought the flame between us might have burnt out over the last few weeks. Outside of our weekly bus ride banter, I hadn't seen or heard from him. But now, curiosity and nostalgia stirred within me. I clicked on the notification.

12:17 p.m.

Ethan Brady: Turn around.

I did, and there he was. As he effortlessly navigated the sea of students, I admired him from afar. His stride across campus was a master class in arrogance, but somehow with each step, I liked him just a bit more. His dark hair was ruffled just enough to suggest a calculated carelessness. But what I liked the most about him was his smile, which was now beaming in my direction. With all of the lingering gazes aimed at him, I couldn't help but feel giddy that at this moment he was fixated on *me*. It was a peek into what life would be like as Ethan Brady's girlfriend. What a tease.

"Hey, Hart," he greeted me, with that stupid grin of his. "What're the odds we both finished our midterms at the same time?"

"Your timing is always impeccable," I joked. "How do you think you did?"

"Not sure, hopefully got at least a B. At least we're done with them now."

"Yeah," I sighed.

"Don't sound so depressed." He nudged me.

"It's not that I'm not excited for midterms to be over. I'm just not doing as well as I'd like in my creative writing class. My professor says I lack sensory details. How am I going to get hired if I can't even write something decent?"

"It sounds like you're being hard on yourself. I'm sure they're good, and as you write more, you'll continue to improve. You know what they say—you're always your harshest critic."

"I'm confident in my work to an extent; I think it's the competition that worries me the most. I've just always felt like I'm meant to do something big, and for some reason, New York has felt like the best place for that, but that's also the city where every other writer is trying to make a name for themselves." I kept going. "God, that sounds so ridiculous when I say it out loud."

"No, it doesn't. Your dreams and ambitions aren't ridiculous. They're what make you you. And for the record, I can see you being a badass Manhattan businesswoman."

I didn't expect Ethan to be good at giving a pep talk, but then again, so far he'd exceeded all expectations I had for him. "Thanks, I needed that."

"What're you doing for fall break?"

"Staying here. Lame, I know," I answered. "I just don't see the point of going home while my mom works the entire weekend and I watch Netflix alone in her living room. I can do that here. What about you?"

"Me too." Ethan shrugged, careful not to let me too far in on his thoughts.

We waited for the shuttle to pull up, and without question sat in our usual seats. Out of all of the routines and traditions I created over the past four years, this had become my favorite one.

• • •

"Sloane?" Lauren called out from her room.

"Yeah?" I replied.

"Can you come here?" She sounded concerned.

I made my way through the kitchen and down the front hall

where her bedroom was. A suitcase was on her floor, and her entire wardrobe was in a pile on her bed.

"What the hell is going on here?" My eyes widened.

"Don't laugh. It's bad, I know." She put her head in her hands. "Graham wants me to meet his parents this weekend, and I don't know what to pack. He said they're chill, but they're literally millionaires. Can you help?"

"Just be yourself!" I sat crisscrossed next to the suitcase and examined what she had packed: six pairs of underwear, two sets of pajamas, and a phone charger.

"Okay, why don't you try on some options? Maybe start with this midi!" I tossed the black dress to her.

Lauren peeled off her sweatshirt and wiggled her way into the dress. "Did you see Ethan today?"

"Yeah, we rode to and from campus together. He said he doesn't have any fall break plans either."

"Oh my god, this is perfect. You guys should *so* hang out! You haven't since the jersey party, right?" She turned to admire herself in the full-length mirror that hung on the back of her bedroom door. "Love this for dinner Friday. What's next?"

I tossed her a pair of skinny jeans and a flowy lace top as I pondered the thought.

"Yeah, besides the shuttle, I haven't seen much of him. Maybe he prefers it that way? I don't know." I groaned. "He's so hard to read."

"I mean…if you're asking for my opinion, I think you should just shoot your shot. Send him a text and see what he's up to tonight! What's the worst that can happen?"

"I'll think about it. I need to do some writing prompts to catch up in my creative writing course though. I swear the professor hates me."

"Sloane." Lauren turned to face me and I could just tell she was about to get on her soapbox. "You have a three-point-five GPA. You're going to land a great job and be an amazing writer. You have a semester and a half of college left. Enjoy it! I can't stand the thought of you sitting in this apartment all weekend alone. Plus, I'm kind of dying to know how Ethan is in bed."

"Lauren!" I picked up one of the tops on her floor and threw it at her. "I hope you're kidding."

"Of course I am. Don't you want to know?"

My face went flush, and she had the answer she was looking for.

"When are you supposed to leave?" I changed the subject. "And where's Jordan?"

"She left while you were at class, something about picking up an extra shift before she goes home tonight. I'm supposed to be at his apartment…" She picked up her phone to check the time. "Shit, five minutes ago."

I threw a casual dress and two extra tops into her suitcase for good measure before zipping it shut.

"Have fun!" I said, sending her off.

"Have sex!" She turned and winked at me before darting down the hall.

I heard the front door shut behind her, and the silence in the apartment quickly became deafening.

What *was* I going to do for the next four days? Surely, I couldn't write that much.

I sat on the couch and put an old episode of *Keeping Up with the Kardashians* on the TV. For dinner, I cooked a box of Kraft macaroni and cheese and poured myself a glass of moscato. Is this what living alone postgrad would be like? I kind of liked it. A few minutes into the second episode, I felt my phone buzzing beneath the couch cushions. When I finally retrieved it, I saw my mom's contact picture displayed on the screen. I loved my mom, but she usually called for one of two reasons: to harass me about my grades or to update me on her dating life. Neither of which I felt like getting into tonight.

Reluctantly, I answered. "Hey, Mom."

"Hey honey, how's your break?" she asked.

"Good," I replied. "How's work going?"

"Work is work. A guy in cardio quit last month, so I've been taking over a lot of his cases until we can find a suitable hire. How were midterms?" Her voice always had a way of sounding both caring and inquisitive at the same time.

"They were pretty good. I'll let you know next week when we get our grades back."

There was a shift in her tone, something I had come to recognize over the years. "Well, I saw on your student portal that your creative writing grade is struggling a bit, so I just wanted to check in. What was the exam like?"

"Mom, I thought we agreed you'd stop doing that." I groaned. "The reason I'm staying here for break is to complete a few online workshops. My professor sent out an extra credit assignment too. I'm fine; you don't need to helicopter-parent my grades."

"Well I'm glad to hear that. I just like to make sure you're not falling behind. Sloane, you're so talented, and I'll always support your dreams, honey, but…"

I felt a familiar knot form in my stomach.

"New York isn't North Carolina. It's cutthroat. You need to be the best of the best to get any job there, especially in editorial. Just focus on sharpening your craft and continue to network. I know you can do it."

I closed my eyes for a moment, absorbing her words. I knew she meant well, but it stung nonetheless. "I understand, Mom. I'm trying."

Her voice softened. "I just want the best for you."

I forced a smile, even though she couldn't see it. "Thanks, Mom." "Take care, okay? Call me if you need anything," she said, her voice returning to its usual warmth.

"Will do. Love you."

As I ended the call, the weight of our conversation lingered in the air. I leaned back, letting out a deep breath I hadn't realized I was holding. That's when my phone buzzed again. It was a text from Ethan. A small unexpected relief washed over me, and for a moment, I forgot about the heaviness of my mother's expectations.

8:01 p.m.

Ethan Brady: Heyo

8:40 p.m.

Me: Hey!

8:42 p.m.

Ethan Brady: Want some company tonight? I think I started to get invested in your nudist show

8:42 p.m.

Me: Sureee you did. Yeah, wanna come down here?

8:45 p.m.

Ethan Brady: Be there in a few

His timing really was impeccable today. I ran into my bedroom to fix my makeup, brush through my fallen curls, and change into leggings and a cropped T-shirt. Fifteen minutes later, Ethan walked through our front door holding a half-empty bottle of American Vodka. I stared at it with a puzzled look.

"I didn't want to come empty-handed, and this is all we had. Graham's usually the one that stocks the fridge, especially when it comes to wine. I don't know the first thing about it," he explained.

"Lucky for us, Jordan opened a double bottle of Barefoot moscato last night, and there's still over half left. If we don't drink it, it'll just go bad," I replied as I grabbed two wineglasses from the cabinet.

"Pour 'em up, Hart, but I have to warn you, wine makes me... you know."

"Sick?"

"Horny." Ethan smirked, and I could feel my cheeks heat up.

"Alright, enough of that. Can you pick something for us to watch?" I motioned over to the coffee table where we kept all of the remotes in a wooden bowl.

"No *Shameless*?" he asked, eyebrow raised.

"I'm in the mood for a movie."

I joined him on the couch and handed him a stemless glass with a heavy pour. Ethan leaned forward to set it on the coffee table, and his arm brushed against my thigh, sending shivers down my spine. He got up to turn off the lights, and the room dimmed, casting a cozy ambiance that made me even more nervous. As he returned and picked up the remote, I watched his hands, the way his fingers moved with grace over the buttons, scrolling through movies on Netflix before landing on a new release.

Halfway through the movie, the wine started to make me feel a little fuzzy, so with the same tipsy confidence as last time, I got closer to him and rested my hand on his thigh. In response he put his arm around me and pulled me in closer, swinging my legs over his. The next thing I knew Ethan's mouth crashed over mine. This kiss was different from the ones that came before. This kiss was pure hunger. His hand caressed my hip and eventually the other hand found its way under my shirt. My heart was pounding, and I knew he could feel it.

He kissed me harder as I moaned into his mouth and felt him grow beneath me. I brought my hand down to the waistband of his shorts. I was insanely turned on and he was too, as I could tell by how hard he was in my grip.

"Sloane." His breath was heavy. "Let's go to your room."

"Whatever you say," I whispered into his mouth.

With a strength I didn't know he had, Ethan picked me up, and I wrapped my legs around him. He continued to kiss me the entire way down the hall. When we got inside, he slammed the door shut, even though we had the entire apartment to ourselves. I expected him to lay me down on the bed, but instead he put my back flush with the bedroom door and pressed himself into me.

I couldn't take it any longer. I wanted, *needed* him.

"Take me to the bed," I begged as his mouth found its way to my neck and then my ear.

Ethan set me down on the mattress and got on top of me. With each kiss, he took off a different piece of clothing until I was completely naked and he was fully clothed. He stood up and took me in with his eyes. In that moment, the most vulnerable I'd ever been, I somehow felt so comfortable. Everything with Ethan came so easily, so naturally, like he was the person I was meant to share the most intimate parts of myself with. I'd never experienced a connection like that before, and I wondered if he felt the same.

"How long are you going to stare before you join me?" I asked.

"Long enough so that I'll never forget this sight." He stripped off his T-shirt, followed by his shorts and boxers in one swift motion. I could see a slight outline of him in the glow that the streetlights casted through the window.

My face was on fire. "You're making me blush."

"I want to make you do other things."

Thank god the lights were off because I swore my face turned crimson red. His body was flush with mine, and he held himself up on his forearms while I crossed my arms behind his neck. He continued to kiss me—my mouth, my neck, my collarbone, my shoulder—and tease me until I couldn't take it anymore.

"Do you have a condom?"

"I thought you'd never ask." He shot up from the bed and dug his wallet from his basketball shorts, where a small purple packet was tucked away. He knew exactly what was going to happen tonight, or at least hoped it would.

Within seconds he was back to his spot on top of me, and I couldn't wait to feel him. He pushed some of the hair out of my face and tucked it behind my ear before kissing me again. He was gentle, and I loved every minute of it. Then he pushed into me with little force, and I let out a small sound.

"Fuck, Sloane," he groaned as our bodies found their rhythm.

Sex with Ethan was better than I expected it to be. Our bodies were made to do this together, like they'd been waiting their entire lives for this moment. And I never wanted it to end.

• • •

In the blink of an eye, fall break was over. I had to find my way out of bed—where we spent the rest of the weekend—and become a functioning member of society before Lauren and Jordan got home. I threw out the empty wine bottles, wiped down the counters, and lit a candle in anticipation of their arrival.

"I'm back, bitch!" Lauren made her grand entrance a little after noon.

"Thank god." I let out a dramatic sigh. "I've been dying here without you!"

"I knew it!" She laughed as she set her bags on the kitchen floor and pulled me in for a hug.

CALL IT WHAT YOU WANT | 51

"I was kidding. Has your head always been that big?" I joked, but before she could answer Jordan walked through the door.

"You're having a reunion without me? That's so sweet!" she said sarcastically.

"What do you guys say we put off our homework just a little bit longer and get lunch and mimosas at Dockside?" I suggested.

"I don't know, Sloane. I just got home, and I have a lot—" Lauren started.

"Come on! It's the perfect weather to sit outside, and before we know it, it'll be offseason. It's senior year; we only have so many of these moments left!" I begged.

"I don't need any convincing for a Sunday fun day," Jordan said. "Let's all change and meet back here in ten minutes."

The afternoon sun bathed the parking lot of Ascent as the three of us piled into my trusty Honda Civic. Salt air mixed with the scent of nostalgia told me to roll down the windows and take in some of the last fall moments in our college town. As we drove through the streets of Wilmington, I couldn't help but wonder where we'd all be this time next year. Change is scary. I wasn't ready to leave this town yet, but even more than that, I wasn't ready to lose the only friends I'd ever had. I hoped that we'd find our way together to a new city with new experiences where we could make new memories. Just like this one.

The restaurant came into view, so I rolled up the windows and turned down the music as we pulled into the parking lot. Over the past four years, Sunday debriefs have become one of my favorite parts of college. We seated ourselves and ordered a bottle of André with orange juice on the side while boats made their way down the channel.

"Alright, Laur, out with it. How'd the weekend with the fam go?" Jordan asked, eager for every detail.

"Yeah, you didn't even text the group chat with updates!" I added.

Lauren's confession came out in a rush. "Don't freak out, but I think I'm in love." Her face turned bright red, and I knew she wasn't kidding, even though she used a playful tone.

"Spill!" Our response was instant.

"I love his parents, especially his mom. I mean she is just so cool. I sat by the pool with her while the boys fished, and we drank expensive wine while she told me story after story. How she met Graham's dad, wild college parties, what she did postgrad, all of it. I literally aspire to be her. Enough about me though; how was everyone else's weekend?"

I drew the focus to Jordan first. "Yeah, what'd you get into, J?"

"I landed a serving gig on a yacht down in Charleston. We made so much in tips, it was insane. Plus, they let us drink whatever we wanted the entire time, and I was with some of my high school friends, so it didn't really feel like work," she recounted.

"Both sound like such glamorous weekends, I'm jealous. Ascent wasn't the same without you guys," I replied.

"Did you get a lot of writing done?" Lauren's attention had shifted back to me as our drinks arrived.

Before I could muster up the courage to answer I poured myself a large glass of champagne, followed by a dash of orange juice.

My smirk betrayed my secret before I could get the words out. "I actually didn't write a single word. Believe it or not, I spent the weekend with Ethan."

"Oh my god. YES!" Lauren's excitement was explosive. "We might need another bottle! I can't believe you didn't text us!"

"I wasn't on my phone much." I blushed.

"Tell us everything! Did you sleep with him? Great, now I'm the only roommate who isn't banging a neighbor!" Jordan's mouth was moving at a million miles a minute.

"Jordan!" I looked around to make sure no one overheard the conversation before I continued. "But to answer your question, yes, I did. Eight times."

"Eight? Holy shit!" She clinked her glass with mine.

"Might I add, me dating Graham doesn't count toward our friend group rule. I started dating him and *then* we became friends with his roommates. Sloane definitely broke the rule though. Next bottle on her?" Lauren turned to Jordan.

"Jordan's the one at the table with a job!" I shot back, my tone teasing yet pointed.

Jordan threw in her own two cents, a smile appearing on her lips. "And the only one at this table not sleeping with a neighbor."

"Hold up. Let's circle back to Ethan. So is this just a friends-with-benefits thing or do you have feelings for him?" Lauren wasn't done interrogating me.

"I don't know yet." I frowned slightly. "For me, it's definitely more than just sex. But for him? I don't know."

"I guess we'll just wait and see how this story unfolds," Lauren said.

"Love story," Jordan added.

I didn't know what to call it, what was happening between us. Whatever it was though, I liked it.

7

Ethan

November 2016

D o you plan on seeing your dad at all while you're home?"
I asked, watching Sloane carefully brush her hair as if it were
her most prized possession. It was one of my favorite things
about her.

"I'll try to. I can't promise I'll stay at his house long though.
Maybe just for like dessert or something."

It surprised me how easily Sloane was able to open up to me. I've
always been the kind of person that hides their emotions. Even from
someone like Graham, who I'd known almost my entire life. I didn't
like to think about my own feelings, much less talk about them with
someone else, so I just avoided it as much as possible. In the beginning, Sloane tried to push. She'd ask questions just to see if I'd answer
them, and when I didn't, she understood. I liked that about her. I
didn't mind being there for her, but I didn't need her to be there for
me. I didn't need anyone to.

"That'll be nice," I said.

"I'm going to miss you." With a gentle smile, she perched herself on the edge of the mattress, her eyes meeting mine. I couldn't resist the urge to reach out and pull her closer.

"You can't miss me if I don't let you leave this bed." I locked my arms around her, and she playfully tried to wrestle her way out of them.

"As much as I'd love nothing more"—she craned her neck so she was looking up at me—"I really have to go. The traffic on the way to Raleigh is always insane the day before Thanksgiving."

"Alright, alright." I unlocked my arms and let her escape. "I'll walk you to your car. I'm gonna hit the gym before Graham and I leave."

"Don't worry. I'll be back before you know it."

• • •

I've always hated holidays. Thanksgiving, Christmas, Easter, birthdays. This year was no different. Usually, I'd join Graham's family for Thanksgiving, but this year he went home with Lauren to meet her family. I didn't tell Sloane that I'd be spending the holiday in Ascent because I knew she'd offer to bring me along, and that was just something I didn't want to do.

I didn't mind a few days alone, since I'd been spending most of my time out of class with Sloane. I got high, ordered takeout, played video games, and watched a shit ton of movies. Sounded like an ideal Thanksgiving to me. I was reaching for the bong that was on the coffee table in front of me when I saw my phone light up.

6:14 p.m.

Sloane Hart: I'm coming back early. Will you be at your apartment in two-ish hours?

6:18 p.m.

Me: Yep. Everything okay?

6:18 p.m.

Sloane Hart: My mom's done nothing but nag me. I'll explain more later. I just want to be back in Wilm with you.

6:20 p.m.

Me: Drive safe. I'll be here 😔

I don't know what came over me, but I felt the need to protect Sloane. Something in me hated that she was hurting. Instead of taking another hit from the bong, I turned off the TV, grabbed my keys, and headed to the nearest convenience store.

As I wandered through the aisles of CVS, I realized I didn't know any of Sloane's favorite things. I pulled my phone out and quickly dialed Graham's number, hoping they'd be done with dinner by now and he'd answer.

"Brady, everything good?" Graham picked up on the second ring. "Usually you text before you call."

"You're more observant than I realized. Yeah, everything's good. Can you put Lauren on the phone for a second?" I asked.

"Uh, sure."

"Hello?" she answered.

"Hey, Lauren, sorry. I would've texted you, but I didn't think about it until I got to the store. What are some of Sloane's favorite snacks or candy?"

"Hmmm." She thought for a second. "Watermelon Sour Patch Kids, a cookies and cream Hershey's bar, and Cheez-Its. That's been her go-to gas station order since freshman year."

"Got it, thanks."

"Are you gonna tell me what this is about, or should I text her?"

"Nah, don't text her," I assured her. "She had a shitty day and is headed back here, so I wanted to do something nice for her."

"Better not forget to give me credit," Lauren joked.

"Enjoy the rest of your weekend. Tell Graham I'll see him Sunday."

And with that, I hung up the phone.

I grabbed everything that Lauren mentioned, along with a bottle of Barefoot moscato—I didn't have to ask to know that was her favorite. I got back to Ascent with an hour to spare, so I cleaned up the apartment and lit one of Graham's candles. I just wanted to see a smile on her face when she got here. I didn't want her to hurt, of course, but if she started talking about her family trauma, I was afraid of the memories that would bring up for me. Maybe all of this would make her forget.

When she walked through the door, I could tell it'd been a long drive.

"Hey." She set her bag down near my bedroom door and nestled herself into me.

"Hey." I wrapped my arms around her.

It was like she'd never left.

"What's this?" She looks behind me at the snacks, wine, and candle set on the counter.

"Just a few things to cheer you up. I'm sorry your day didn't go as planned."

"It's so much better now." She smiled and then reached up to run her fingers through my hair.

In one swift motion, I picked her up, walked her to my bedroom, and, even though no one was home, kicked the door shut behind me.

8

Sloane

December 2018

The last day of the fall semester fell on a Wednesday. It was one of those December nights that felt cold enough to snow, even though it never would. Classes were finally over, which meant there was only one semester of senior year left. Only fifteen short weeks until I would be catapulted into adulthood. It was equal parts exciting and terrifying.

Things with Ethan were good. Dare I say great? Besides one small thing…

We still weren't dating.

As far as I was concerned, we were exclusive. We spent every night together, so we had no room to hook up with other people. I knew that wasn't the issue. It was him. I'd learned through sound bites from Lauren and Graham that Ethan had a traumatic past. I didn't question them because I wanted him to be the one to tell me—when he was ready. I wasn't sure if his past had anything to do with his fear of commitment, but that's what I decided to chalk it up to for now. It had only been about two months of us consistently seeing each other, so it didn't seem *that* crazy that we weren't official yet. Right?

Pike's first-semester LDOC party was always holiday themed, so wearing an ugly Christmas sweater was a tradition. I borrowed one of Lauren's and paired it with some over-the-knee boots and a choker necklace. For someone who didn't have anything to wear twenty minutes before the pregame, I was impressed with the outcome.

"Are you almost ready?" Lauren peered through the doorway, a smile plastered across her face. "Oh my god, you look gorgeous! Ethan is going to lose his mind when he sees you tonight. Things seem to be going really well with him, huh? How are you feeling about everything?"

"Have I ever told you how annoying you are?" I teased. "We're good, I think. We haven't defined anything just yet, but there's something there—I can tell."

Lauren leaned against the doorframe, her curiosity obvious. "And that doesn't bother you? Not knowing, I mean. I'd be so anxious to know where things stand. Aren't you?"

I paused, considering her words. "I guess part of me does want to know. But he's made his feelings clear—he likes me, and for now, that's enough. It's not just physical; it's more…you know?" I looked at Lauren, seeking some semblance of understanding.

"I just want you to be careful, Sloane. Graham mentioned that Ethan's not the type to date, historically speaking. It's been a decade of bachelorhood for him. I'd really hate to see you end up hurt." She bit her lip, concern shining through.

"And why can't I be the exception to his rule?" I shot back with a half smile.

"You're right. I shouldn't have assumed. Forget I mentioned it. Let's make tonight about having fun, okay?" Lauren replied, her expression softening.

"Absolutely. I'm happy with where things are at with Ethan. There's no rush to label it." Part of me agreed with the words that were coming out of my mouth, but another part knew that they weren't necessarily true.

Lauren nodded, her earlier hesitation replaced with a supportive grin. "If you're happy, then that's all that matters to me." I felt a rush to my head as I slid out of the car behind the girls. I didn't mean to get that tipsy at the pregame, but I forgot to eat dinner, and by the time I remembered, it was too late.

"Remind me again why we couldn't ride with the guys?" Jordan asked.

"They said they needed extra hands for the party setup tonight," Lauren replied. "Whatever that means."

"Sloane, you good?" Taylor looked back to check on me, and instead of replying I just held two thumbs up.

"Let's make sure to find you some water when we get inside."

The bass-heavy Christmas music filled the air as we walked through the back door. The entire house had been enveloped in an illusion of winter. Mimicking snow, a sea of white packing peanuts crunched beneath my feet as I moved through the crowd. Strings of colorful lights adorned the low ceiling, casting a warm and somewhat cozy glow for a disgusting frat basement. Some of the younger brothers were even dressed as elves and played bartenders for the night. The boys had truly gone all out for their last Christmas party.

"Can I get you girls something to drink?" Graham greeted us. "We have candy cane cocktails and keg beer."

"Sloane needs water, but probably a beer too. Can you make the rest of us cocktails while I run upstairs to grab her some?" Lauren kissed Graham's cheek and then disappeared into the sea of people.

"Ladies, follow me to the bar."

In a drunken haze, I did what I was told. As we approached the bar, I scanned the basement for Ethan without any luck. Graham handed me a Solo cup full of beer, just as Lauren returned with a bottle of water.

"Where's Ethan?" Lauren turned to Graham. "I'm not sure how long she'll last. She hasn't eaten dinner."

I finally spoke. "I'm gonna be fine!"

"There she is!" Taylor threw her arm around me. "Jordan and I can stick with her for the night. I'm sure Ethan's around here somewhere though."

"Chug this," Lauren said.

Just as I was halfway through the bottle, the DJ started playing "This Is What You Came For," and I about lost it.

"Let's dance!" I pulled Lauren, Jordan, and Taylor into the crowd.

"This is how I know she's drunk."

"She hates dancing!"

I ignored their comments and let myself enjoy the moment. As the pulsating rhythm washed over me, I felt a familiar tingle of exhilaration, a sensation that had carried me through the best moments of my college life. Surrounded by my best friends, I lost myself in the intoxicating melody of a song that I never wanted to forget.

After an hour on the dance floor, we needed to use the bathroom and refill our drinks. Waiting in line for the bar, I noticed Ethan out of the corner of my eye.

"Can you guys stay in line? I'm gonna go say hi to Ethan!" I said.

I made my way across the basement, and as I got closer to Ethan, I noticed he was talking to another girl. I saw her take what I assume was her phone back from him and continue whatever conversation they were having. A mix of anger and alcohol caused me to do something that was usually out of my comfort zone: confront them.

"Hi." I fake smiled at Ethan and then turned to the mystery girl. "I'm Sloane."

"Hey, I'm Olivia," she responded. Her reply was polite, unaffected by the tension that had arisen.

I could tell Ethan was getting uncomfortable, but I didn't care.

"What are you doing?" I turned back to him.

"Sloane, not here," he replied, his tone a low but firm warning.

"I'm gonna go," Olivia interjected, quickly excusing herself. "It was nice meeting you."

"Who was that?" I asked as she walked away.

"No one. Just a girl I met a few minutes ago." He offered a nonchalant shrug, trying to downplay the encounter.

"I didn't know you were talking to other girls."

"I'm not really," he said.

"So what was that?" The question hung between us.

"Can we not do this here?"

Before I could respond, Ethan took my hand and led me outside. I felt nauseous, and I wasn't sure if it was from the alcohol or the sinking feeling of seeing him with a girl that wasn't me.

The back door slammed shut behind us, and goose bumps immediately covered my entire body. The cold air bit at the exposed skin on my thighs between the oversized sweater and knee-high boots. We took a seat on an old leather couch that sat in the corner of the patio underneath some twinkling lights. The winter chill seeped into my bones, making me shiver as I wrapped my arms around myself. Even though I was mad at him, as Ethan's warmth radiated beside me, I couldn't help but feel a contrasting warmth in my chest.

"Why'd you act like that?" He turned to face me.

"I hadn't seen you all night, and then when I finally did you were talking to another girl. What was I supposed to think?" I defended myself.

His reply was dismissive. "It was nothing, Sloane."

Something about hearing him use my first name felt wrong.

"She was clearly interested in you and you gave her your number. How is that nothing?"

"I was being nice. What was I supposed to say when she asked?

No? It's not like I have a girlfriend," he said so casually, which only fueled my frustration.

I stood up, angry and eager to remove myself from the situation. "There it is." The words were bitter on my tongue. "That was what I was waiting for. So I'm good enough to hang out with, I'm good enough to fuck, but I'm not good enough to date?"

"You're putting words in my mouth," he deflected.

"Because you're not actually saying anything! You're running me in circles. I might be drunk but I'm not stupid, Ethan." I spat his name like it didn't belong in my mouth anymore.

"Let's just go." He pushed himself off the couch abruptly. "I'm not in the mood to party anymore."

"Who said I wanted to go home with you?"

"Sloane, you're being ridiculous right now. You're drunk. Let's just go back to Ascent and talk about things tomorrow when we're both sober." His reply felt condescending.

The thought of going home without him made me feel empty inside, so reluctantly I agreed. He pulled out his phone to call us an Uber and then wrapped his arms around me. As mad as I may have been at him, the warmth his body brought me was something I couldn't do without in that moment. And even though I hate to admit it, his arms were the only place I wanted to be.

• • •

Light just barely seeped through his broken blinds, which meant it was still early. I rolled over to face Ethan as he wrapped his arms around me and pulled my body as close to his as it could get.

"I'm sorry," I whispered.

He stopped my apology. "You don't need to be."

"I was just drunk and upset," I explained, tilting my head so I was looking up at him.

"You had every right to be upset. I shouldn't have done that."

"I didn't want to ask this question but"—I gulped—"I feel like I have to after last night."

He waited for me to continue.

"What are we doing?"

"I don't know, Hart." Ethan pulled me in closer. "I don't know." I laid my head on his bare chest and admired the freckles that covered his upper body. We started kissing easily, like waking up together was something we'd done hundreds of times before.

"Whatever it is, I like it though," he whispered. His mouth was practically touching my ear, which sent shivers down my spine.

I relished the words. They were all I had wanted to hear for months. They let me know that maybe I wasn't making a mistake by taking a chance on him.

"Me too." I smiled.

That moment was my undoing. Ethan Brady had me and he knew it. As much as I didn't want to admit it, he was holding my bare heart in his hands. I was so afraid of what he might do to it, but I also couldn't wait to find out.

9

Sloane
January 2017

Just like that, it was our final semester of college. Four years had come and gone in the blink of an eye. It felt like just yesterday when my parents, who weren't on speaking terms at the time, dropped me off at Moore Hall and I cried while eating microwaveable popcorn for dinner. I wasn't much for regrets, but I wished that I could rewind time. I wasn't ready to leave Wilmington, or Ethan. The only thing I could do was make the most of the time I had left.

We had a long weekend for Martin Luther King Jr. Day coming up, and Graham invited us to spend it at his family's cabin in Asheville. It was like our own little mountain weekend. The drive there was long and terrifying. I closed my eyes the entire way up the Blue Ridge Parkway, not only because I thought Jake might run us off the road but also because I was terrified of heights. When we finally pulled into the driveway, I opened my eyes and was blown away by the sight in front of me.

When Graham said his parents owned a cabin in the mountains, I was expecting just that—a cabin. The house was perched on a slope, surrounded by a sea of trees. It was three stories tall with a warm wooden exterior and large windows, which I'm sure offered gorgeous views.

"Wow," I said to Ethan as he grabbed my bag from the trunk.

"Nice, right?"

Nice was an understatement. The house looked like it was taken straight out of a magazine. We entered through a recreational area on the bottom floor. It was an open and inviting space with a bar and pool table on one side, and a stone fireplace and sectional couch on the other. In the middle was a massive TV, which I already knew the guys would be watching the playoffs on.

"You guys made it!" Lauren ran down the stairs to hug us.

"I was almost positive we were going to die on the drive up here." I laughed. "I kept my eyes closed for the last thirty minutes."

"Oh, I did the same. Let's put your bags down and make some drinks!" Jordan and I followed her up to the main living area while the guys finished unpacking the car.

I took in every detail as we made our way through the house. The ceilings were stained wood with low-bearing beams, and the walls were off-white. Sliding glass doors and windows covered the back wall, opening the view for miles upon miles of mountaintops. All I could think about was what it would be like to be that successful one day. My parents never struggled, but we were never well-off enough for a second home or international vacations.

"Should we make some Bloodies?" Lauren asked, waving around a bottle of Grey Goose.

"You know I love a good Bloody Mary!" Jordan was practically drooling.

"I have a love-hate relationship with them. I love the first few sips and then hate the rest." We made a pitcher anyway and sat at the island that was at least ten feet long, while we went over the agenda for the weekend.

"Okay, so we'll spend today at the house. We're having groceries delivered. We can drink, play games, and go in the hot tub. Tomorrow we're skiing, Sunday is football, and then Monday we'll be on our way home!" Lauren recited from a note in her phone.

• • •

By the end of the night, the six of us found our way into the hot tub, each with a glass of whiskey—which was very uncommon for me.

"Should we play Never Have I Ever?" Lauren asked.

"Sloane's favorite game!" Jordan laughed. The boys rolled their eyes before willingly holding up ten fingers.

"Never have I ever smoked weed," I started off the game, and everyone put down a finger.

"Come on, that's always your go-to!" Lauren argued.

"Well, it works, doesn't it?"

"Maybe we should change that. Jake, get the bong," Graham ordered.

I declined. "I'm good." Jake passed it around anyway, and everyone else took a hit.

"Never have I ever been a high school athlete." Lauren knew that would get all the guys and Jordan. Somehow, I almost always ended up winning this game. Did that make me boring?

It was Graham's turn. "Never have I ever cheated on someone."

Jake and Ethan both put down a finger, and I could feel my stomach turn as a pit started to form in my throat. After that scene at the LDOC party, I didn't need another reason not to trust Ethan. I needed to remove myself from the situation, stat.

"I'm gonna go use the bathroom." I quickly grabbed a towel and made my way inside.

I locked the door and leaned over the sink until I felt tears rolling down my face. Why was I so upset? It wasn't like he cheated on *me*.

I mean he couldn't cheat on me since we weren't dating; it was just something that happened in his past. It made me feel like I didn't know him though.

"Sloane?" Ethan knocked. "Open up."

"I just need a second." I sniffled.

To conceal the fact that I was crying, I flushed the toilet before letting him in. When I turned the doorknob, I avoided looking at him until he took hold of my chin and directed my gaze towards him.

"I'm sorry." His thumb brushed my cheek, wiping away a tear. "I didn't realize you'd get so upset. I was in high school, like fifteen or sixteen; you can imagine how young and stupid I was back then."

"It just reminded me of the way I felt when I saw you give your number to that girl at the party a few weeks ago. It makes it hard to trust you, especially when we're not dating."

He didn't say anything.

"I really don't want to get hurt," I continued.

"I wouldn't hurt you, Sloane." He pulled my body into his and rested his chin on my head.

I didn't know if I should believe him or not.

"I think I'm just going to go to bed. Can you tell the group I don't feel good?"

"Seriously?" He rolled his eyes. "Why do you always have to make everything into a bigger deal than it is?"

"You're kidding, right?" I asked, my eyes widening. "I've given you literally so much leeway. I don't know why you can't or don't want to date me, and even though that's what I want, I've put my needs aside. You can't turn this around on me."

"That's not what I'm trying to do."

"Well, it sure feels like it."

And with that, I took the back staircase up to our bedroom and closed the door behind me. I hoped that Ethan would be convincing enough that no one would come looking for me. I didn't want to admit to Lauren that she was right about my relationship with him. I needed to define it, because it was no longer fun and free. Was it ever though?

The thought of him with other girls sent me spiraling. Maybe my innermost fears were true. Maybe he wasn't dating me not because he wasn't ready, but because he didn't want it to be me. How could I get him to see that it *should* be me?

I felt Ethan climb into bed an hour later. He didn't say anything, and I wondered if he was pretending not to know I was awake. He didn't try to cuddle me; he didn't even try to touch me. We were lying in the same bed, but it felt like we were hundreds of miles apart. I tried to close my eyes and tell myself things would be better by morning. If only I believed it.

• • •

In the middle of the night, I rolled over to readjust my sleeping position and realized that Ethan wasn't next to me. I reached for my phone to check the time and see if he'd texted to tell me where he was going. No new notifications except for a comment from a classmate on my discussion board post. I got out of bed and grabbed a T-shirt and a pair of sweatpants from my duffle bag before heading downstairs to find him.

After a few minutes of scoping out the main level, I noticed one of the back sliding doors was ajar. I found him sitting in a rocking chair, staring at the electric fire he must've started.

"Hey," I said sitting down in the chair next to him. "Are you okay?"

Ethan's response lingered in silence before he finally murmured, "I needed some space."

"From me?"

"No, Sloane."

"Are you sure?" I pressed. "I know I got a little carried away earlier. I didn't mean to make the whole night about a stupid game. I should've just brushed it off and rejoined the group."

"I said it wasn't about you." He seemed to be getting angry. "Not everything I do or say directly involves you."

"Oh, okay." I shifted uncomfortably. "Sorry, I didn't mean to make it about me. I just wanted to apologize for earlier."

"Sorry," he replied. "I didn't mean that. I just feel overwhelmed."

"Do you want to talk about it?" I asked gently.

"Not really," he admitted, his voice a low rumble of buried pain.

I got up, but instead of retreating, I wanted to be closer to him. In a quiet, fluid motion, I pulled a blanket off the back of my chair and sat on his lap. I draped it over the both of us and laid my head between his collar and jaw. Nestled against him, it was almost like I could feel the tension release from his body.

"You know you can tell me anything, right? I don't mean now, but when you're ready," I said softly.

"I know."

Ethan wrapped his arms around me and pulled me in closer. It was then, in the security of our cocoon, that he started to really talk.

"It's this house, that bedroom. It can be suffocating, coming back here," he confided, the words heavy.

"Why does it feel suffocating?" I asked, sensing there was more he wasn't saying but hoping that he would.

With a deep breath, he opened up even more. "It's just…it's full of memories I'd rather not revisit. I spent so much of my childhood here, holidays especially. It's ironic that the holidays are what I've come to resent, because those memories weren't all that bad. We'd ski, build fires, play manhunt. Looking back it was good," he admitted. "The Clarks are great people, but it was hard to be surrounded by this perfect family that wasn't mine. It was just a constant reminder that I'd never have that."

I sat in silent empathy. My initial intention to offer comfort through words shifted as I realized maybe he didn't want a reply. Maybe he just wanted someone to listen. "I'm sorry," I finally said, my voice a soft echo on the quiet porch.

He shook his head slightly. "It's not your fault," he reassured me. "Go back to sleep. I'll be there soon."

Reluctantly, I nodded, squeezing his hand in assurance before standing up, leaving him with his thoughts and the crackling of the fire.

When I got back to our room and was nestled under the covers, I wondered what really happened to him when he was younger. How bad could it have been? Clearly bad enough to scare him out of falling in love. Even though my parents were divorced, I still believed that love existed. It was never perfect, never secure, and sometimes never forever, but it was something that I believed everyone should experience at least once in their life. My heart hurt at the thought of him feeling alone and unloved. I wished he could see that all I wanted was to love him, and if he'd let me, I'd never leave.

10

Ethan

January 2017

I stared at the ceiling fan and followed it with my eyes as it went around and around and around. Something about being back in a bedroom I grew up in always gave me insomnia. The only thing that was different this time was that I wasn't lying in the bed alone. I looked over and Sloane was fast asleep with her back facing me.

When I was younger and spent holidays here, I didn't expect the traditions to carry into adulthood. I thought that one day my parents would come back, and we'd be a family again. I only gave up on that hope a few years ago. As much as I hated to admit it, this house was as much mine as it was Graham's. I'd officially reached the age where I lived with his family longer than my own.

I carefully slid out of bed, making sure not to wake Sloane in the process. As I entered the hallway, I stopped to look at the wall of photos that I usually tried my hardest to avoid. One that caught my eye particularly was of Graham and me on the morning of our high school graduation. At first glance, we looked like a totally normal family. You'd never suspect that was the worst day of my life, at least so far. I spent it hoping that my mom would show up to the ceremony.

She never did. I had to hide how much it hurt as I went to dinner with the Clarks and then got the most wasted that I'd ever been at our friend's party. I slept in a bush in front of the house until noon, when Graham finally found me.

Passing the rest of the memories I'd tried so hard to forget, I went into the kitchen, poured myself another glass of whiskey, and opened the sliding doors that led to the back porch. I took a seat in one of the large rocking chairs and reached for the remote that started the fireplace. As I looked out into the vast snowy mountains, I wondered what my future would look like. This house wasn't really mine, as much as it sometimes felt like it was. My kids wouldn't have grandparents—not biological ones anyway. What kind of dad would I be? Would I be the kind that played football in the front yard? Taught them how to ride a bike? Maybe I wouldn't even have kids. I tried to turn off my thoughts and drown them in whiskey when I heard someone approach from behind me.

"Hey," Sloane said. "Are you okay?"

I didn't want her here. Not to be a dick, but I'd never leaned on anyone my entire life, so why would I start? She couldn't fix me so why was she trying?

"I needed some space," I muttered, my gaze fixed on the fake flames. "From me?"

I knew Sloane had her own issues, but how could someone like her ever have understood mine? Her parents might not have loved each other anymore, but they loved her. I could see it in the way she carried herself and hear it in the way she spoke about them. I didn't want to open up to her. But I knew if I didn't give her some sort of answer, it would become a fight, and that was something I really didn't care to deal with right then.

I shook my head slightly. "No, Sloane."

I struggled to explain to her how I felt.

I could feel her eyes on me, could sense her urge to comfort, but I didn't want her pity. I didn't want her to look at me and see a project or a lost cause. People looked at me that way for longer than I cared to admit. It would have been nice to start over in a place where no one knew me or my sob story. Being back here made me realize that it wasn't just familiar people that stirred up those feelings, but places too. Maybe a fresh start was what I needed after graduation.

Sloane made it easier than I'd expected to let down some of the walls I had meticulously built. For most people that would be comforting, but instead, it made me want to run.

I'd known for a while that she was falling in love with me—it was written all over her face and melted into every interaction I had with her. I felt bad knowing that I'd never be able to love her the same way she loved me. It wasn't that I didn't want to. I just knew I couldn't. I also knew that stringing her along wasn't fair. I knew what I needed to do.

11

Sloane

February 2017

than pressed his foot to the gas, and my Honda Civic accelerated down College Road. I watched as he sang along to the radio while his hand rested on my thigh. A little over six months ago was the first time I'd ever laid eyes on him. Before him, I was afraid I'd never meet the right person. I wanted so badly to believe what people said about soulmates—that one day I'd meet someone who everything fell into place with, and I'd realize why it never worked out with anyone else. I'd like to think that someone for me was Ethan.

He wiggled his hand into one of the holes of my jeans and looked over at me from the driver's seat like he wanted to have me right then and there.

"Stop it!" I laughed.

"Come on, not even a quickie? I can find somewhere to pull over," he pleaded.

"I thought this was supposed to be my birthday dinner," I argued.

"You know I'm always hungrier after sex." He winked.

"Key word: *my* birthday dinner."

He turned his attention back to the road. My least favorite love language was physical touch, and that was Ethan's preferred method of communication. It wasn't that I didn't enjoy it, but the way he'd touch me sometimes felt like he only wanted me for one thing—sex. Even though I knew our relationship was deeper than physical intimacy, it was still a thought that lingered in the back of my mind often.

The car pulled into an Outback parking lot, which wasn't a terrible restaurant choice for a college student on a budget. The past few months that we've been hanging out, Graham has been getting us to try wine other than moscato. While he and Lauren preferred white, Ethan and I leaned toward red.

He ordered a bottle of pinot noir, and even though I preferred cab, I didn't say anything. I was just glad he was taking me out, considering most of our "dates" were just drive-throughs, frat parties, or sleepovers.

"So, why don't I know when your birthday is?" I asked as the waiter brought over our bottle and two glasses.

"It's in July," he started. "I don't like to celebrate it though."

I didn't even try to pry. I wanted to keep the conversation light, because I knew he hated talking about his past. The last thing I needed was for something to change his mood or for him to push me away. I didn't want a repeat of our weekend in the mountains. I actually wanted to enjoy the night.

When we got back to the apartment, it was dark and quiet. As I approached the end of the hall that connected our entryway to the kitchen, I turned on the lights and was shocked at the scene in front of me.

"Surprise!" A sea of my closest friends stood in front of me. "Happy birthday, Sloane!"

I turned around and glared at Ethan, who was still only halfway down the hall as if he were avoiding being a part of the grand entrance.

I wasn't turning twenty-two until the following week, but Lauren always made a huge deal out of birthdays, so knowing her we'd celebrate every day until the real thing.

"I put an outfit on your bed. The bodysuit and skirt you were eyeing at Vestique a few weeks ago!" Lauren whispered. Sometimes I wondered if she could read my mind, or if we were just that in tune. I squeezed her and excused myself so that I could change.

We went downtown to Front Street instead of the usual beach bars. It was unusually warm for a February night, so we took full advantage of the weather and spent the next few hours on the back patio of a dive bar buying rounds of green tea shots and requesting throwbacks from the DJ.

"On to the next!" Graham motioned for us to all chug so we could make our way to the next bar.

I wanted to feel remotely excited about going to Reel for late-night karaoke, but I didn't. Ethan had barely said two words to me since we got out of the Uber, which only made me more anxious and less fun, two things I shouldn't have felt on my birthday. I drank my vodka soda too quickly as I listened to Lauren blabber on and on about how Graham invited her on his family trip to Key West this summer. They hadn't even been dating six months and were already planning vacations together; meanwhile most days I wondered if Ethan felt the same way about me as I did about him.

I watched from behind him in line as he talked and laughed with his friends, wishing he would motion for me to come to stand with him and put his arm around me. I would do anything for him to give me just the slightest bit of attention. The bouncer scanned my ID and fastened a blue band tightly around my wrist before telling me to have a good night. When I found our group, Ethan was waiting with a shot and a drink for me.

"What is it?" I asked, referring to the shot.

"Cheers." He winked and lifted his glass up to mine, ignoring the question.

We took our shots simultaneously, and immediately I could feel the cheap vodka coming back up. I quickly ran to the bathroom, and for the next half hour, I didn't leave the handicap stall, which I'm sure the groups of girls in line were thrilled about.

"Sloane, it's me." Lauren banged on the stall door. I wiped my mouth before flushing the toilet and collecting myself.

"Let's go home," I said as I opened the stall.

"Graham is in a car out front." She led me through the crowd and out of the bar.

"Where's Ethan?" I asked when she opened the car door, and the only people inside were the driver and Graham.

"He didn't want to leave," she replied. I could sense the disappointment in her tone of voice. She didn't want to upset me, but she wasn't surprised by his actions.

When we got back to the apartment, I thanked them for taking me home and went straight to my room. I managed to wash my face and put on an oversized T-shirt before getting into bed. The room felt like it was rotating, and the remnants of vodka stung the back of my throat. I rolled out of bed and miraculously made it to the toilet where I let it all out. Again.

• • •

The next morning my mouth tasted like a mixture of sour liquor and stale cardboard. As much as I was glad that I woke up to an empty bed considering my current state, I was pissed at Ethan. How could he treat me that way? And on my birthday? Sometimes I felt like I didn't know him at all, and maybe I didn't. How he could go from one extreme, like planning a dinner date, to completely ignoring my existence a few hours later was beyond me. Moments like these made me realize that I was the one in the relationship who had more feelings, and that was never a good thing.

My hand smacked the nightstand a few times before finally locating my phone. I held it close to my face as I pressed the home button and scrolled through dozens of notifications. I kept searching for the only one I cared about: a text or call from Ethan. There it was.

2:22 a.m.

Ethan Brady: 1 Missed Call

Before I could decide whether or not I wanted to call him back, there was a knock on my bedroom door.

"I literally just opened my eyes, Laur. Can you give me at least an hour before the lecture?" I croaked.

"It's not Lauren." I was surprised to hear a guy's voice. "Are you decent?"

"Depends on if you consider dried vomit in my hair as decent or not," I replied.

The door opened, and Graham smiled. He was holding a brown paper bag, which I could only assume had a bagel inside, a bottle of ibuprofen, and a blue Gatorade.

"The hangover breakfast of champions." He set everything next to my bed, and just as I thought he was leaving, in one swift motion, he effortlessly flipped my desk chair around and straddled it backward. "How're you feeling?"

"Not great, but this should help." I held up two small capsules before I popped them into my mouth, followed by a long sip of electrolytes.

"You know that's not what I meant. Have you talked to Ethan?" Graham asked.

"No," I sighed. "He called me last night, I'm assuming on his way home. I just hate that he thinks he can do whatever he wants and then come and crawl into my bed at two a.m. like nothing ever happened. Who does he think he is?"

"That's Brady for ya. Not that I'm sticking up for him by any means, but he's an only child, pretty much grew up on his own, so he's a selfish guy. I don't think he sees anything wrong in it," he said.

"Neither of us know what we're doing when it comes to a relationship, but treating someone the way they treat you isn't hard. I would've never done that to him. I'd spend every day with him if he'd let me." I threw myself back onto the pillow, knowing exactly how desperate that sounded.

"For what it's worth, I'm rooting for you guys. You just have to keep in mind that this is who he is to his core. I don't know; maybe he'll change. Just be careful. I didn't like seeing you hurt last night." And with that, Graham left my room.

As I sat there, my thoughts wandered to Lauren and Graham. They seemed almost like carbon copies of each other. I mean, I've truly never met a guy like Graham. People always say opposites attract, but I think there's something wrong with that theory. Ethan and I, we're like night and day. Maybe that's our problem.

I stared at my phone's call log, Ethan's name glaring back at me. With a bit of hesitation, I decided to call him back.

"Hey," he answered after the third ring.

"You called?" My voice came out sharper than I intended, irritation lacing every word.

"I'm sorry I didn't leave with you last night. I just…wasn't ready to leave yet." Ethan's apology sounded genuine, but it didn't fully soothe the sting.

"Yeah, Graham told me. It was really shitty of you, Ethan." I couldn't help but let my disappointment and hurt show.

"I know, and I'm really sorry," he replied.

We fell into an awkward silence, the air thick with things left unsaid.

I found myself asking the question that was always haunting me. "What are we doing, Ethan?"

I didn't have to elaborate; he knew exactly what I meant.

"I don't know, Sloane," he admitted, his voice heavy with uncertainty.

Another silence enveloped us, deeper than before.

"Obviously, I like you." Ethan finally broke the quiet. "I just… need some time to think. Is that okay?"

"Yeah," I sighed, feeling a mix of sadness and exhaustion. "I'm going to try to get some more sleep. My head is killing me."

"I'll text you later. Hope you feel better," he said gently before ending the call.

When I finally decided I was ready to wake up for the day, it was nearly time to eat dinner. I checked my phone, expecting to find messages from Ethan, but frowned when I had no new notifications. I dragged myself into the bathroom and blasted Taylor Swift on shuffle to put myself in a better mood. There was nothing that a hot shower and "All Too Well" couldn't fix. By the time I got out of the shower, I heard Jordan and Lauren in the kitchen, so I threw on some clothes and joined them.

Jordan's laughter greeted me first. "Wow, we thought you were dead," she joked, not knowing how close to the truth she was.

"Very funny." I offered a tight-lipped smile while I fetched the Brita from the fridge.

"So the elephant in the room…" Lauren broke the ice. "Have you heard from Ethan?"

She was always the one to confront uncomfortable truths and, even knowing I had a slight hangover, didn't miss a beat.

"We talked on the phone earlier. It didn't help though; I think it might've made me more confused. This whole situation is just—*ugh*. This is exactly what I didn't want to happen."

"Like it or not, it's happening, babe. You and Ethan? You need to DTR."

"DTR?" Jordan asked.

I shut the refrigerator door with a bit of force, not wanting to admit that Lauren was right. I sighed, "Define the relationship," and the weight of those words felt as heavy as the pitcher I was holding.

"Yeah, I know, I know."

The sad thing was, I did know. I just didn't care. I was afraid to have that conversation with him because there was a chance it would mean losing him for good. And while I didn't love what was going on between us now, I wasn't ready for it to end.

• • •

I hadn't heard from Ethan, and I was spiraling. After we got off the phone, I waited around for a text from him—it never came, and as much as I wanted to talk to him, I knew what him not reaching out meant. So I was avoiding him in the same way he was avoiding me.

For the weekend, my bed had become a sanctuary. Jordan managed to coax me out, promising a Sigma Chi party would make me feel better. It didn't. I wasn't in the mood to sip on cheap beer or interested in frat house banter. I missed Ethan—missed the simplicity of us just being together. So after enduring an hour of hollow conversations and forced smiles, I made my escape back to the quiet of my room.

I wanted to show up at his apartment and let myself inside, but I knew I shouldn't. I wanted to call him and tell him that I took everything back, but I knew it was too late. Maybe if I'd just continued to play it cool and not force him into a relationship yet, he'd be here right now, lying beside me in bed. Instead, I had no idea where he was, who he was with, or what he was thinking. I'd have given anything to get into his head sometimes.

Sunday morning rolled around, and I managed to stay in my room undisturbed until close to noon, when my phone vibrated somewhere in between the sheets.

11:47 a.m.

Ethan Brady: Sorry I've been MIA. Just needed space to think about things. Can we talk in my car?

He was ending it before it even had a chance to begin. My hands started to shake as I replied with one word.

11:50 a.m.

Me: Sure.

I walked out of my apartment a few minutes later and found that it had started to rain. Ethan's tone via text, my anxiety, and the weather presented the perfect formula for a breakup. Could I even call it a breakup if we were never dating?

All I knew was that conversations in cars were never a good thing. Everything big that had ever happened to me in love happened in a car. My first kiss with Carter, the time he told me he was seeing someone else, and—as much as I hated to admit it—most of our intimate moments happened in the back seat of his Toyota.

Ethan's familiar headlights appeared in the parking lot and pierced through the curtain of rain. He pulled up to the curb and glided to a stop in front of me. Before reaching for the handle, I took a deep breath to try and calm my nerves.

I slid into the passenger seat, my clothes already damp and goose bumps covering my entire body. Ethan reached to turn up the heater as if he knew what I was thinking and then pulled around the back of the building into an empty parking spot. I noticed that he was wearing the same Yankees T-shirt that I met him in. Nostalgia seeped through my veins as I prepared myself for the end of something that never got a chance to begin.

"Hey," Ethan greeted me. His gaze remained fixed on the steering wheel, his knuckles white against it.

"Hi," I replied. I stole a glance at his profile, his jaw clenched and his brow furrowed. I was so fearful of what was about to come. I wish I could've done something, anything, to stop it.

The rain continued to pour outside, obscuring everything beyond the windshield. The drumming of the raindrops seemed to echo the pounding of my heart. I watched as he wiped his palms on his thighs nervously.

I couldn't take the silence any longer. "Is everything okay?"

Finally, he turned to look at me, his eyes filled with sadness and regret. "I don't know how to say this," he said, his voice trembling just slightly.

"What's going on?" I swallowed hard, my throat dry.

"Things between us escalated so fast and became something I can't do. I should have never let it get this far. I think we should stop seeing each other."

"Do you not have feelings for me?" My bottom lip quivered.

"I do," he said so matter-of-factly, confusing me even more.

"So then why can't we make this work? Why would you want to let me go?" I replied with a lump in my throat as I fought back the tears threatening to spill over.

Ethan avoided eye contact with me. "I wish it were that simple," he said, his voice filled with regret. "I care about you more than you realize, but I can't give you what you deserve right now. If I'm being honest, I don't know that I'll ever be able to."

The tears I had been holding back finally broke free, coursing down my cheeks as I stared at the person I thought I might have loved. The rain outside mirrored my emotions, a relentless downpour that seemed to have no end.

"Why do you get to decide what I deserve?" My sadness suddenly turned into anger.

"Sloane, we both know that you want and deserve a relationship. Someone who will put a label on things, show you off, meet your parents—all of it. I'm not that guy. I'll never be that guy. Not for you, not for anyone." His words stung.

"We don't have to date. I told you I wasn't sure if I was ready for a serious relationship yet either." I tried to lie. "I'm happy with how things are going right now."

"We both know that eventually this is going to have to be something more. We can't stay in the in-between forever," he said. "The longer we continue this, the worse it's going to hurt in the end. I really don't want to hurt you."

"Am I not enough?" I managed through tears.

His face dropped. "Please don't think for a second that any of this is your fault. It's not at all. You're too good for me. I don't deserve this. I don't want to take you down with me."

I couldn't look at him. I wanted to get out of the car and run into my apartment, but I couldn't move. I was frozen in his passenger seat. Half of me never wanted to see him again, and the other half couldn't bear the thought.

There were so many things I still wanted to say. We could have worked out, I knew we could. If he just put in a little more effort and I gave him a little more space. I could be the one if he just let me. I couldn't change his mind though. You can't love someone into changing—you shouldn't have to. I knew that. So why didn't I believe it?

My hand was shaking as I reached for the handle. Stepping out of the car, I slammed the door shut, trying to make a statement. I trudged through the parking lot without looking back, no matter how much I wanted to. I had to accept that we were never going to get a chance. How was I able to fall in love with someone who wasn't sure about me? What was so wrong with me that every time I got close to love, it ran from me?

The apartment was empty when I stepped inside, sopping wet from the rain. In the middle of the hallway, I peeled each piece of clothing off of my body one by one and threw them into the washing machine. I wrapped my hair in a towel, got into bed, and buried myself under the sheets. Within seconds I was uncontrollably sobbing. I'd never been hurt like that before. If I knew loving him would have hurt this badly, I would've never laid my eyes on him.

12

Ethan

February 2017

No part of me wanted to hurt Sloane. The day we met, I knew things would be different with her, which is why I tried to stay away. I wasn't looking for a relationship, but something about her made me want to try. It just wasn't enough. I realized that eventually I was going to end up hurting her one way or another—even more than I already had. Seeing her cry last night made me want to tell her everything. I wanted to lay it all out for her so she would understand, but I couldn't. I didn't want to be this way, but it was who I was after a life of heartbreak and disappointment.

I unplugged my phone from the charger and scrolled aimlessly for a little while. My thumb wavered over the Facebook icon before I decided to tap it. In the search bar, her name was recently viewed: Laura Brady. She still hadn't changed her last name, even though she'd remarried. I clicked on her latest profile picture, which said it was posted two weeks ago. The Christmas tree in the background told me the photo was taken around the holidays. She was smiling and posing with her daughter—the half sister I'd never met and likely never would.

I closed out of the app before I spiraled down that rabbit hole any further, and rolled over. As much as I hated to admit it, I missed Sloane. I missed the comfort of sharing a bed with her every night. Knowing she was next to me made it easier to sleep. That was something I never thought I'd say.

• • •

The next morning, I wandered out of bed and into the kitchen, where Graham was making a huge stack of protein pancakes while Jake played video games. In the two years we'd been roommates, absolutely nothing had changed.

"Hey, man, want some?" Graham motioned toward the plate of food.

"No bacon?" I asked as I took a seat at the counter.

"In the oven. I'm too lazy to deal with a mess this morning," he replied. "So were you gonna tell me about Sloane?"

"Shit. It's barely been twelve hours since our conversation. News travels fast around Ascent. Lauren, I assume?"

"Yep. So what happened?"

I turned around to see if Jake had paused the game to hop into the conversation, but he still had his headset on, which meant I could be a little more honest. I didn't mind talking about things with Jake; there was just a lot he didn't know about me that I didn't want to have to explain.

"I didn't want to string her along anymore. It's not fair."

"Well yeah, we all knew that. I thought you liked her. At least it seemed like it." Graham pulled the tray full of bacon out of the oven and set it on the stove.

"It's not that simple," I said. "I'm not ready for a full-on relationship. Do I have fun with her? Yes. Do I like her? Yes. Do I want the responsibilities and expectations that come with a relationship? No.

That's what made me realize I needed to end things before they got too deep."

"Seems like you were a little too late, buddy." He handed me a plate of bacon, and I took a handful before Jake devoured the rest.

"What time should we hit the gym today?" Jake asked.

"I have class until four. Do you want to meet then?" Graham replied.

"Works for me." I shoved a piece of bacon in my mouth and patted Graham on the back as a thank-you before going into my room to shower and head to campus earlier than usual to avoid any shuttle run-ins. I didn't want to upset her more than I already had.

13

Sloane

March 2017

At first, no contact seems impossible, like quitting an addiction cold turkey. There's no slowly weaning yourself off of them. One day you have them, and the next day it's like they don't exist.

As time goes on, you start to remember your life before them. You stop reaching for your phone when you see something that reminds you of them. You take the songs that they showed you off of your playlist. Eventually, you start to forget them completely.

One month without contact, and I was becoming a different person. Winter had slowly turned into spring, and the extra freckles I got from the sun were starting to come out again. I had stories Ethan had never heard and memories he wasn't present for. One month without contact. and I was finally starting to feel okay again.

Lauren was dragging me to Pike's formal. Last week I'd put up a fight because I wasn't sure that I was ready to see Ethan yet, but I realized I had to stop putting my life on pause for someone who was no longer a part of it. Usually, formal was a whole weekend down in Savannah, but since the chapter was on probation, fraternity standards required them to host an event monitored by the university.

"Think of it this way—running into him at formal is better than running into him at a bar. Here you'll have a date to distract you. Plus, Reese is hot. That never hurts." Lauren winked.

"Fine, you're right, I guess. Which shoes?" I held up two pairs of heels.

"Black. You can never go wrong with an all-black moment."

"Ladies, you ready?" Graham knocked before entering.

We took a group tequila shot before heading to the bus pickup lot. The closer we got to campus, the more uneasy I started to feel. All I needed to do was make sure I didn't throw up or cry when I saw Ethan. Simple enough.

When the pledge driver pulled up, the parking lot was already full of people. Luckily, no sign of Ethan as far as I could tell. My stomach started to feel uneasy, but I did my best to hold it together.

"Let's find Reese," Graham said. "Sloane, you've met him before, right?"

"A few times," I replied.

"He's cool. Good guy," he assured me.

"Reese!" Lauren waved him down.

Reese Thompson was tall, well over six feet. He had short hair that was dirty blond, and I could tell he had recently shaved, though he didn't look like the type that grew much facial hair. When Graham gave me the lowdown on Reese, I learned he should've graduated last year but had to stay for an extra semester after he missed a few credits.

"You made it!" Reese reached out to side-hug me. "Ready to get wasted?"

"Am I ever," Lauren replied, grabbing a water bottle full of vodka from Graham's back pocket, proceeding to pass it around.

I scanned the crowd one more time for any sign of Ethan before we piled onto the party bus. Maybe he wasn't coming after all. I felt myself begin to relax and start to try and enjoy the night. It was a little over a forty-minute ride to the venue, but thankfully we brought plenty of roadies. I took a seat halfway through the drive, and by the time I stood up to get off the bus, I could feel the Smirnoff rush through my entire body. Vodka was never my friend.

"Woah there." Reese grabbed my arm and helped me balance. "I've got you. Let's go inside." He took my hand and guided me off the bus, which I was thankful for because I wasn't sure I could feel my legs.

"This is a really nice place," I observed.

I expected the restaurant to be a slight step up from our usual dive bars but was surprised to see white tablecloths, a live band, and a buffet with chicken tenders and mozzarella sticks. It reminded me of a low-budget wedding planned by a former fraternity event chair. Reese gripped my hand tightly and led me to the bar, where a huge line had already formed. I wrapped my hands around his forearm to keep my balance. From the back of the crowd, I could see Lauren and Graham had almost made their way to the front.

"Should we cut the line?" I asked.

"It'll move fast; they have four bartenders," he said. "Are you ready for graduation?"

"Yeah, I guess," I replied. "I'm still not sure what I'm doing."

"It'll happen; you still have plenty of time. I'm moving to New York right after finals." Reese was trying to make conversation with me in the middle of the loud and crowded bar. I couldn't tell if it was because he was interested in me, wanted to sleep with me, or was just being nice. Either way, I played along.

"Oh yeah, I think Graham mentioned that. I love New York. It's always been a dream of mine to move there and become a writer."

"What kind of writer?"

"I don't know. I just love to write." I shrugged, not wanting to get into it.

"Well, if you do end up in the city, I'm sure you'll love it. I've interned there every summer since freshman year and never want to leave. Well, once I move there in August, anyway. I finally got offered a full-time role when I left this past summer."

I listened to Reese as he told me about his new boss, the apartment he and another fraternity brother signed a lease for, and his favorite spots there to go out after work. As we got closer to the front of the line, I became less and less interested in what he had to say. I looked across the bar to see if there was a drink menu or specials. I reached over to the girl next to me to grab a laminated card from under someone's hand, accidentally brushing it.

"Can I see this?" I said, looking up at the person whose hand was resting on the cocktail menu.

Our eyes met and my stomach dropped.

"Oh, sorry," I quickly replied.

"All good, you can have it." Ethan lifted his arm off the bar, and I watched his eyes glance over at Reese. I grabbed the menu and quickly turned back around.

"What do you want?" Reese asked.

"Vodka soda, please,"

"Two double vodka sodas," he ordered.

I tried to enjoy the night with Reese. Even though when my incoherent mind could form thoughts, the only thing I could think about was Ethan.

• • •

Like most mornings after I drank, my head was pounding and my mouth was dry. I managed to open my eyes to the sight of gray striped bedsheets and a Carolina Panthers poster on the wall adjacent to me. Whoever's bedroom I was in, I was semifamiliar with it.

I turned over, and there was Reese, lying on his back, breathing so heavily it could've been confused with light snoring. I inched my way out of the covers and down to the foot of the bed without waking him and tiptoed to the bathroom. The toilet paper roll was empty, which seemed unlike him. I searched around for a second before I decided to just give up. I'd thought if these guys went out with the intentions of bringing home a girl, they'd at least ensure it was a place she'd feel comfortable in. Or maybe that was what they did when they didn't want them to return. Either way, I had to get out of there. Quietly, I made my way out of the bathroom and searched Reese's room for any sign of my phone or purse.

"Morning," he said groggily. "Do want me to take you home?"

Shit. I woke him up.

"It's okay. Once I find my phone, I can call an Uber or Lauren."

"Your stuff is on the coffee table downstairs. You fell asleep on the couch last night, and I put you here. I offered to take the couch, but you told me to sleep here. I'm not sure how much you remember..." He trailed off.

"No, totally, I remember," I lied. "Thanks so much. Sorry that I got drunk; I shouldn't have pregamed so hard."

"Seriously, just let me drive you." He got out of bed in just a pair of boxers. His body was more toned than I expected.

"Here." I handed him a T-shirt that was hanging on the back of his desk chair. "I'll grab my stuff and wait in the hall."

The car ride home was silent.

"This is me." I pointed to building number three.

"Would you want to get dinner sometime this week?" he asked.

"Oh, um," I stuttered.

"Why don't you put your number in here, and you can just think about it?" He handed me his phone. I did as he asked and placed it back in the cup holder.

"Thanks again for driving me."

"No problem."

I got out of his car and headed towards the stairs without looking back. I made it into the apartment without running into Ethan, which I considered a win.

Lauren catapulted from the couch as I shut the door. "Oh my god, look, it's our ghost bestie—finally haunting us with her presence!" She threw her arms in the air dramatically.

"We were about to send out a search party. Are you good?" Jordan seemed concerned for once.

"I got a little too drunk. Reese took me back to his place so I could sleep. Somewhere along the way my phone died. Sorry for the scare!"

"Did you guys hook up?" Lauren asked.

"Are you into him?" Jordan followed.

Still in my dress from the night before, I sank into the couch, feeling the weight of their stares.

"No, we didn't hook up. Reese is nice, and yeah, there's an attraction," I confessed. "But I'm not there yet, not really," I murmured, resting my head on Lauren's shoulder, seeking solidarity.

As much as I wanted to be over Ethan and move on, seeing him last night only reminded me that I wasn't.

Jordan, scrolling through her phone, dropped a bombshell casually. "Ethan was asking about you and Reese," she said, her eyes not leaving the screen.

"Jordan!" Lauren hissed.

My head snapped up. "He was? Laur, why weren't you going to tell me that?"

Lauren's sigh was heavy. "You've been doing so well. I didn't want

Ethan's...whatever it is, to mess with your head. He noticed you with Reese while he was there stag, and I think it caught him off guard."

"He didn't bring a date?" I lit up inside.

"Yep. But don't read into it, Sloane," Lauren warned, but the caution in her tone couldn't cancel out the relief that washed over me. A bit of frustration quickly followed though. I didn't want Ethan to think I'd moved on so easily, or at all. I wanted him, not Reese; if only he knew that...

I stood up, stretching. "I need to charge my phone and wash off the night," I declared, walking to my room.

"We're going to get bagels. Want your usual?" Jordan offered.

"Definitely."

I connected my phone to the charger, its battery as drained as I felt, and then headed for my ultimate hangover cure: an ice-cold shower. After those ten minutes of torture were over, I wrapped myself in a towel and checked my inbox, eager to see what messages awaited me.

10:15 p.m.
Lauren Ellis: Did you leave??

10:45 p.m.
Jordan Coleman: Where are you?!

12:07 a.m.
Ethan Brady: Hey

9:58 a.m.
Unknown: Hey, it's Reese!

Seeing his name in my inbox felt comfortable, like life was back to normal again, though I knew it wasn't. I knew the right thing to do was leave Ethan on read and go on that date with Reese. *Why is it always so hard to do the right thing?* I wrote back to Ethan and left Reese unanswered for now. When it came to Ethan I had absolutely no self-control, and the sad part was, I think he knew that.

• • •

An hour later, we were sitting in his car—the same place he'd broken my heart only a few weeks ago.

"I guess I'll just go for it," Ethan started. "This thing between us scares me. I don't know how to deal with it. I thought that ending things with you was the right thing to do, for both of us. But when I saw you with someone else...I realized I didn't want that. I know you deserve more than what I can give you, but I owe it to us to at least try."

Relief washed over me, and a smile emerged on my face.

"I still need to take things slow. No title yet, okay? I'm not saying we won't get there; I just don't think we need to rush into it."

I didn't care that I was settling for a fraction of a relationship with him when I knew I deserved so much more. I was willing to settle for whatever he would give me, because a fraction of him was better than nothing at all.

I reentered the apartment dreading having to explain where I had been. It wasn't that the girls didn't like Ethan; it was that they didn't like what he was doing to me. Stringing me along was what they liked to call it. They didn't know him the way I did though. I knew that he wanted to try; he just said it himself. I could tell that he was scared that he'd fail, or he wouldn't live up to my standards. None of that mattered though, because what he didn't know was that I was already in love with him. I was afraid to tell him, because once I did, it would be game over. That was the only move I had left, and I wanted to keep it in my back pocket.

"Where'd you just go?" Lauren was sitting at the counter doing schoolwork.

"Ethan and I talked," I said sheepishly.

"Sloane!" Jordan inserted herself into the conversation without moving from the couch. "We just talked about this!"

"He texted me a few times last night, and I didn't see them until earlier because my phone was dead. I just wanted to hear what he had to say."

"So…what did he have to say?" Lauren asked.

"The TLDR is that he wants to try again. I feel bad for him. I know this is all new to him, and me I guess, and I feel like I put a lot of pressure on us. We're going to take it slow and try to work up to a relationship."

"Come on. Do you hear yourself? A relationship isn't supposed to be this hard. Sure, every couple has arguments and makes compromises but the lead-up shouldn't be this long. He should know what he wants, and if he doesn't, maybe that should be a sign that it's not you."

I knew she was trying to protect me, but those words cut deep. While I'd never been one to get angry with Lauren, that instance was the closest I had ever come.

"I'm sorry, I know that sounds harsh. All I'm trying to say is that you need to stop losing your mind over someone who doesn't mind losing you."

"He does know what he wants; he just doesn't know how to give it to me."

"And that's any better? Why him? What's so special about Ethan?"

"I wish I could put it into words. I think he's my first love, which sounds weird because I'm twenty-two. For a while I thought I loved Carter, but the more I thought about it, what I had with him wasn't love. It was an attachment. He was just a distraction when I needed it the most.

"Things with Ethan are different though," I continued. "Right off the bat, I knew there was chemistry between us, and then it started to grow into this confusing but sort of beautiful connection. He's the first person that I've ever been this close to, and I know that's not saying much, but to me it's something."

"We want you to be happy," Jordan cut in.

"Seeing you hurt just hurts us," Lauren said. "I'm all for second chances, but he better not fuck it up again."

And I completely agreed with her.

14

Sloane

April 2017

wanted to feel even remotely excited about graduation, about interviewing for jobs and touring apartments in new cities—but the truth is, I was dreading all of it. This once lifelong goal of mine to move to New York and become a writer had somehow taken a back seat to my relationship with Ethan. I didn't expect to fall in love. Honestly, some days I thought I never would. But then he came along, and I couldn't (and didn't want to) imagine a life without him in it. So I tried my best not to, until I couldn't avoid the future any more.

"I got it!!!" Lauren shouted. Jordan and I ran down the hall to find her jumping around her bedroom.

"Got what?" we asked in unison.

"The teaching job in New York! They just called and are sending over my contract by the end of the week!"

"Congratulations!" I hugged her.

"This is huge, Laur!" Jordan concurred.

"You're next!" She turned to me. "Once you get an offer letter, we can officially start to apartment hunt. Have you heard back from any of the places you've applied to?"

"Not yet. I probably need to get more serious about searching though." I shrugged, trying to act like it wasn't a big deal, even though I knew it was.

While I was so happy for Lauren, I couldn't help but feel defeated that I still had no promising leads. I'd been lying to my mom for months—telling her interviewing was going well and I was getting better with each one I had. The truth was that I had only applied to three roles, none of which had reached back out to me. My grades were great though, which is probably why I hadn't heard from her in a while.

"Jordan, are you sure you don't want to try being a city girl? Just for a year?" Lauren pouted.

"Let's face it, I'm never leaving Wilmington." Jordan laughed. "And marketing coordinator at the yacht club really isn't a bad gig. Think about it—hot guys, hot rich guys, hot rich guys with boats..."

"Okay, okay, don't make me jealous." Lauren laughed. "I'm going to call my parents to tell them the news!"

For the rest of the day, I searched high and low for any job in New York that I had enough experience for, which wasn't as many as I'd hoped. If you know anything about job hunting right out of college, you know that most entry-level positions require three years of experience. How that made any sense, I wasn't sure.

In the editorial world, entry-level positions were almost impossible to come by. Everyone was looking for new young voices, but a person had to stand out or be connected because the pool was massive. My mom was right: to make it as a writer in the city, it was sink or swim. I wasn't even there yet, and I was already drowning.

After a few hours, my laptop died on me. I didn't have the energy to search for my charger, so I gave up on my job hunt for the night.

9:22 p.m.

Ethan Brady: Heyo, how was your day?

9:35 p.m.

Me: Could have been better. Just applied to what felt like a hundred jobs. Lauren got one today and I'm worried I won't 😞

9:37 p.m.

Ethan Brady: Stop saying that. You're so smart and talented. You're gonna get something, I just know it. And don't settle either.

9:37 p.m.

Me: Ugh, it's just exhausting. I should've started applying months ago.

9:39 p.m.

Ethan Brady: Stop being so hard on yourself. Seriously, Hart. Be less hard than I am every time you walk into a room 😜

9:40 p.m.

Me: You're the worst.

9:40 p.m.

Ethan Brady: You like it. Night, Hart.

As annoying as Ethan could be at times, his lighthearted energy and advice instantly put a smile on my face. I fell asleep that night dreaming of New York and what life would be like there. My subconscious left Ethan out of every single one.

• • •

"You broke up with him?" My voice was raised as I set my to-go bag down on the table in front of Lauren. "Why? Did something happen? Graham has been a picture-perfect boyfriend. Literally he's Prince Charming."

"Nothing happened. Long distance just doesn't make sense for us." Lauren said.

"I don't get it." I truly couldn't wrap my mind around the thought of Lauren breaking up with Graham. One minute they were perfectly fine; the next they were no more.

"If I'm being honest"—she took a bite out of her chicken sandwich before continuing—"he just started to feel like my friend. I think we jumped into things extremely fast, and while I have no regrets, I don't want to keep putting effort into a relationship that I'm not sure about, especially while we're hundreds of miles apart."

Sometimes I wondered how Lauren was wise beyond her years. I wished that I had her confidence and sense of security. Even in the most unsure moments, she always seemed to know what she was doing.

"Well, how did he take it then?" I sipped my Dr. Pepper.

"He, uh, didn't take it well at first. I don't think he saw it coming honestly." I could tell she felt bad. "But hopefully we can move past this and be friends one day. Especially if you and Ethan stay together."

If. I hated hearing that word, but I knew she was right. *If* we stayed together. The odds were slim, but I was taking my chances. When it came to Ethan, I was all in.

"Yeah," I nodded. "Are you still going to the luau party tonight?"

"We talked about that too. He said he didn't want to make these last few weeks weird and that we can still exist in the same room but just keep to ourselves. I'll come, but maybe we can just do a girls-only pregame at our place?"

"Of course." I said. "After we finish lunch, I told Jordan I'd pick her up from Ascent so we could go to Goodwill and Target to get outfits and accessories. You in?"

"Well, now that I'm single, I have to look extra hot. So yes, I'm obviously in."

I gave her a playful glare.

"Sloane! I'm kidding. I'm not gonna go whoring myself around twenty-four hours postbreakup. Especially not in front of Graham."

"Just making sure. Let's get out of here. We have a lot to do in the next few hours, and we can't be late for our last LDOC party."

. . .

We walked into the split-level house, which was covered in any and every decoration needed for a luau. Blow-up palm trees stood in each corner, lanterns hung from the ceiling, and leis were on the banister for people to grab as they walked in. Girls were dressed in bikini tops and cutoff shorts, guys in swim trunks and tank tops. Somehow, they had even managed to cover the dining room in sand. I felt bad for whatever brothers had to clean that up in the morning.

I spotted Ethan almost immediately and waved to him and Graham. As much as I hated the idea of not pregaming my last college party with him, it was a really special way to close out four years with the girls that got me through them.

"Sloaney bologna!" Graham picked me up and spun me around. I could tell he was already wasted based on the new nickname he'd just given me.

"Put me down!" I demanded.

"Okay, okay." He obeyed. "Ladies, what'll you have to drink?"

"PJ works," Lauren replied. "Thanks, Graham."

He half smiled at her and found his way into the kitchen.

"Well, that wasn't too bad," Ethan whispered.

"I can hear you, you know," Lauren pointed out.

"Laur, let's go to the basement," Jordan said. "Sloane, wanna meet us with the drinks when Graham gets back?"

"Sounds good!" Once they were out of my line of sight, I turned to Ethan. "How's he doing?"

"He's fine. Just drunk now." Ethan shrugged.

"That's it?" I knew I wasn't going to get much else out of him.

"Here you go, ladies!" Graham returned before he could answer.

"Where'd they go?"

"To dance. I'll take their drinks downstairs. Thanks again, Graham." I side-hugged him. "You know you can always call me, right?"

"Right."

And with that, I disappeared down the creaky wooden staircase that led into the basement, praying I didn't drop one of the three drinks.

By 1 a.m. the kegs were kicked and the coolers full of PJ were dry. I scanned the basement full of sweaty twentysomething-year-olds until I located Ethan near the bar with Jake.

"Should we call an Uber?" Lauren asked.

Before I replied, I looked over to Ethan again. I wanted to stay there with him instead of babysitting Lauren, but I knew if roles were reversed, she would do it for me.

"Yeah, can you?" I handed her my phone. "I'm gonna go say bye to Ethan." As I walked in his direction, I watched his eyes take me in.

"Hey," he said. "Are you leaving?"

"Yeah, I'm gonna get Lauren home."

"Where's Jordan?" Ethan looked around the room.

"She went to Sigma Chi an hour or so ago."

"Why don't I get a sober brother to take you guys? You can make sure she gets home okay, and then he'll drive you back to the house."

"You're sure?" I asked.

"Yeah, we're gonna postgame, and I don't want you to go home yet," he reassured me.

Then, he kissed me. I felt on top of the world.

A freshman drove us back to Ascent and waited in the parking lot until we saw Lauren reach the second floor. She waved to us, and he started driving back in the direction of the postgame.

"So you're Brady's girlfriend?" he asked.

"I wouldn't say that," I replied. "I mean, I don't know."

Even after all of this time, I never knew how to describe us. Technically, we weren't dating, but we were exclusive. At least, that's what I thought. I hated how a title held our entire relationship in its hands. To me, we were very much in love. The most in love I've ever been. But to him? Well, I didn't really know how he felt. All I knew was what his body language told me and what I felt. I knew he loved me. Deep down, I knew. Even if he hadn't told me yet. He didn't have to say it out loud for me to know. That was the best part about us.

"That's cool," he replied.

This guy probably wouldn't even remember this conversation when he woke up in the morning, yet the question he asked would loom over me for days, maybe even weeks.

I got out of the car and thanked him for the ride. I couldn't wait to see Ethan again. Walking into the fraternity house alone was always so nerve-wracking. I entered through the front door and walked through the foyer to find the guys settled in all the old leather couches in the living room.

"Sup, Sloane," one of them greeted me.

"There she is!" Graham echoed.

I took a seat next to Ethan, and he squeezed my thigh. I was so glad I came back. I loved how it felt when he showed me the slightest bit of attention. The boys passed around slices of pizza, which they ordered once the party died down. They offered me some, but I declined. I hated eating in front of people, especially when I drank.

"Let's go home," Ethan whispered in my ear. *Home.*

Brothers had stopped driving once everyone from the party got home, so Ethan called an Uber and I shuffled into the back seat behind him. He pulled me so close to him that I was almost sitting on top of him. He kissed me, and his breath tasted like whiskey. Fireball, to be specific. I relished it. I parted my mouth to let him in, and I let the happiness flood in too. We got dropped off in the parking lot, and he held my hand up the entire three flights of stairs to his apartment.

As I opened the refrigerator and reached for the Brita, Ethan pulled the string on the back of my bikini top, and it fell to the ground.

"Ethan!" I gasped and covered myself.

"No one's home." He smirked. "Let's do it here."

"In the kitchen? What if Graham or Jake walks in—"

He put a finger over my mouth, picked me up, and set me on the granite countertop. With the force of his lower body, he spread open my legs and stood between them.

His mouth came so close to mine that I could smell the Fireball again, but he wouldn't let me taste it yet. His hands found their way to the button on my denim miniskirt, while his lips lingered on my neck.

He lifted me, managing to wiggle my skirt and underwear off so that I was completely naked before sitting me back down on his kitchen counter. Within seconds his swimsuit was on the floor, and he pressed into me.

It was in moments like that when I was in control. I knew how he felt about me when we were intimate; it was written all over his face, but I could never get him to say it. I knew it was more than just sex to him. You don't make love to someone that you don't love, and what we were doing, that was making love. You couldn't convince me otherwise.

• • •

The next morning the hangover was enough to swear off PJ and vodka for the rest of my life. I guess it was a good thing that yesterday was my last day of undergrad.

"Finally." Ethan's voice made my head pound even harder. "Your phone's been going off for like twenty minutes."

I snatched the phone off the nightstand and sat up as fast as I could without getting too lightheaded. When I unlocked it, I had two missed calls and a voicemail from a 212 area code. Did I even know where that area code was from? I held the phone up to my ear as I played the message.

"Hi, Sloane, this is Annie Walker. I'm a senior editor at *The Gist*. I reviewed your application, and I'd love to talk with you about a few positions we have open here. If you have time today, give me a call back on this number. Thanks!"

"Oh my god!" I screamed.

Ethan darted back into the room, grasping a bottle of Advil and a glass of ice water. The look on his face told me that he was extremely worried to hear whatever I was about to tell him.

"I have an interview!" I jumped out of his bed. He wrapped his arms around me, and I felt the condensation from the glass seep through my shirt.

"That's amazing, but you almost just scared the shit out of me." Ethan laughed and handed me two blue tablets. I put them in my mouth, followed by a large gulp of water.

"It's for a company I literally didn't think I'd hear back from. I was applying as a shot in the dark. I can't believe she looked at my application! I need to call her back." I kissed him, grabbed my purse, shoes, and clothes from the night before, and made my way down the single flight of stairs and into my apartment.

I pressed the callback number for Annie, my fingers nervously tapping against the cool surface of my phone as I shut my bedroom door behind me. The room was adorned with my cap and gown, graduation tassels, and scattered textbooks, a testament to the chaos of finals week.

"Hello?" Annie answered.

"Hi, Annie, this is Sloane Hart. I just got your voicemail!" I replied, trying to keep my voice steady.

From the other end, I could hear the subtle ambient sounds of an office—the distant hum of conversation, the clatter of a keyboard.

"Sloane, thanks for calling back so soon. Apologies for the craziness. I leave on a weeklong trip tomorrow, so I was hoping to touch base with you before then," she explained.

"No worries at all. Sorry I missed it. It's finals week, so life is a little overwhelming with that and graduation right around the corner," I lied, glancing at the pile of books and notes on my desk.

Annie's voice softened slightly. "This is such an exciting time for you. So listen, I'll just cut right to it. I know you applied for a staff writer position, and while I thoroughly enjoyed some of your work, I'm afraid it's lacking some emotional depth," she said.

My heart plummeted into my stomach, and a wave of disappointment washed over me as her words sank in. I absently twisted a strand of my hair, my gaze dropping to the floor.

"But," Annie continued, "I wanted to see if you were interested in an assistant role that just opened up. We finally got budget to hire an assistant for our senior editors here. The position reports to me. You'd mostly be organizing calendars, handling travel, chasing down writers who are late on deadlines—those kinds of things. I know it doesn't sound too glamorous, but there's potential to grow. Your resume is impressive, and like I said, I like your work, and I think you have potential to grow as a writer, which I'm willing to help you with.

If this sounds like a position you'd consider, I'll connect you with HR to start interviewing while I'm gone."

I didn't know what to say. It wasn't the position I'd been dreaming about, but it was a step in the right direction. It was also the only interview I'd been offered, so could I really have turned it down?

"Yes," I finally answered, a tentative smile beginning to form. "That sounds great! Thank you so much for considering me."

"Amazing. Be on the lookout for an email from me this afternoon. You send over your availability, and then you'll receive calendar invites for Skype interviews with each of our senior editors. If all of those go well, your last round will be with me in a little over a week. Sound good?" Annie's tone was upbeat and encouraging.

"Sounds great! Thanks, Annie. Enjoy your vacation," I said with a newfound sense of optimism as I ended the call. I stood there for a moment, phone still in hand, wondering what my mom would think. I guess I'd cross that bridge once, no *if*, I got to it.

15

Sloane

May 2017

Although my childhood was filled with so many what-ifs, one thing was for sure—I wanted to be a writer. It didn't matter that there wasn't much money in it. I knew that I had to make a career out of a passion, something that I loved, or else I'd never survive decades of a nine-to-five. That passion was writing, an ambition ultimately fueled by my loneliness. Without many friends, siblings, or a steady place to call home, journaling became an escape for me. I was putting the words I was too afraid to say out loud down on paper, in hopes of understanding them myself. When there was no one to turn to, there was always a pen and a notebook beside me. Words had become my sanctuary. My journal would never leave me. Writing would always be there, or so I thought.

Annie offered me the assistant position at *The Gist* not even ten minutes into my final interview. Even after weeks of rigorously applying to other writing gigs in the city, nowhere was interested in hiring me. I'd really underestimated how hard finding a job would be. Luckily, every editor I'd interviewed with was kind and encouraging. They all knew it wasn't the position I wanted, but they reassured me that this was a step in the right direction. In my final interview, Annie mentioned the potential to freelance as well. She said I could pitch her one piece a month; no promises they would make it online, but she would give me feedback and help mentor me when she had the time. While it wasn't the dream postgrad life I'd envisioned for myself, I was excited. An assistant title wasn't comparable to staff writer, and *The Gist* wasn't as reputable as the *New York Times* or as popular as *Cosmo,* but it was a start. It was the beginning of my story, and I couldn't wait to see how the rest of it unfolded.

I looked around my bedroom at what still needed to be done. I'd managed to fit my entire closet into two large suitcases. Lauren and I decided to sell our apartment decor on Facebook Marketplace, agreeing it wasn't worth the hassle of shipping to New York. This was a fresh start for us, and we wanted it to feel like that. I just needed to pack the rest of my toiletries, which I couldn't do until after I showered that night.

I checked the time on my phone; it read 10:54 a.m. Today was my last day in Wilmington, and I was going to spend it with Ethan. He was picking me up in a few minutes, and I was dying to see what he had in store for us.

When I got to the parking lot, Ethan was waiting near our building in Graham's car. He had the top off and was blasting the new Migos album, his favorite.

"Get in, Hart!" He lowered his sunglasses and reached over the console to open the passenger-side door for me.

"Where's your car?" I asked, pulling myself up into the lifted Jeep.

"It's not suitable for today's activities." He grinned.

I fastened my seat belt as he took off, one hand on the steering wheel, the other resting on my thigh. Out of the corner of my eye, I took him in. His hair, which had grown longer than usual, was flowing in the wind, and he had a huge smile on his face as he recited every word to "Get Right Witcha." He'd memorized the whole album within a week of its release in January, and it was all I'd heard since then. He and Graham had already gotten in a few beach days this season, so the freckles on his arms and face were peeking through more than usual. I placed my hand over his and squeezed it, hoping he would know what it meant: I wanted today to last a lifetime, because come morning, I wouldn't see him for a month. Our lives were about to change; I was just unaware of how much.

We drove south for what seemed like miles until we reached the end of Kure Beach. I didn't ask questions, though I wanted to. Instead, I chose to live in the moment and soaked in every second I had left with Ethan.

He parked in front of a small office building nestled between sand dunes, then walked around to my side to open my door.

"Is this where we're going?" I looked at him, puzzled.

"Not quite. We're driving onto the beach. Let me show you how to take some air out of the tires while I go inside and get the day pass."

I jumped out of the car and sat with him on the curb.

"So you'll just unscrew each tire cap and then stick my mailbox key in there to let out the air. The tires should be around twenty PSI; you can check their pressure on the dash. I shouldn't be more than a few minutes, so when I'm back I'll help," Ethan explained.

"Got it." I nodded.

"You're sure?"

"Yes, Ethan. It's not rocket science. Go get the pass. I'll be fine!"

As I sat there waiting for Ethan's return, my mind drifted back off to the big move. I took in my surroundings, salt air, blue cloudless skies, sand in the cracks of the cement underneath me. I was going from one extreme to the next. Even though moving to New York City had been a lifelong dream of mine, I couldn't escape the sinking feeling in my stomach. Was I ready for this?

"Secured the pass," Ethan shouted from behind me a few minutes later. "How're the tires coming?"

"Two down, two to go," I replied.

"You can get in the car and take a break. I'll get the rest," he offered.

"It's alright. It'll be quicker if we both do it."

Five minutes later, we were back in the Jeep.

"Buckle up and watch your head. The drive in can get bouncy, and I don't need you to get a concussion on our last day," he said.

Our last day.

I did as I was told and watched out the passenger window as we maneuvered our way onto the beach. A tear fell down my cheek. I tried to wipe it away as fast as I could so that Ethan wouldn't see. I didn't want to look back on our last day and remember tears. I did my best to get it together and look forward to the time that we did have left.

"This spot seems good," Ethan said as he put the car in park and took the keys out of the ignition. "Wanna help me unload?"

I looked into the back seat, where I saw a tote bag that was packed to the brim. A smile immediately appeared on my face. I couldn't believe how much effort he put into this; the least I could do was not ruin it by crying.

"What is all of this?" I asked.

"You'll see." He winked.

I grabbed the tote bag as he lifted the cooler I'd painted him for beach weekend from the trunk.

"You wanna know something, Hart?" Ethan asked.

"Always."

"This is probably one of my favorite gifts I've ever gotten," he said, referring to the cooler.

Painting coolers is a tradition most fraternities have—their dates for mountain or beach weekend are supposed to paint and fill coolers, in return for the guys paying for the weekend. I wanted mine to be perfect, so I spent over a month slaving over it. To hear he loved it made all of those hours more than worth it.

Ethan laid out a blanket in the sand and then continued to unpack everything while I sat back and watched. He brought us sandwiches from Jersey Mikes, a bottle of prosecco with a little container of orange juice, and watermelon Sour Patch Kids for dessert.

"This is really nice of you," I said. "Thank you. I needed this."

"Anytime, Hart." He smiled in return. "Do you want to pop the bottle, or should I?"

I started uncontrollably laughing.

"What?" he asked.

"Ethan," I continued, barely able to breathe. "It's a twist-off."

He looked down, and to no one's surprise, I was right. We laughed as he opened the bottle and made us each a mimosa.

He tried to defend himself. "You know I don't really drink wine."

"I know, I know. That was just too funny."

"So you guys have all weekend to settle in before you start work Monday. What're you gonna do?" Ethan changed the subject.

"Lauren's parents are driving up with the stuff we weren't able to fly with, so I think Friday, they're taking us to IKEA, and then we'll go to dinner somewhere in the neighborhood. I can't imagine we'll do too much besides get settled in."

"Are you excited for your first day?"

"I don't know if *excited* is the right word. More like extremely nervous. I keep having nightmares that I'll get on the wrong train or miss my stop and be late. So I'm making Lauren practice the commute with me on Sunday."

"There you go! I'm sure it seems intimidating, but once you do it a few times, you'll be a pro. You're good with directions. Remember when I took that wrong turn on our way home from the mountains? You navigated us back to the highway," Ethan reminded me.

"Oh my gosh, yes." I chuckled. "That was scary, but then funny, but then scary again when I thought I might puke from all of the twists and turns. I still can't believe you couldn't figure it out. Didn't you guys grow up going there?"

"Graham mostly drove. I didn't have my own car for a while." Ethan shrugged.

A pang of regret came over me. Sometimes it's easy to forget how different his upbringing was than mine.

• • •

Once the sun was setting, Ethan took me to dinner at my favorite Mexican restaurant, and a few margaritas later, I was feeling tipsy and ready to go home. I'd managed to make it all day without bringing up the dreaded topic of what would happen to us after I moved. I'd also managed to make it all day without crying. Until we drove over the bridge.

I tried to keep it to myself, but as soon as he lowered the volume, I knew he knew.

"Sloane?" He never used my real name. "Are you okay? Do you want me to pull over?"

"I'm okay." I sniffled.

"So why are you crying?"

"I'm scared."

"Of what? Moving?"

I nodded before adding, "Of what's going to happen to us."

Ethan reached over and grabbed my hand, trying to navigate his gaze between the road and me. "Don't worry about that right now. I'm not going anywhere. You'll go to New York, and I'll be here, and I'll visit in a month. How does that sound?"

"Good," I managed to say.

"There's no use in being upset over the unknown. Let's see how this first month goes. We can book my flight when we get back to Ascent," he offered.

"Really?" I lit up a little.

"Really. I think you even have time for one Taylor Swift song." He handed me his phone as I scrolled through Spotify until I found the only one he knew. We sang "You Belong with Me" the rest of the way home.

When we pulled into the parking lot, Ethan shut the car off and turned to me.

He ran his thumb over my cheek and then under my eye, I assume to wipe off any mascara that ran.

"Promise me something, Hart?" His tone was sincere. "No matter how much you miss me or Wilmington, you won't let that bring you down. You've wanted this your entire life. You finally have it. Grab New York by the balls and enjoy it. I'll be cheering you on, no matter how far away I am."

"I'll do my best."

"Now, I need to get you in my bed, because there are some things we just can't do hundreds of miles apart."

"You're always so horny," I joked.

"Only for you."

Was that Ethan admitting that we were exclusive? They were words I never thought, or expected, to hear. But they were also the only words that made me feel somewhat better about moving hundreds of miles away the next day.

16

Sloane

May 2017

The wheels of the train steamrolled under me as I made my way to Midtown for a half day at work. The subway came to a halt, and I quickly got off at my stop, which was conveniently right across the street from *The Gist* HQ. Just like most in Midtown, the office was in a standard high-rise that lacked any sort of charm. When I entered the building, I pressed the button for floor sixteen and stared down at the Gucci mules my dad had gifted me for graduation. I know he probably spent a significant chunk of his alimony check on them, so I wore them every day this week. When the elevator doors opened into lobby, I was greeted by a bright neon sign and a sleek modern workspace.

"Morning, Kim!" I waved to her as I headed into the bullpen.

Kim was the CEO's executive assistant but doubled as the front desk secretary because, according to her, she was the most personable employee in the office.

"Week one down! Not so bad, right?" she called after me.

"Right!"

I wasn't lying. This time last week, I had let my anxiety get the best of me. I was trained to hate change; it had always been forced upon me. I had to remind myself that this change was my choice. I'd give the city a year, and if I hated it, I could move back down south. If I loved it, I could stay forever. I was in control now. That was a change I just needed to get used to.

"You're here!" Mila spun around in her chair as I stood in the doorway of her cube.

"You're early." I laughed.

Mila had started at *The Gist* the same day as me, except she got the job I originally applied for. She brought the essence of New York in her stride—okay, technically Long Island—and as a writer on the lifestyle beat, she had this vibrant energy that was infectious. And there I was, an assistant, juggling schedules and supplies, with a secret hope of one day seeing my byline on our website. When Annie had the time, she'd give me writing assignments and critique them to help me better my craft. She didn't have to mentor me, but I was more than grateful for the offer.

"I was up at five a.m., thanks to a cockroach in my sheets. I've never gotten out of bed faster. I grabbed breakfast and have just been simmering on some topics before the editorial meeting next week. Will you be sending out the agenda for it soon?"

"Yeah, Annie and I are sitting down later this morning to review it, so it'll hit your inboxes before the end of the day," I replied. "Have you been looking for new places to live?"

"My only other option right now is my parents. We'd have to pay a few grand to break our lease, so I can't afford anything else."

The apartment she lived in was on top of a convenience store that routinely left mountains of trash in the alley. In the past week, her roommates had killed eight cockroaches and trapped two mice.

"I envy your courage. If a single mouse dares to cross my path, I'm hightailing it back to Wilmington," I joked, only half kidding.

"It'll happen to you eventually. It's a rite of passage in the city."
She laughed while I shuddered at the thought.

"I'm about to make a coffee; do you want one?" I offered.

"Oh my gosh, will you? I need all the caffeine I can get today."

"Cream and sugar?"

"Perfect."

As I waited for the coffee to finish brewing, I admired the view
from the hall near the break room. I was surrounded by sprawling
windows that framed the cityscape, and I remembered why I decided
to brave this concrete jungle in the first place.

"So are you coming to happy hour today?" Mila inquired when
I returned to our cubicles.

I frowned slightly. "Ah, I've got dinner plans with Lauren."

"It's early, like two p.m. Think you can do both?"

"That could work. Is there an occasion?" My frown turned into
a smile.

Mila laughed lightly, "Nope, just the usual Summer Friday vibes.
You know, Sarah from entertainment mentioned it's a thing here—
unofficial happy hours every Friday during summer."

"Summer Friday?" I furrowed my brows, clearly confused.

"Annie hasn't told you?!" She lit up. "Basically, every Friday from
Memorial Day to Labor Day, we get to leave the office at two. The
happy hours aren't mandatory. I guess it's just *The Gist*'s way of giving
us a bit of a summer break."

• • •

"Cheers to your first week and first Summer Friday, ladies," Annie
said with a warm grin. "Welcome to the team."

The golden sunshine danced on the sidewalk, and we found ourselves indulging in conversations that reached beyond the walls of
HQ. A round of cocktails later, I was starting to feel a warmth—both

from the summer sun and the alcohol—course through me. Laughter filled the air as office tales flowed freely, and I was swept up in the camaraderie.

"One more for the road?" Mila suggested, raising her glass.

"Who said we have to stop at one?" I winked. "Especially when they're on the company's tab."

Mila's question came out of nowhere, casual but loaded: "So your boyfriend, how'd you guys meet?"

I skirted around the technicality that Ethan wasn't officially my boyfriend, because let's face it—one, it was mildly humiliating, and two, in my heart, we might as well have been.

"College!" I blurted, a little too excited to talk about him. "We were neighbors."

"Oh god, that must have been fun. All four years?" she asked.

I shook my head, laughing at the memories. "No, just senior year. My roommate started dating his roommate, and then the rest was history."

Mila nodded, her smile indicating she was all ears. "I stayed with my parents during my time at NYU. Missed out on the dorm drama. I mean, New York's one big campus, but it's not the 'college experience' you expect."

"You're lucky though," I countered, my voice a bit too loud as the room began to spin gently. "Growing up here must've been amazing! But yeah, our little neighborly saga didn't start off on the best foot. Right after we all met, they threw a party and didn't invite us. The music was so loud that it literally vibrated our ceilings and shook our furniture. We debated crashing, but ended up calling the cops instead. Petty? Maybe. Effective? Absolutely."

Mila laughed. "You didn't! So they just…invited you over after the cops showed up?"

"Yep, right after the party got busted." I nodded. "They had no idea it was us. His roommate asked mine to be his girlfriend that night, so I took full credit for that. As for Ethan—if he ever found out, he'd probably think I'm insane."

As the happy hour continued, the stories got louder, the laughter richer, and my sense of discretion looser. Even Annie sprinkled in a few of her very own dating escapades.

It wasn't until I was nestled in the back seat of an Uber, the city lights blurring past, that the weight of my words hit me. The anxiety bubbling up inside. Did I cross the line between colleague and friend? The last thing I wanted was to be the office oversharer—or worse, the one who spilled enough to jeopardize her career. I could already hear my mom's "I told you so" in my head. That ride home was longer than any walk of shame I'd ever taken.

17

Sloane

June 2017

think he's here!" Lauren shouted from the other side of the apartment.

I ran to her room and joined her in looking out of the window. Ethan was wearing a navy T-shirt and the gray Lululemon shorts I helped him pick out. His hair was tucked into a baseball cap, but I could tell it had gotten longer by the way it stuck out of the back.

"I'm nervous," I admitted.

Butterflies filled my stomach—it felt just like the first time we met.

"Go get him." She nudged me. "I'll join you for a drink, and then I'm off to my date."

The week we moved, Lauren started swiping her way through several dating apps, trying to fill the quiet gaps that a lack of friends left in our new life. It was an adjustment going from knowing everyone in a small town like Wilmington to knowing no one in New York City.

I picked up the pace as I walked down the stairs of our third-floor walk-up. Through the frosted glass door, I could see Ethan's silhouette. I couldn't believe he was finally here. It didn't feel real.

"Hey, you." His smile filled his entire face as I opened the door to let him in.

"Hi." I smiled back, feeling my face go flush.

The door closed behind him, and he dropped his bag to the floor so he could pull me in for a hug. We stayed like that for a minute before he grabbed my face with both of his hands and stared at me.

"You have more freckles," he noted.

"So do you." I ran my finger over his cheeks and nose.

Then he kissed me.

God, I missed kissing him. His lips were home, and I didn't realize just how homesick I'd been until I got to kiss them again. I knew we had to pull apart, but I wasn't ready yet. How do you let go of someone who feels like home?

"I've missed you," I said when our lips eventually separated.

But instead of replying, Ethan just kissed me again.

"Show me the way, Hart."

"Lauren's home, but she's leaving for a date in a little. Knowing her, they'll be out all night," I joked, sort of.

We walked through the front door, and I watched as Ethan took in the sight before his eyes. Our apartment wasn't the nicest, but we made it work. It had a large living room and a small, closet-sized kitchen. Luckily, we didn't cook much.

"Hey guys, hope you don't mind I poured myself a glass to take the edge off." Lauren stood at our makeshift bar, which was just a tall console table and barstools that backed up to our couch.

"Hey, Lauren." Ethan gave her a side-hug. "How's the city life treating you?"

"It's been good! I'm pretty sure the boys I nanny are spawns of Satan himself but other than that, life's great. You can't really be too sad about anything when you live in Manhattan. You know?"

"I hear ya." He laughed, then turned to me. "Where's your room? I'm gonna shower and change if that's cool."

"Down the hall to your right. And the bathroom is the door straight ahead between both of our rooms. There's a towel on my dresser for you."

Once Ethan had disappeared down the hallway, I turned to Lauren and shot her a huge smile. I loved that his presence did that to me.

"Alright, stop making me so jealous," she mocked.

"So where's the date?" I asked.

"Some bar in the West Village." She shrugged. "I think it's close to his place. I'm not trying to crash with you two tonight."

"Don't feel like you can't come back!" I reassured her.

"I know, I just really don't want to." Lauren laughed. "Okay, I'm out of here. Have fun tonight!"

Once Lauren was gone, I made my way down the hall to find Ethan. The shower wasn't running, but the bathroom door was still closed. I knocked lightly and then peeked my head in before he could answer.

"Hey, hey!" He quickly covered himself up.

"Oh shush, can you get ready so we can actually spend time together?" I wrapped my arms around his torso and pressed my cheek up to his back. I didn't care that my clothes were getting wet from the spots he didn't fully dry.

"Anything for you." He grabbed my hand and kissed it.

"Seriously." I led him into the bedroom so he could change.

"Is Lauren gone? What if we just—" With one swift move, my body was flush against his bare chest.

"We have a reservation!" I frowned, even though a part of me wanted to.

"Alright, alright."

• • •

Summer in Manhattan was surprisingly hot, especially underground. By the time we got off the subway, we were five minutes late for our dinner reservation. The top restaurant to try that summer, according to *The Gist*, was The Smith. We got seated at a two-top in the back of the restaurant, surrounded by other couples. I ordered us an appetizer and a bottle of wine to share.

"I hate to ask but," Ethan started, "do you mind if we split the check? I had to dip into savings for the plane ticket, and I'm not getting as many hours at the golf course as I'd hoped."

"Stop," I cut him off. "I wanted to get tonight's dinner anyway, but we can split everything else this weekend. I'm just glad you're here."

"Thanks." He half smiled.

After we finished our main courses and the bottle of wine, I paid the check and texted Lauren to see where she was so we could meet up. I wasn't ready for the night to end.

"Lauren said they're still out," I said. "I was thinking we could stop in for a drink?"

"I'm exhausted. Could we just go back to your place and turn on a movie?"

"Sure, yeah, that's fine." I sighed, trying to make my disappointment evident.

"Sloane." He picked up my hand and held it in his. "I just need a breather. Let's pack it all in tomorrow."

When we got back to the apartment, I changed into a big T-shirt and pajama shorts while Ethan poured us each a glass of wine. By the end of the movie, we'd finished a bottle of red and he was playing with the drawstring on my shorts. A small part of me was mad and didn't want to give in to the temptation, but I reminded myself how much I'd missed him in the month we spent apart, and the next thing I knew I was sliding my hand under the waistband of his boxers. I wanted to make him realize how much he missed me and how much he needed me. Maybe then he'd consider moving here.

We made our way to my bedroom, kissing and stumbling the entire way there. I pushed him onto the bed and got on top, both of us still fully dressed. I continued to kiss him and take off his clothes, piece by piece. It turned me on more than anything to know that I was getting him off.

He quickly took control, and in one swift motion, he was on top of me.

"Want me to fuck you like I missed you?" he whispered.

It was soft at first, but then became more urgent. My legs wrapped around his waist, a motion I was all too familiar with. I liked when he was on top; it felt more intimate. I could see his face, look into his eyes, and feel him in more ways than one.

He squeezed my throat as his tongue found its way back into my mouth. My back arched, and I let out a small moan when his teeth sank into my bottom lip.

For the next few minutes, I forgot what it was like to miss him and remembered what it was like to have him.

• • •

Before my alarm went off, I woke up nestled under Ethan's arm while he lay on his back snoring. It was a small insignificant moment, but it was one that made me appreciate just how badly I wanted to wake up like that every day. After a few minutes spent daydreaming about a future with Ethan, I crept out of bed and headed to the bathroom to freshen up. I took a quick glance into Lauren's room to see if she had returned, but her bed was untouched and empty. I quickly got dressed, putting on a sports bra, shorts, and sneakers before heading out to our favorite bagel shop.

When I returned with breakfast, Ethan was lying on the couch in nothing but his boxers, scrolling on his phone. I set the brown bag on the coffee table and handed him a small hot black coffee. Just the way he liked it.

"You might want to put some clothes on. Lauren will probably be back soon."

"It's just so hot in here. This window air-conditioning unit sucks."

I rolled my eyes. It was like he was trying to hate everything about the city without even giving it a chance. I didn't respond and instead decided to decompress with a shower. Ethan made his way in a few minutes later, and I let him because I didn't want to miss another minute with him.

"Why have we never done that before?"

I planted a small kiss on his lips and wrapped the towel around my shivering body. Showering with someone else was one of my least favorite experiences, but I'd never let him know that. I'd do almost anything to please him. I wanted to make him realize that I was more than enough.

"What's on the agenda today?" His mood seemed to have lifted.

"I was thinking we could walk around SoHo and grab lunch. I haven't been down there yet. Then we'll head back here to change before the Yankee game."

"What?"

"I got us tickets to the game tonight. I know it's not a big one, but I got us good seats. I get a discount through work."

"Sloane, that's awesome. Thank you so much." He grabbed my face and kissed it all over. I loved making him happy.

• • •

It took us over an hour to get into the Bronx. The subway ride was rough, but we brought a water bottle with vodka in it, so that at least made it bearable.

When we got through the line and into Yankee Stadium, we waited in another line for beer before making our way to section 103.

"These seats are sick!" Ethan said as we sat down.

"You can thank *The Gist*. My salary might be entry-level, and my position might not be the one I wanted, but at least I get some perks."

"Do they need any new employees?" he joked.

"Very funny. Before the game starts, can we take a picture for my story?" I opened the app, pointed the front camera at us, and tilted my head closer to his. We both smiled as I snapped the photo.

He followed it up with, "Don't post that."

I took off my sunglasses and looked at him. "Are you serious?"

"You can save it. But just don't post it."

"Why?" I was starting to get pissed off.

"I don't know. I just don't understand why every time girls do something, they have to post about it."

"God forbid you come and visit me in New York, I take you to a Yankee game and want to post about it. I really don't see the big deal. I used to post pictures of us."

"Whatever, just do what you want."

I saved the photo and never posted it. At that point, I didn't want to. Why did he have to be like that? Was he trying to hide that he was visiting me? Was he trying to hide *me*? The entire game that was all I could think about.

At the bottom of the fifth inning, Ethan went to find us food and more drinks. I stayed at our seats and texted Lauren to complain because I knew she'd understand.

"Here you go." Ethan handed me a hot dog and a Blue Moon. "Hope these are okay."

"How much was everything?"

"Don't worry about it."

I passive-aggressively enjoyed my hot dog and waited for the game to end. I wanted to be anywhere else, but even with the discount, the seats weren't cheap. So I sat in silence until they won. At least we had that going for us. After the game, we went to a dive bar down the street where I drank too much, so Ethan called us an Uber back into the city. My last memory of the night was falling asleep in the back seat.

Morning came, and I was upset that I let a small argument get in the way of Ethan's last night in the city. He would be leaving a few hours later, and I wished that I could press rewind and start the weekend over again.

"I wish you could stay." I rolled over and positioned my body closer to his.

"Me too." He stroked my hair.

"This weekend felt different." The words escaped my mouth before I could stop them.

"Yeah, it did kind of."

To avoid the subject further, I got on top of him and started kissing him. I wanted him to know how much he meant to me, and I knew how much he loved morning sex, so I did just that.

I peeled off his T-shirt, followed by his boxers, and within seconds he found his way into me.

"Just like that," he groaned. "You feel so good."

"Kiss me," I murmured.

He did more than that. Ethan flipped me over so that he was on top. He kissed me, and I relished every second of it. His pace quickened as my breaths became shorter, and I could tell we only had a few seconds left.

I wasn't ready.

I wasn't ready for him to leave.

"I'm close." He pressed his mouth up to my ear.

I wasn't, but I couldn't focus on anything besides the thought of how he wouldn't be in my bed tonight. I let out a few quiet moans, and that was all it took.

"Fuck, Sloane." He rolled over onto the pillow beside me and let out a deep sigh. "Maybe we can go one more round," he offered, but we both knew we didn't have time for that.

An hour later he stood in the living room, freshly showered, bag packed, and Uber ordered. I walked him downstairs as we waited for the car to pull up. Neither of us were talking because we didn't know what to say. I hated goodbyes, and this one was proving worse than I'd expected.

I think Ethan could tell I was on the verge of tears because he pulled me toward him and wrapped me in his arms. The warmth of his body gave me comfort until his ride pulled up. He waited another minute before pulling away.

"See you soon, Hart."

I watched the car drive away, and a tear fell down my cheek. Why did this have to be so hard? Our relationship had always been hard, and I was ready for it to be easy. Didn't we at least deserve that?

• • •

It was getting dark out, and I hadn't heard from Ethan. I assumed that he had made it home safely but sent a text to be sure. He didn't fly too often, so maybe he just didn't realize what texting etiquette was like when it came to taking off and landing.

Time ticked by—two hours and three unread messages later, my phone finally buzzed. I braced myself as I glimpsed the length of his response, the longest I'd ever seen from him, and felt a sudden pit forming in my stomach.

10:18 p.m.

Ethan Brady: I'm sorry to do this over text, but I couldn't find the words earlier. I don't think this is something I can do anymore. I feel so bad saying that, but you deserve someone who's ready to go all in with you. I'm just not there yet. I don't know if I'll ever be. I never pictured myself in a relationship or getting married, but when you came along, I was confused. I still am. I want what's best for you, and I'm not it. I have problems that you don't want to get involved in, and as much as it kills me, I know I have to let you go. You deserve so much more than me.

Ethan's words felt cold and final on my screen, but they were nothing I hadn't heard before.

I'm sorry to do this over text... The message echoed in my mind as I read it again, disbelief and anger bubbling up inside me. With my heart pounding hard against my ribs, I hit the call button, each ring sending shivers down my spine.

The moment he answered, I let it all out. "Are you kidding me, Ethan? Over text?"

"Sloane, I—"

"No, just don't," I snapped, cutting him off. "You spend the whole weekend here, and you can't even say it to my face? *That* was your exit strategy?"

"I know," he sighed heavily. "I wanted to. I just—I couldn't. I knew how emotional it would be, and this relationship was already hard enough on both of us. I didn't want to make it worse."

"Well, you managed to make it so much worse. I hate you, Ethan. With every fiber of my being, I hate you for this. This entire year. How could you do this to me? You let me fall for you. You let me believe you'd eventually get there. You even let me believe things were okay all weekend. You had every opportunity to end it, and this is how you chose to do so? I should've known..." My voice was sharp.

I might have sounded tough, but on the other side of the phone I was falling apart.

He spoke again, his voice low. "I'm sorry, Sloane. I'm so, so sorry." I ended the call with a click and hurled my phone against the wall, where it left a mark. How could someone I did nothing but love do nothing but hurt me in return? The arteries around my heart tightened, making it harder to breathe. I'd never known a heartbreak like this, one that caused physical pain.

I spun around to find Lauren in the doorway, her eyes wide. I was sure she'd heard everything. She walked towards me and wrapped me in a hug, which made me cry even more. For the girl who was finally starting to be in control of her own life, I sure felt pretty powerless.

"I'm so sorry." She broke away from the hug to pick up my phone and make sure it wasn't broken.

Unfortunately, it wasn't.

"Do you want some space? Some wine?"

"Wine, definitely wine," I said.

"Of course."

We sat on the couch as a mindless reality show played in the background until I was ready to rehash the weekend's series of unfortunate events with Lauren.

"I really thought things were different this time," I said. "I feel so stupid, delusional even, for thinking we could make long distance work when we couldn't even have a functional relationship as neighbors."

"Sloane, you're not stupid. Love just blinds people. You were blind and hopeful, never stupid."

"I really thought he was ready this time. Or I hoped that he was anyway."

"Some people just aren't ready, no matter how much time you give them. Nothing will change until they decide they're ready," Lauren explained. "You can't wait for them though."

"But I love him." I started crying again. "I've never loved anyone like this before."

"You're gonna hate to hear this, Sloane, but we're so young. Your person is out there, and they're going to be your person for the rest of your life. You won't have to worry about this one-foot-in, one-foot-out situation with them. You don't want someone who comes back; you want someone who never leaves."

"I just wanted it to be Ethan."

"I know you did."

I crawled into bed, burrowed myself under the covers, and tried to sleep. Even then, when I closed my eyes, all I saw was him. Isn't it funny how that happens? One day you don't know someone exists, and the next you can't imagine life without them.

18

Ethan

June 2017

Sloane hung up on me. I didn't blame her, I guess. Why did I have to be the world's biggest dick and do that over text? Why couldn't I, for once in my life, just be vulnerable and honest? I owed that much to her, I knew that. I just couldn't give it to her.

Graham said there was a party at a brother's house in Wrightsville he wanted to go to, so I decided to join to take my mind off things. I'd love nothing more than to be drunk or stoned right now. After I showered, I threw on a Pike T-shirt, khaki shorts, and Nikes, and found Graham cracking open a beer.

"You ready?" I asked.

"Grab a beer first." He pointed at the fridge. I cracked open a Miller Lite and took a seat next to him on the couch. "So what happened with Sloane?"

"Did she call you?" I asked.

"Dude, I could hear you on the phone. You weren't necessarily being quiet."

"I ended things with her." I knew Graham wouldn't give up until I told him. "I just felt like it was unfair to her."

"What was?"

"Leading her on when I can't date her. Not to mention the fact that we were long distance when we weren't even dating."

"Haven't we been here before? Why didn't you want to date her? I get the long distance thing, but I feel like it's more than that."

"I don't know. I really don't wanna talk or think about it anymore tonight."

Graham didn't press me any further. We finished our beers, and once Jake got home from work, we headed to the party. Like most Wrightsville party houses, this one was a run-down shithole, but it was unusually packed for a Sunday summer night.

Before Sloane there were other girls. Of course there were other girls. A lot of them, if I'm being honest. I was constantly surrounded by attractive girls—classes, pregames, parties, you name it, there were at least five girls in the room I'd be willing to sleep with. But that was it. It was always a one-time thing. A one-night stand. I'd go to her apartment, we'd hook up, and then I'd make up some excuse as to why I had to leave so I could sleep in my own bed. Until I met *her*.

Sloane was different. I couldn't explain it, but I had this instant connection with her that I hadn't experienced with anyone else before. She was funny, smart, and cared about everyone around her. Not to mention she was also hot. I enjoyed spending time with her, so much so that I allowed her to get closer than I'd ever let anyone before. She knew almost as much about me as Graham did, except for the reason why I was the way I was. You might be thinking that this was a good thing—opening up, being vulnerable, letting someone in—and sure, maybe to some people it was, but not to me. I let Sloane get too close, and I knew I'd never be able to be the kind of person she wanted, the kind of person she deserved.

I tried to get out of my head and guzzled down two cups full of keg beer before joining Graham at the pong table on the back patio.

"Think we could take you on next?" Two semiattractive girls bounced over, flipping their hair like that would make any sort of difference. They knew we'd let them play.

"How about we switch it up so you have a chance of winning? One of you with each of us?" Graham suggested. "What're your names?"

"I'm Jamie," the taller one said.

"And I'm Marissa."

"Jamie, you're with me," I blurted out, trying to channel some sort of alpha vibe. Girls loved a guy who took control.

"Hi, Marissa. I'm Graham." He was much smoother in his delivery.

"And your name is?" Jamie asked, eyebrow raised.

"Ethan." Just Ethan, no need for last names at a party, especially with a girl I had no intention of seeing again after tonight.

We played, we won, and then we got comfortable on the couch, where we passed around a bong. When Jamie and Marissa hit the bathroom, Graham and I hit the whiskey—hard. Not my usual scene, but tonight I didn't want to feel a damn thing.

"Hey." Jamie slid next to me later, her voice low. "I'm kinda over this party."

"Same here. Crash at your place?" I tossed out, casual.

Her eyes lit up. "Thought you'd never ask. Let's walk; it's close."

That was easier than I thought.

In my drunken haze and the glow of the streetlights, I tried to take note of Jamie as we walked down the block to her house. She was much taller than Sloane, had medium-length blond hair that had a sort of frizzy curl to it, and dressed like she went to that party asking to be fucked. Cutoff shorts that her ass pretty much hung out of and a white crop top that you could see her nipples through. I wasn't complaining, but I knew exactly what kind of girl she was.

"This is me." She pointed to a little white house.

We stumbled in, and some tiny furball started yapping. "Want a drink or something?" Jamie was already halfway to another room.

"I'm good. I'll just be right here." I plopped onto her couch and wrangled my phone out of my pocket. I checked my text messages, wondering if any were from Sloane. None. That was to be expected, I guess.

Jamie didn't play games. She came back, grabbed my hand, and it was straight to her room. I tried not to think too hard as we started kissing. It felt off, kissing someone who wasn't Sloane, but I was trying to scrub her from my mind, one beer, one shot, one kiss at a time.

I lowered her onto the bed and stripped her clothes off, quickly and efficiently. I wanted to get this over with. I thought this was what I needed, and maybe it was, but something about it still didn't feel quite right. It was all so mechanical. Nothing had felt right since the Uber drove away from Sloane's apartment. But it would. It would all make sense one day.

19

Sloane

June 2017

No one talks about the morning after a breakup enough. Swollen eyes. Waking up—if you were lucky enough to sleep—wondering if it was just a nightmare. Realizing that it wasn't. The pain in your heart reappearing. No *Good morning* text. No *I'm sorry I fucked up* voicemail. Nothing. That was your new reality. A cold bed, an empty stomach, and an ache in your chest that you fear will never go away.

I looked at myself in the front camera on my phone, because I didn't know if I'd be able to get out of bed. My eyes were the size of golf balls; I'm surprised I could even open them. There was no way I could keep my composure for an entire day in the office, and even if I could, my appearance would scare off all my new coworkers.

"Can you call in sick today?" Lauren stood at the end of my bed.

I hated lying, but I knew that was my only option. I handed Lauren my phone so she could send a message to Annie for me. I watch her type away, hit send, and place the phone back on my bed.

"Do you want me to stay home?" she offered.

"We can't both lose our jobs." I let out a slight laugh.

"You know I'd stay if I could. Call me if you need anything—and don't start drinking until at least four. Okay?"

The silence after the front door clicked shut felt heavy, loaded with the weight of finality. My fingers trembled slightly as I reached for my phone, scrolling to the one person who always seemed to have the answers. Well, about Ethan anyway.

"Hello?" he answered groggily.

"Hey, Graham," I replied.

"Everything okay? You never call this early." His voice was thick, and I knew he was hungover. I wanted to ask what he did last night, but it probably involved Ethan, and unfortunately, he was none of my business anymore.

I pressed my free hand against my forehead, willing back the tears. "I'm... How are you?"

"Sloane, cut the shit. What's going on?" He was more awake now.

With a deep breath that did little to calm me, I confessed. "Ethan dumped me. Over text. I just don't get it. Was I not enough for him?" I started to sniffle.

There was a pause, and I could almost hear Graham's gears turning, trying to find the right words. "Look, Sloane, it's not about you being enough or not. Ethan's got issues, like...with letting people in. To be honest, I'm kinda shocked you got past his walls as much as you did.

"Wow, thanks, Graham." I couldn't help the slightly sarcastic laugh that escaped me.

"No, no, I mean—" He cleared his throat. "Sorry, I'm not really firing on all cylinders yet. What I'm trying to say is, Ethan's never opened up to someone like he has with you. Maybe he just needs a bit of space... He might come around."

"I shouldn't want someone who comes back. I should want someone who never leaves. Right? I mean, that's what Lauren's been saying this whole time. I should be with someone who's sure about me."

There was a heavy sigh on the other end, the kind that said he was weighing his next words very carefully. "Okay, I'm gonna tell you something, and Brady would absolutely lose his shit if he knew I told you…"

"What is it?" My curiosity was piqued.

"This is between us. Got it? Not even Lauren can know."

I gulped, my anxiety surging. He knew I was horrible at keeping secrets.

"Okay?" he asked again.

"I won't say anything," I promised.

"I still don't really know all the details, just what's been relayed to me through him, my parents, and some news articles," Graham started. "When he was thirteen, both of his parents were arrested. They were drinking and driving, and they killed someone on a bike."

I was speechless, so he continued. "Brady's dad had a few prior DUIs. He owned a hole-in-the-wall bar in Carolina Beach, so I think he'd drink a lot while he was there. Apparently, there was a party at the bar the night of the accident, which is why Ethan's mom was also in the car. She was sentenced to a year, mostly for hiding information about the case, and his dad was sentenced to ten. When his mom was released, we all expected her to come back for him. That was the plan, according to Brady. She never showed up, and it broke him. He never said it, but we all knew. We could see it in everything he did. My mom tried to get in contact with her a few times, but she acted like that part of her life never existed. As far as my family knows, his mom moved somewhere like Oklahoma or Texas, I forget which one, but she got remarried and has another kid. His dad gets out next year, but I don't think they're in contact."

"Oh my—" I couldn't even finish my sentence. I truly didn't know what to say. What could I say to that?

"Yeah, so, I mean, I think that's everything. Brady's a good guy; he just has a lot of baggage, which is why I wanted to tell you this. It's not that he can't be with you; it's that he can't be with anyone. He doesn't know how to. Does any of this help? Or did I make things worse?"

"It helps a lot. I just feel bad that I didn't see it. How could I not see it?"

"You can't blame yourself. Remember, you know none of this. It's not something you need to address, but I was hoping it would make you see his side of things. He has a lot of work on himself to do, but I like you for him."

"Thanks, Graham." I wiped a tear from my cheek. "Miss you."

"Miss you too, Sloane."

My thoughts were racing at a million miles per minute as I tried to make sense of the situation. I felt bad, horrible actually, and I wanted to understand it, but I couldn't.

If you loved someone, I mean really loved them, would you be willing to just let them go? Especially over something from your past that you couldn't control? My parents' divorce did a number on me. For a little while I wondered if I would ever truly love someone, and if I did, would I live in constant fear wondering if they'd just leave one day? Then I met Ethan, and those thoughts didn't cross my mind once.

So no, I didn't want to let him go. But I knew once the shock and initial pain subsided, I'd have to, because that's what he did to me. He let me go without thinking twice, and I think that was what hurt the most—thinking I meant something to him, just for him to show me that I didn't.

• • •

The next morning I felt okay enough to go back to work. I walked down the long hall from the elevator to my cube and wondered if I'd be able to focus on anything besides Ethan. I stopped in the doorway of my workspace and admired the bouquet that was placed in front of my monitor. I set down my bag and pulled out the note that was tucked in between the peonies.

Sloane, a card and flowers can't make this better, but I'm giving them to you anyway. XO, Annie.

How did Annie know about the breakup? I sorted through my tote bag until I found my phone and immediately pulled up the message Lauren had sent to her yesterday on my behalf.

7:08 a.m.

Me: Hi, Annie, this is Sloane's roommate. To be completely honest, she got broken up with last night and isn't doing too well. She really needs to take the day. Hope you understand, and please don't fire her for this!

"Got a sec?" Annie appeared at my desk.

"I'm so sorry about this." I held up my phone, which was open to our text conversation. "I had no idea."

"Don't be sorry. I appreciate the honesty. You have a great roommate." She leaned on the edge of my desk. "Your twenties are hard, and breakups are no joke. Why don't you try writing about it? Maybe you can pitch me some bylines next week? Or whenever you're ready. No rush! Just don't be afraid to be vulnerable and put these feelings into words. You'd be surprised at how cathartic it is. Plus, it might just help you find that depth you've been searching for."

Annie was right. I plugged my laptop into the monitor and sent Mila a meeting invitation for that afternoon.

"Breakup brainstorm?" Her head popped up over the half wall that separated us. "What happened? I thought you were so excited for your weekend together."

"Long story short, he's not ready. Too much too soon. Do you think you have some extra time this week to help me on a pitch to Annie? It seems like she's interested in something I have to say... I just have to figure out exactly what that is."

"Of course! I'm sorry though, about the breakup. That sucks. Well, I've never actually been dumped, but I can imagine that it sucks."

"You've never been dumped?" I envied her.

"Nope, I end it with them before they have the chance to do the same. Saves me a whole lot of heartbreak."

"Save it for the brainstorm sesh." I laughed and shooed her away.

• • •

"Let's start with some topics." Mila stood in front of a whiteboard.

"If we want the readers to follow the journey of the breakup, I'm thinking we start with something small and work our way into the deeper stuff," I explain. "Maybe like, *We've made a postbreakup playlist, so you don't have to?*"

"Genius," she said. "What's next?"

"*Our best breakup advice, before you get into an 'almost relationship,' read this, an open letter to the guy who didn't want to date me.*"

We sat in that conference room until well past 5 p.m., spewing off advice, stories from past relationships, and things we've read or watched in movies that stuck with us.

I spent the entire subway ride home writing articles piece by piece in the notes app on my phone. I swore, if anyone ever had access to these, I'd have personally dug my own grave and buried myself in there. Midnight thoughts, drunk rants, things I'd never have told anyone. Good thing they were password protected. Hopefully Annie would like at least one of them. Maybe this could finally be my big break.

20

Sloane

September 2017

I n the months that followed our unofficial breakup, I threw myself into work. I stayed late at the office, wrote article after article, and Annie loved them. *The Gist* published three of my pieces, one of which seemed to be resonating with hundreds of thousands of people: "An Open Letter to the Guy Who Didn't Want to Date Me." Annie had taken a chance on me, allowing my voice to rise from my notes app to the spotlight of a byline, and it paid off.

I started to realize how common almost relationships were. So many people had that one person they loved but never truly dated, but hardly anyone ever talked about it. Slowly, I started to feel at peace with the fact that Ethan and I were meant to be but weren't meant to last. It hurt to think of us that way, but it was true.

"Sloane! Your article from last week hit a million reads!" Annie shouted from her office, followed by cheers and shouts of congratulations from the surrounding cubicles.

I couldn't help but cry. Mila handed me a few tissues and hugged me. "I'm so proud of you," she said.

"Thank you, Annie," I managed to say, "for the opportunity."

"Wanna pop into my office?" Her tone was casual, but there was a twinkle in her eye that hinted at something more. I nodded, dabbing at my eyes, and made my way over.

Inside Annie's office, the buzz from the editorial corner was a distant hum. She gestured to the chair in front of her desk with a smile. "I'll cut right to the chase," she began, her hands clasped together as if she were containing her enthusiasm. "A million reads is no small feat. It's exceptional. And it's clear to me—and to the readers—that you have a lot more to say."

I sat, waiting for her to continue, as the remnants of my tears dried on my cheeks.

"So how would you feel about a promotion to staff writer?" Annie's question hung in the air. I couldn't believe it was finally within reach.

I blinked, the weight of the offer settling on my shoulders. "I—that would be amazing, but I…"

"You'll still need to handle your current tasks for now. We're aiming to hire someone by year's end. But Sloane, your writing"—she paused, her gaze steady and sure—"it's raw, it's real, and it's what we need."

The office suddenly felt too small for the enormity of the moment. Staff writer. It was all finally happening. Maybe I didn't have Ethan, but I had everything else I wanted. My emotions were a cocktail of fear and excitement. Would I be able to live up to these newfound expectations?

"Thank you, Annie. I won't let you down." The words came out of my mouth before I could stop them.

Annie's smile widened. "I know you won't. Now, go celebrate. You've earned it."

As I left her office, the reality of her words began to sink in. My new title felt like a badge, a testament to surviving heartbreak and turning it into something that moved a million souls. And maybe, just maybe, it was the first step toward finally moving on myself.

• • •

"Can we get a bottle of prosecco?" Lauren asked the bartender and then turned to me. "So how does it feel?"

"How does what feel?" I arched an eyebrow.

"To turn this heartbreak into something good."

"It's hard to explain." I sat back in my seat. "I read those words, and sometimes I believe them, but other times I can't even believe I wrote them. It's only been three months, so I know I'm not fully over him yet, but I'm getting there. These comments and posts from girls who are reading and relating to my article are helping to accelerate it though. They're giving me the closure he was never able to."

"I'm so proud of you."

We lifted our flutes and *cheers*ed each other. After finishing the bottle, we ended up at a piano bar on the Upper East Side, right around the corner from our apartment.

"We really need more friends in the city," Lauren sighed as we settled into a two-top near the window. "This would be the perfect night to go out, like *really* out! Not just to a bar close to our apartment."

"Who else do we know here?" I said, scrolling through my contacts.

"No clue." Lauren rolled her eyes and took a swig of her vodka soda.

My phone vibrated, and though I'd usually try to be respectful and not check it, I picked it up immediately in hopes that it was someone that I'd been waiting on. As confusing as it was to admit, I think part of me wrote this article hoping that Ethan would read it. I mean, it was an open letter to him after all. The romantic in me hoped that maybe he'd digest the words, feel the same way, hop on a flight, and confess his feelings, his trauma, his every waking thought. I knew that only happened in the movies though.

Instead of being greeted by a text from Ethan, it was the last person I'd expect to hear from.

8:37 p.m.

Reese Thompson: Hey there. Heard you moved to the city, also happened across your article earlier. Congrats on everything! Are you free for drinks or dinner this week?

"Oh my gosh."

"What?" Lauren asked. "Ethan?"

"No…Reese Thompson." I set my phone back on the table.

"Stop! You're gonna answer right? Wait, I bet he has roommates. Tell them to come out tonight!" Lauren begged.

I played along. "Fine."

What did I have to lose?

An hour and a half and two more vodka sodas later, Lauren and I were waiting in line at The Gem Saloon. Since we only moved to the city a few months ago, we hadn't explored many places outside of our neighborhood yet. According to Reese, Gem was one of the better weeknight spots.

"I'm nervous," I said to Lauren as the line slowly inched forward.

"Don't be! Reese is great. Plus, he was like obsessed with you, so that's a plus," she said.

"Oh, was I?" a voice replied from behind us. I spun around and there he was—Reese Thompson in the flesh.

"Kidding! Hey, Reese!" Lauren hugged him and proceeded to introduce herself to his friends.

"Hey, you." He side-hugged me.

"Sorry about all of that." I blushed.

"Don't worry about it; it was flattering. Now follow me; I know the bouncers." Reese took my hand, confidently guiding us past the waiting crowd. The bouncer, a broad-shouldered guy with an easy smile, chuckled as Reese slipped him cash. With a friendly nod, he ushered us through the door.

The Gem Saloon was just like any other hole-in-the-wall bar except it was decently sized and had a ton of windows, which seemed rare for New York. As we followed Reese through the lively chatter and clinking glasses, he steered us to the bar in the back—well stocked, with a much shorter line. He ordered with a familiarity that told me he'd spent many nights here. The bartender lined up our drinks, and after distributing them to the group, Reese grabbed my hand. Before I knew it, I found myself hoping that he wouldn't let it go.

The DJ started to play a mix by Calvin Harris, a favorite of Lauren's. Reese's eyes met mine, a silent question hanging in the air between us. I nodded, and without a word, he led me to the dance floor. His friends followed suit.

With every beat, the space between Reese and me seemed to dissolve. My heart raced, not just from the movement, but from a crush I tried to deny I ever had. Reese was the nice guy, the one I knew would've treated me right, had I given him the chance. Instead, I chased someone who barely gave me the time of day. Somehow months later I was hundreds of miles away from Wilmington, dancing with Reese and not Ethan. It was funny how life worked.

As the song wound down, our movements slowed, and we found ourselves in a quiet corner of the bar. Reese's gaze was intense, more intimate than the dim lighting of the bar warranted. He leaned in, his voice low over the fading music.

"You know, I've always thought there was something between us," he confessed.

"Maybe there's still something there," I whispered back.

And then, in a moment that felt both like the end of a journey and the start of another, his lips met mine. The kiss was soft, hesitant at first, like a question. But I kissed him back, affirming what we both felt.

That night I realized that losing someone doesn't necessarily mean losing. Every time someone walks out of your life, someone new eventually walks into it. Losing someone means you'll eventually gain someone even better.

An Open Letter to the Guy Who Didn't Want to Date Me

By Sloane Hart

Dear ex-"something,"

I'm writing you this letter in hopes that it'll give me the closure that you were never able to.

September first is this week, which means it'll be the third month without you. Three months without you in my bed, in my inbox, and in my heart as someone who didn't break it. It's weird seeing the seasons start to change. It's like time is moving so quickly yet so slowly. I think back to that night in June, the night you ended things. Sometimes I feel like it was a year ago; sometimes I feel like it was yesterday. The days are easy, but the nights are hard; that's when I miss you the most.

What I don't miss, though, is the hurting. I mean, I do still hurt, but not in the same way I did when we were together. The constant wondering: *Am I not enough for him? Why am I not good enough? Why doesn't he love me the way I love him? Will he ever love me?* Even just typing out these questions hurts my heart so badly.

Somewhere along the line of loving you and then hating you and then missing you and then hating you again, I realized that you did all you could. We weren't made for each other, no matter how much I tried to convince myself we were. Although this isn't me making excuses for you. I deserved so much more than you were ever willing to give me. So why did I used to think that I wasn't deserving of *any* of it? I thought I wasn't worthy of love, and I feel so sorry for the version of myself that believed otherwise. I deserved a title. I deserved a label. I deserved honesty. I deserved clarity. I know that now.

I didn't want this to be a lesson; I wanted it to be love. But if we weren't meant to last, then the best I can hope for is that you use our time together as a learning experience, a source of wisdom, a reason to change. I never asked for much from you, but I need to ask this one thing: please, don't treat someone else the way you treated me. I hate that I'm saying this—my stomach turns at thought of you with someone else—but I know eventually you will move on to another relationship, and I hope it's different than this. I hope you meet a girl one day that changes the world for you. I hope you love her enough to lay down your armor and give up the fight. I hope that you finally realize you deserve to be loved in a way you never were before, in a way that you couldn't return to me.

Thank you for giving me a story to tell my future daughter one day when she is going through her first heartbreak.

xx,

The girl who would've loved you through anything.

PART 2

NOW

21

Sloane

January 2018

I turn over on my side and, with my eyes, trace Reese's profile. He sleeps on his back almost exclusively, which only contributes to his snoring. I watch him sleep and I recount the past several months we've spent together.

Reese was a breath of fresh air when I needed it the most. I remember thinking as early as our first date: *This is what it should feel like.* So I clung to it; I intertwined my hand with his and never let it go.

"Where are you taking me?" I asked after he insisted on picking me up before our first *official* date.

I say *official* because I slept with him the night we reconnected at Gem. I didn't think it would go anywhere, and I wanted to get my first post-Ethan hookup over with. I definitely didn't expect him to ask me to be his girlfriend two weeks later. It felt a little crazy and rushed. Lauren even thought so, but it also felt right.

"I can't tell you that," he bantered. "What I can tell you is that I know you'll love it."

"Not to be that girl, but how do you know? You've known me all of two weeks," I argued.

"Well, if you want to get technical… I've actually known you for about six months. Just trust me on this one."

He insisted on walking to dinner, and we stopped at a cocktail bar on the way. It was one of those fancy no-menu places where they ask what kind of alcohol you enjoy and make you a drink based on your answer.

"What kind of food are we having at least?"

"Italian." His mouth curled into a smile.

As if I could read his mind, I immediately knew his thought process behind the choice. After Gem we went back to his place, had a glass of wine, and talked for over an hour. About anything and everything, including family. Which was a topic that was hardly discussed in my conversations with Ethan. I shared with him that one of my favorite things about my dad is his penne with vodka sauce recipe. Right before the divorce, a few months before I was due at college, he taught me how to make it. The recipe is stored in my notes app for safekeeping, and I make it when I miss him. Reese not only wanted to try it, but also insisted I teach him how to make it one day too. Chicken parm, sub vodka sauce, was his "secret order" at Italian places.

"If they have both on the menu, most places will do it. Especially if I flirt with the server a little bit," he said.

I love that he listens to me, like really listens, and puts thought and effort into every interaction—no matter how big or small.

On our third date, he took me to a Yankee game because he knew they were my dad's favorite team. Unbeknownst to Reese, it was my second game. I didn't have the heart to tell him I'd been once before, and I was ready to make new memories there that didn't involve Ethan.

"Our seats are right on the first base line," Reese said as we waited in line for hot dogs—which were the best in the city according to him. "Nothing hits like a ballpark dog."

At first, I was scared to go to the game. I worried I'd think about Ethan the entire time, that I'd miss him too much. Maybe even send him a text that I'd regret the next day. But Reese proved me wrong. I thought of Ethan only once, when I passed the section we sat in, and the vivid memories of anger, confusion, and embarrassment washed over me. Ethan kept me at arm's length like he was hiding me, and Reese puts me on his shoulders like he's parading me around town. The two feelings could not be more different.

Reese rolls over like he knows I'm thinking about him and pulls me in. My face is pressed up against his bare chest, and I inhale, taking in the exact scent of him—subtle notes of pine just lingering from the cologne I bought him. His soft hands glide up and down my back; his gentleness always has a way of calming me down. I take inventory of every part of him because I never want to forget it.

"Baby," he whispers. "Why are you awake?"

"I can't sleep." I'll never tell him that it's his snoring that wakes me up most nights.

"What can I do?" He opens his eyes.

"How are you real?"

He chuckles. "What are you talking about?"

"I couldn't sleep, and you were just lying here, so peacefully, and I thought about our last few months together. They don't feel real sometimes. I've waited my whole life for a guy like you," I spoke into his chest.

"Better get used to it, because I'm not going anywhere." He presses his lips to my forehead, and then they find their way down to mine.

It took some getting used to, sex with Reese versus sex with Ethan, like the relationships were complete opposite experiences. Ethan and I had this unexplainable chemistry, like our bodies were magnets and they'd attract each other even in the most crowded of rooms. With Reese, it took some getting used to. I had to teach him what I liked— *slow down, speed up, keep going, don't stop.*

Reese was gentle in everything he did. He'd kiss me for hours until I'd tell him what I wanted next, much like he was doing now.

"Take my clothes off," I whisper.

"If I do, I won't be able to go back to sleep."

"So don't. Sleep is overrated anyway."

He follows my directions and pulls the baggy T-shirt over my head. I graze my hands up and down his neck, then into his hair as his disappear in mine. Eventually making their way down to my underwear, his fingers find their way inside of me, and I moan into his mouth.

"Sloane, you're so—" He doesn't even have to finish that sentence.

"I want you, Reese."

"And I never want you to stop saying that. Tell me again, baby."

He presses into me, and I feel my eyes roll back into my head. When I finally open them, the sun is starting to rise, the light peeking its way through his blinds and onto his duvet cover.

His groans intensify until he's a puddle beside me.

"I want to wake up like this every morning."

"Me too," I reply, planting a gentle kiss on his lips.

22

Sloane

January 2018

The subway is nearly empty on my way home from work. Our office has been open since the day after New Year's, but everyone knows that people with kids don't go back to work until the second week of January, when school starts back up again.

Annie sent me a text asking me to cover an event tonight because she wouldn't make it back from New Jersey in time. Now that they've hired an assistant to replace me, she's taken me under her wing. The event is a launch party for a new skincare company, so I know there's guaranteed to be a lot of free samples. I agree and start typing the details into my calendar when the crosswalk brings me to a complete halt. I shove my phone into my bag and watch for the walk signal— that's when I see it.

Through the crowd of people in front of me, I notice a backward navy-blue New York Yankees hat poking out. I haven't thought about him in a while—weeks, maybe months even. But seeing that hat, just like the one he has, just like the ones thousands of other people in the city have, brings back a flood of memories that I thought I buried. Apparently, not well enough.

Now that I remember, I can't seem to forget. The touches, the kisses, the laughs, the tears, the time, the emotions, the energy. I remember everything. How can you make yourself forget? I want to forget. I want to forget him and every dreaded memory that comes along with him. Can you ever really forget your first love? The rest of my walk home is a silent one. My thoughts are consumed by him, all because of a silly little baseball cap. Imagine if I had seen *him* though? Unlike the beginning of the summer, I'm grateful for all of the miles between us.

I walk into our apartment, and Lauren is already home, nestled on the couch watching reality TV, per usual.

Our new apartment is about the same size as the last but with a bit more living space, which means we spend more time together. After living in a walk-up, we knew we wanted a more modern building, preferably one with a doorman and an elevator. A lot of my coworkers encouraged us to look in Murray Hill and Kips Bay, saying they were popular neighborhoods for postgrads, and Reese's roommate, Blake (also a Pike at Wilmington), pointed us in the direction of a good building. And that's where we landed.

It couldn't be more perfect, honestly. We're walking distance from any bar in Murray Hill, we have laundry in the building, and we have AC that actually works. We're finally living the postgrad life we dreamed of.

"Welcome home!" Lauren greets me. "How was work?"

"Quiet. I can't believe we're one of the only offices open this week. How are the boys?"

Lauren accepted a job as an elementary school teacher in the Bronx when we first moved to the city. She knew it would be hard; she'd make just above minimum wage, and the commute wasn't the best. But the reason she majored in education obviously wasn't for the money; it was to have an impact on underprivileged children.

To pass the time until the school year started, she found a full-time nanny job with the Bauer family. She spent the entire summer with their two five-year-old twin boys, and come Labor Day, she resigned from the teaching job to continue nannying. They feel like her home away from home—on most days anyway.

"Annoying. It's full days with them until school starts again. What do you wanna do for dinner?"

"Will you actually go with me to a work event tonight? It's a launch party for a new skincare brand, and I'm covering it. They'll have passed apps, and I bet their swag bags will be good," I offer.

"You already had me at free food and drinks, but merch? Now I'm a thousand percent in. I'll go get ready."

In my tiny bedroom, I'm able to fit a vanity, which is a necessity since we share a bathroom with a pedestal sink. I take a seat on the stool and look at myself in the mirror. I think back to when I would get ready in college; my face was a little fuller and my eyes a little brighter. After the move and breakup, I lost a little bit of weight. You can tell the most in my face—my cheeks and jaw are more defined now, which I think makes me look more mature. I turn on a playlist as I reapply mascara, blush, and a light coat of lipstick. What seems like seconds into the first song my phone starts vibrating.

Incoming call: Reese Thompson

"Hey," I answer a bit coldly.

"Hey! Busy tonight? I got off earlier than I expected to and was thinking we could try that new cocktail lounge around the corner from my place." I could hear the hustle and bustle of the city in the background, which told me he likely just stepped out of the building.

"There's a collab event tonight I'm roped into. Lauren's coming too," I say, the words clipped.

"Shit, I'm sorry, baby."

Baby. God, I hate pet names. "It's okay, I'll manage."

"Some other time then? Maybe Friday?"

I pause, a beat too long. "We'll see."

"Everything okay?" he asks. "You seem upset."

"Yeah, sorry," I sigh, knowing my feelings *toward* him aren't *about* him. "It's been a long day, and I'm not looking forward to it getting even longer. Let's plan for Friday."

"Well, I hope it gets better. Have a drink to lighten the mood. I'll text you later," he says before hanging up.

I feel a little bad treating Reese like he's done something wrong, because he hasn't. I haven't thought about Ethan in a while until today, and now that I have, it's hard not to. It's hard not to compare my relationship with Reese to the one I had with Ethan. Both are so different. Both guys are so different.

Reese is like no one I've ever met. He's attentive, always makes plans for us, and he's great at communicating. Almost too good at it. Reese is the opposite of Ethan. Things with Reese are simple and fun, which is why I like him. I think that I could maybe love him one day, but I'm just not there yet.

• • •

The party is stunning. Upon arrival, a server hands us each a glass of champagne and a branded card with the night's agenda on it. It's being held at a bar in the Moxy Hotel, and the room is full of life-style, beauty, and fashion editors. I already know it'll be all I'll see on Instagram for the next forty-eight hours.

"I would kill for your job," Lauren says as she reaches for another glass of champagne from the display wall. "Tonight, I'll pretend I'm a big-shot fashion editor. Tomorrow, it'll be back to running around Tribeca with two little gremlins."

"Oh, stop it, they're not gremlins."

"I know, they're so cute. William won his soccer game yesterday and was so proud of himself. I'm sure it will be all he talks about tomorrow." She manages a quick eye roll, followed by a smile. Even though some days are tough, I know deep down she loves her job—it's so very Lauren.

"That sentence just made me feel like we're forty-year-old moms having our monthly ladies' night." I laugh.

"Touché. Let's get martinis and mingle. Who should we talk to first?"

We approach the bar and order two extra dirty martinis, mine with olives and Lauren's without; then I scan to see if I notice any familiar faces.

"I see the head of marketing over in the corner. I'm going to grab a few pictures and a statement from her for our Instagram. Make us some new friends!"

I leave Lauren and nervously walk toward the group of people I only know by association. After an hour of small talk, I find Lauren sitting at the bar wrapped up in conversation.

"Hey, are you ready to go home?" I say, tapping her shoulder.

"I think I'm gonna stay, I have a late start tomorrow morning." She turns to me and throws a slight head nod to the guy sitting next to her. "Text me when you get to the apartment!"

I hand her the rest of my drink, knowing it'll go to waste otherwise, and pull out my phone to call an Uber. There's no way I'm taking the subway this late alone. I'm not that much of a New Yorker yet. The car pulls up to our building, and I notice our doorman perched right behind the double doors. Doormen are one of my favorite things about the city—they make me feel safe, like I'm coming home from a date to my dad waiting up for me on the couch.

"Thanks, Phillip!" I greet him as I step through the open door and into the lobby.

"Pleasure's all mine, Sloane. Want me to get your mail while you're here? Unit 405, correct?" he asks.

"Sure, that'd be great." I pull out my phone to text Lauren that I've made it home when I hear the buzzer that signifies someone is entering the building. Out of instinct, I look up, and my heart immediately sinks to my stomach.

Are my eyes deceiving me? Did someone spike my drink? Am I going insane?

"Hey, Hart."

Something about hearing him speak makes it real. I'd know that voice anywhere. He isn't just a figment of my imagination. Ethan Brady is standing right in front of me, in Manhattan, in my apartment building. I want to run. Turn around and run right back through the front door, or escape into the elevator and stay under my covers for at least five business days. I want to be anywhere but here right now.

"I guess now would be a good time to tell you I moved to New York, and by the looks of it, I moved into your building," he says, barely able to look at me.

"You live here?" I stutter.

Phillip returns and realizes that he interrupted something. He sets my mail at the front desk and walks back to his office.

"I thought you were on the Upper East Side? But yes, Sloane, I live here." I hate how he says my name like he's using it against me.

"That was only ever a six-month sublease until we figured out what area we wanted to be in long term," I state. "How did you end up here?"

I have so many questions, but that's all I can manage to get out.

"Do you know Blake King? He was an older Pike, might have graduated before you started coming around."

Of course I know Blake. He's my boyfriend's roommate. I nod as he continues.

"He suggested it, said he lived here last year before moving to the West Village. I met some guys at work who have been dying to get out of Brooklyn, and we got lucky. We took the last three-bedroom they had available until summer. I really had no idea you lived here."

Anger boils inside of me, but so does something else. Sadness? Heartache? Nostalgia? All of the above? I wasn't quite sure.

"You didn't think to reach out when you accepted a job offer here?" I ask. "A text? A call even? Didn't I deserve that much?"

"I was going to." He sounds genuine. "I wanted to. I didn't know what to say."

"*Hey, Sloane, just wanted to let you know I'm moving to New York?*" I suggest.

"I'm sorry, you're right. I should've said something. I didn't want to open this up again and make it a whole thing." He looks to the ground.

"Well, it's definitely a whole thing now."

This time he looks at me. He finally *looks* at me. It's funny how people don't change. I mean, not really. He still has those same piercing brown eyes that somehow both comfort me and break my heart at the same time. When I stare into them, I see the cotton candy skies that drenched the windows at the mountain house. I see streetlights glistening through the windshield on our drives over the bridge. His eyes make me feel like I'm back in those places, in those exact moments. I miss those moments. I miss him. Even when I know there are a million reasons I shouldn't. How did we end up here?

I turn my back to him and hightail it to the elevator. I feel a lump of emotion work its way to the back of my throat and tears form in my eyes. When I finally reach the fourth floor, I can't hold it in any longer, and I start sobbing. Until Lauren gets home, I sit on the couch in the dark replaying the entire run-in over again in my head. I debate pouring myself a glass of wine, but know that more alcohol will only make the situation worse.

"Oh, Sloane," she says as she walks through the door. "I'm so sorry."

"Why can't I just forget him already? Why does he have to keep popping up in places like our fucking apartment building? I can't be neighbors with him again, Lauren; I can't do it. I can barely stand to see his face without wanting to cry. How is this supposed to work?" I cry.

"Listen to me." Lauren plops down next to me. "I'm gonna be brutally honest here. He's your first love, so you're never going to forget him, not really anyway. A part of you will always love him, but not in the way you used to. In the way that you love an old friend you no longer talk to, in the way you love a restaurant that you can't return to because it closed—it's an empty kind of love. You're happy to have experienced it, and maybe you're sad from time to time that it's over, but you know it wasn't meant to last forever."

"Thanks, Laur." I wipe a tear from my cheek. "Do you think Graham knew? I would've thought he'd warn me."

"At the end of the day, Graham only cares about himself. He's probably too wrapped up in his new girlfriend to think about you and Ethan. But if you're asking me, I'm sure he knew. They're best friends." She stands up.

"You're right." I reach my arm out so she can help me do the same. "I hate both of them so much."

"As you should," she says, only half kidding.

23

Ethan
January 2018

*F*uck.

How are we living in the same building? Isn't this supposed to be the most populated city in America? If she didn't already, she for sure hates me now.

I set my takeout on the counter and don't even feel like eating anymore, which is very unlike me since I never pass up a meal. My roommates, Noah and Alex, are still out, so I strip down to just my boxers in the hall and head into the bathroom. The scalding hot water hits my back as I stand in the stall shower and think about everything Sloane and I have been through the past two years.

After I finish recounting the weirdest two years of my life, I heat up the Chipotle bowl and sit on the couch to eat it. Scrolling Netflix, I realize there's nothing new I haven't watched, so I decide to FaceTime Graham.

"Look who it is!" he answers.

"Is it Ethan? How's the city?" Emily appears from behind Graham with a huge smile.

"Hey, Em," I greet her. "It's fucking cold."

"It's January. Besides that, everything good?" Graham asks. "How's work? Roommates?"

"Work's great; roommates are cool." I pause. "There is one thing though…"

Graham readjusts the phone as if he's now completely dialed in. "What?"

"So, uh, Sloane lives in my building." The name feels like a weight on my tongue.

His mouth hangs open. "You're fucking with me, right?"

"Dude, I wish. King suggested this place to me; must be pretty popular."

"Wait, Blake King?" Graham asks, still in disbelief.

"Yeah, I hit him up before I moved here, asking for apartment recs."

"No way… King is Sloane's boyfriend's roommate, you idiot."

"Blake King and Reese Thompson are roommates?" I'm confused. "I knew Sloane and Reese were a thing, but I didn't realize the boys still keep in touch."

He laughs, shaking his head. "You really need to start using social media more. You wouldn't have even known known she had a boyfriend if I hadn't told you. So are you and Sloane gonna talk about it?"

"Probably not." I shrug.

"I don't get you, man."

I throw him a smile, "Neither do I."

We hang up and I stare at the blank TV screen. I wonder where Noah and Alex are. I shoot a text to our group chat, hoping if they're out they'll stay there for a while. I could use a drink.

• • •

"There he is!" Noah waves me down. "Grab a beer from the bucket; you've got winner."

Darts are such a New York City thing. I don't think even one bar in Wilmington has them, at least none I've been to.

"So how's your first official week in the city? Work kicking your ass yet?" Alex asks.

"It's going. Luckily not yet," I reply.

"Screw you, Alex," Noah says, pulling the darts from the board. "Brady, you're up."

"Anyone ever tell you that you're a sore loser?" Alex mocks Noah.

"Every damn day."

Despite living here for exactly eight days, I can already tell I'm going to like it. I never pictured myself as a city guy, but I also never thought I'd land a job like this. I was grateful to the Clarks for providing me with a family and a life I didn't think I was worthy of. I've always been afraid of it, but I think I'm realizing that change is a good thing. A really good thing.

24

Sloane

February 2018

Reese smiles at me from across the table and then takes a sip from his wineglass. I move around the lettuce on my plate while he rambles on about new clients. I'm surprised that he hasn't realized how checked out I've been all night.

It's Valentine's Day. I've never celebrated this day with anyone, except Lauren of course. He made this reservation three months in advance, sent a dozen roses to my office, and was waiting outside of my building when I got off work. I can't help but feel like I'm betraying him.

Since I found out that Ethan's my neighbor, I've been questioning my relationship with Reese. He has no idea about any of this, because I wanted to give myself time to process it all. It's been a little over a month, and I still can't bring myself to tell him. Things with Reese are easy in a way they never were with Ethan. Our relationship is secure and predictable. So why doesn't it feel like enough?

"After this deal closes, I want to take you out of the city for a weekend," he says. "We haven't been on a trip together yet."

"That would be nice," I say as I put my napkin over the hardly eaten salad.

"Where should we go? Somewhere warm?"

"Yes! Somewhere with a beach. I miss the beach."

"Did you not like your food? Order something else," he offers.

"I'm not that hungry; I had a late lunch." I hate lying to him. Reese has become familiar. I've gotten used to falling asleep next to him at night. I like the way he smells fresh out of the shower and how it feels when he wraps his arms around me. We spend weeknights ordering in and weekends exploring the city. He gives me the kind of relationship I convinced myself for so long that I wasn't deserving of.

"I was thinking we could go back to Wilmington. My parents usually spend the spring at our rental in Kure Beach, and I'd really like you to meet them."

The wine, mixed with my overwhelming sense of shock, causes me to swallow wrong, and I start coughing. I can't go back to Wilmington with him. I haven't even been back there myself since graduation. That entire town has Ethan written all over it. It's where I fell in love for the first and last time.

"Sorry, wrong pipe I guess." I lift the napkin to my mouth. "That could be fun."

"Think on it. I'll go wherever you want." He smiles and motions for the server to bring the check. "Should we stay at your place tonight? I feel bad that you've been coming to mine a lot. Work should slow down soon."

"We can do yours again; my sheets are still in the dryer." Here I go again, lying.

I can't bear the thought of sleeping under the same roof as Ethan with Reese in my bed. Something about it just feels…wrong.

On the few-and-far-between nights that I've slept at my own apartment, I've lain in bed wondering if he's staring at the same ceiling fan that I am. It's like looking at the stars knowing the person you're missing shares the same sky as you, wondering if when they look up, you come to their mind too.

I just can't seem to comprehend how this has happened. Over eight million people live in this fucking city, and I wind up living in the same building as the only guy that's ever broken my heart. How is that possible? At first, I thought maybe it was a sign. Maybe we were meant to be. I quickly realized that sometimes not every coincidence or run-in at the grocery store must mean something. Sometimes, you really do end up in the same place at the same time as someone you don't want to see by chance. And there are two ways to handle it.

Option one: convince yourself this was on purpose and try to figure out said purpose.

Option two: realize it was a coincidence and continue with your life.

I sleep at Reese's for the rest of the week to avoid the thought of Ethan. When I'm in this bubble, alone with Reese, things are great. When I'm by myself is when I start to spiral.

• • •

"Brought you coffee, baby." I open my eyes to Reese sitting on the edge of his bed, stroking my arm to wake me. "I've gotta get to that cycling thing with the guys, but let me know what you get into tonight. We can all meet up."

He leaves a key on the counter for me, and I roll over in his bed. Sometimes, it feels wrong to be here. To know that he likes me more than I like him. I reach over to the nightstand for my phone as it starts vibrating in my hand.

"Hello?" I answer without looking at who it is.

"I haven't seen you all week! It feels like I live alone now. Brunch?" Lauren asks. "A few of the girls from my nanny group are meeting in Midtown and added us to the res. Can you be home and ready in an hour?"

"Yeah, I'll see you in a few." I hang up and quickly get out of bed. I brush my teeth with the pink electric toothbrush Reese bought for me, which matches his blue one. I'm wearing one of his T-shirts paired with the leftover mascara that I was too lazy to take off last night. I sigh as I stare at the confused girl who looks back at me in the mirror.

Why can't I just be content with him? Is love being content with someone? I know that love isn't settling just because the person you're with loves you the way you've always loved other people. I fully believe that for a relationship to last a lifetime, you both need to be infatuated with each other. And as much as I try, sometimes I worry that I'll never feel that way about Reese.

Lauren and I walk into brunch less than five minutes late, which is record time for her. Usually, whatever time Lauren says we're leaving is delayed by at least twenty minutes. That time consists of at least four outfit changes, misplacing her phone or ID, and touching up her makeup. I don't consider myself a patient person, but with Lauren, I have to be. I don't mind waiting on her, well, most days anyway.

"Here they are!" one of the girls announces our entrance. "Brunch officially starts now."

In the city bottomless brunch gets timed. Typically, you have about one and a half to two hours per table, so you can't sit there all day with a fifty-dollar tab. Servers have to make money somehow, and bottomless brunch and tips from drunk patrons is how they do it. Not even a few minutes into brunch, I get a text from Annie, which is out of character for a Saturday afternoon.

1:07 p.m.

Annie Walker: Hate to ask but any chance you can go to Boston this week to speak on a panel for me? Kids are sick. LMK.

A wave of relief washes over me. I can't wait for a few days away from the city. I can't think of a better way to clear my head. I've never been to Boston. I'd love to explore the city on my own.

"Who's that? Reese?" Lauren gushes over him.

"No, it's work. I have to go to Boston this week to fill in for Annie at a conference."

"Boo." She pouts and furrows her eyebrows.

One of the girls interrupts us. "Let's hit the Lower East Side next! I bet we can find some good live music there."

We head to the subway after hitting our time limit at brunch. I've already had a lot to drink but figure one or two more couldn't hurt. Besides Lauren and Mila, I don't have any friends in the city. When we first moved here, I was putting all my effort into work and long distance with Ethan. Once that ended, I was focused on work and getting over Ethan. I wish I realized the importance of making friends in such a big city.

We find a dive bar and spend the next few hours playing darts and listening to cover bands. I'm a few more drinks in when I feel my phone vibrating in my back pocket. I let it go to voicemail and see that I have three unread text messages from him.

7:39 p.m.

Reese Thompson: We're pregaming Gem in a bit

9:17 p.m.

Reese Thompson: In the back by dance floor

9:45 p.m.

Reese Thompson: Miss you baby

Those texts make me want to take a shot. Something about the amount of alcohol I'm drinking makes me want to think of Ethan and forget about Reese. It's fucked up, I know. I can't help it. Before putting my phone away again, I check social media to see if Ethan's posted any stories today. Nothing. Maybe I should just reach out to him? I'm fighting an internal battle that I know I can't vocalize to Lauren because she'll tell me not to text him. Which is exactly what I shouldn't do.

Yet, I hit send anyway.

• • •

Less than an hour later, I'm in Ethan's apartment, which is just a few floors above my own. Stepping inside feels like crossing into a past life—it's Ascent all over again. I settle on the couch, its worn leather cold against the bare skin of my legs. Even though it's the height of winter, my favorite going-out outfit combination is a skirt, tights, bodysuit, and tall boots. Thank god for New York City coat checks. I survey his apartment, the mismatched furniture that he probably snagged off the curb, two TVs set up for a football fanatic's dream, and blank walls that I'm sure will never be filled.

"Want a drink?" Ethan's voice, calm and familiar, calls out from the kitchen.

"Sure," I answer, my voice steadier than I feel. My limit was several drinks ago.

"All I've got is whiskey," he says.

I accept the glass and give myself a moment to watch him. He chooses a spot on the opposite end of the sectional—making us feel worlds apart in the tiny universe of his living room. It's as if he's respecting the boundaries that have grown between us, yet everything in me leans towards erasing them. I take a sip, and it burns all the way down.

"I'm sorry again, for all of this," he says, breaking the silence that has settled comfortably around us.

"It's okay; you didn't know," I reassure him, as I always do.

"I mean, I knew you lived in the city. The least I could've done was text you."

"You're not wrong." I nod.

"So why'd you text me?" he asks. "Was that all you wanted? An apology and a free drink?"

I hesitate, the truth swirling in my glass. "Can't answer that."

"Why not?" He raises an eyebrow.

"This isn't my first drink tonight, Ethan." I laugh and playfully wave around my drink until a few drops of whiskey wind up in my lap.

"Alright, alright. Give me that." He scoots closer and reaches for the glass. For a moment, everything but us falls away.

"No way!" I protest.

I tilt my body away from his, holding the glass as high and as far away from his reach as I can get. Ethan grabs it and places it on the coffee table while positioning his body on top of mine. He's closer now, his presence a gravitational pull that I'm not sure I want to escape.

"Can I ask you something else then?" he inquires, sitting back a little.

"Sure," I answer with more of a question than a statement.

He hesitates before continuing. "So…the article."

A lump starts to form in the back of my throat.

"You had to assume I'd read it. I mean, that's why you wrote it. Right?" Ethan continues.

"I don't know." I sit back onto the couch, hoping to sink in between the cushions and escape this conversation. "It started off as a way to stop myself from reaching out. I wrote to you all the time. In my journal, in the notes app, in texts that I would just backspace. It was like therapy. I didn't intend to publish it ever, but one day I just decided to pitch it to Annie, and well, I'm glad I did. I just didn't think that many people, or you, would read it."

"Yeah…" His voice trailed off.

"I'm sorry."

"Sloane," he whispers. "You have nothing to be sorry for. I'm the one that's sorry. I've hated myself for so long for what I did to you. I never wanted to hurt you."

"I know. The sad part is, as much as I tried, I couldn't hate you. I don't think I'll ever be able to hate you."

In an instant, his hand grips my thigh, and his face is within inches of mine. My cheeks go flush, and my heart rate quickens. This is what Ethan does to me every time.

"Hi," I say nervously.

"Hi," he says into my hair. "Is this okay?"

I remember when I was his and he didn't have to ask if what he was doing was okay—he could just do it because he knew that I wanted him to. I also remember that now I'm someone else's. Someone who's kind. Someone who's caring. Someone who would never do what Ethan did to me. Someone who loves me.

"No," I find the strength to say, pulling back from him. "I'm sorry. I don't know what I'm doing here. I should've never come."

The space between us grows, not just in inches, but in the realization that some distances can't be measured. The whiskey remains on the table as I stand to leave, the taste of regret and what-ifs lingering on my tongue. I grab my purse and walk towards the front door, waiting for him to tell me to stop. He doesn't. Of course he doesn't. I reach for the handle and still nothing. As it closes behind me, a tear falls down my cheek. How am I back here again? After months of moving on, and I am right back to feeling the same way I did the morning he left for the airport.

I head down the single flight of stairs that lead to my apartment and pull out my phone to call Reese.

"Hey!" he shouts over loud music.

"Can you come over?"

"I thought you'd never ask. Unlock the door; I'm on my way." He hangs up.

I change into my favorite matching sweat set and freshen up so he can't tell that I had been crying. As I wipe the mascara from under my eyes, I stare at my reflection in the same way I did this morning and wonder who I've become. I'm in love with someone who can't love me back and has told me that more times than I can count. Reese is sure about me. His feelings for me have never wavered, and that's all I've ever wanted. I remind myself of that until it's engrained in me.

"Sloane?" Reese calls out.

"In here!"

He sits on my bed and reaches his arms out, motioning for me to join him. I stand in between his legs and place both of my hands on his shoulders. His hands rest on my waist, and he looks up at me, waiting for me to kiss him. Kissing Reese is different than kissing Ethan. It's more gentle and less passionate.

I kiss him harder and wait for his mouth to follow. He catches up and slides one hand under the front of my shirt. Then I feel his other move up my back and unclasp my bra before maneuvering it and my sweatshirt off me. Finally, he takes charge. I move from his lap and lie on the bed, wiggling my pants and underwear past my ankles as he leans over to grab a condom from my bedside table. I never used condoms with Ethan, but Reese almost always insists.

Sex with Reese is fine. Just that—fine. Sometimes I think about Ethan while I'm having sex with Reese. It's fucked up, I know, but I can't help it. Tonight is one of those times.

I often wonder if I'll ever feel the things that I felt with Ethan ever again. Is that the kind of love you only get once in your life? I reinsert myself into the present moment right as Reese is about to finish, and I almost wish I hadn't.

"I love you, baby," he whispers between breaths. This is the second time he's told me without waiting for me to reciprocate it. I grasp his body tighter and lightly dig my teeth into his shoulder to avoid having to respond right away. I need to delay a response for as long as I possibly can.

He pulls back and kisses me before plopping his body next to mine. We lie there for a few minutes before I get up to go to the bathroom.

"Wait, not yet." He grabs my arm and tries to pull me back towards him.

"I have to pee."

I apologetically kiss his forearm and search for a shirt to wear before heading to the bathroom. I run the faucet water so Reese can't hear that I'm not using the bathroom as I stare at myself in the mirror. Partially ashamed but mostly confused.

"You good?" Reese asks as he knocks on the door. I flush the toilet and turn the doorknob to let him in.

"Had to wash my face," I said, hoping the water had erased more than just the physical traces of a night I'm not too proud of.

"Come to bed," he says, not a command but a plea wrapped in two words.

He grabs both of my hands and pulls me so that my body is flush with his. His hands then find their way to my hips and then my butt. He hoists me up and carries me the entire twenty steps to my room. I think I could love him. But as we nestle into the warmth of my sheets, the inches between our bodies feel like miles.

"Is there something wrong?" Reese asks.

"No, why would there be?" I'm a little too quick to answer, wondering if he has any idea where I was just an hour ago.

The bed shifts as he turns, the streetlights outside casting stripes across the room, revealing a hint of concern on his face. "I didn't want to bring this up, but I've told you I love you twice now, and you haven't said it back. I was giving you some time, but I feel like we should talk about it."

I turn around so that I'm facing him. Even though the room is dark, the streetlights shine through the blinds, allowing us to somewhat see each other's faces. I don't know how to answer his question, so I rely on yet another lie.

"Both times have been during sex. I want to say it when I feel it in a different moment."

"Shit, I'm sorry, baby. I love you all the time, not just during sex." His hands cradle my face, his thumbs tracing the line of my jaw as he pulls me into a kiss filled with the words I'm not ready to say.

• • •

"Where should we go for breakfast?" Reese wakes me up by rubbing his fingers over my cheek.

"I'm not that hungry." It's true. Since Ethan's been back, I haven't had much of an appetite. My anxiety doesn't let me.

"What if I said I was able to get us reservations at La Mercerie in an hour?" he says.

"Seriously?" The word escapes me in a half whisper, half gasp, as I prop myself up on my elbows.

There's a playful twinkle in his eye as he responds, the corners of his mouth lifting into a smile. "Go get ready," he laughs.

We've been trying to get a reservation there for weeks now. In college, Reese studied abroad and said that La Mercerie was the closest thing on the East Coast to French bakeries. So of course, I need to make sure he isn't overexaggerating.

As the elevator doors glide open, a moment I never wanted to experience unfolds in what feels like slow motion. Reese's hand is warm in mine, until my gaze lifts—and there, like a statue, stands

Ethan. The air thickens, and I feel my stomach cramp up. I don't do well in awkward situations, especially not ones in which I'm lying to someone I care about. I never did find the right time to tell him about my new neighbor.

Our steps are synchronized as we silently pass by Ethan. I'm holding my breath and still holding on to Reese's hand, hoping that this bout of silence never ends. But silence, much like the truth, is a fragile thing.

Reese's grip tightens imperceptibly, the edges of his fingers pressing into my skin—a silent indicator of the anger he clearly feels. We step out into the crisp morning, and the city sounds rush to fill the void between us. It's only when Reese drops my hand and his voice cuts through the air that I realize how upset he truly is.

"Really, Sloane? You're kidding me, right?" His voice escalates as he opens the car door for me.

"I can expl—"

The interruption comes quickly, his words cutting me off, "I'm not doing this with you. This is fucking pathetic. Why is he here?" He hammers me with questions in the confined space of the Uber.

"Stop." I nod subtly towards the driver, whose discomfort is palpable.

"Stop trying to distract me from the fact that we just ran into your ex in the building that you live in. Why was he there Sloane?" He's yelling now.

"I guess your bestie, Blake, didn't tell you?" I match his tone because now I'm mad too. If it weren't for Blake, none of us would be in this mess. "He helped Ethan find a place."

"Shit." He hangs his head in defeat. "I don't think Blake knows about you two having history. How long have you known? Why haven't you told me?"

"I just found out. I ran into him in the lobby a few days ago," I lie.

Days, weeks, what's the difference? In the rearview mirror, I catch a glimpse of the driver's wary eyes, and I wonder what he's thinking.

Silence settles over us and I focus my eyes on the city as it passes us by. Coffee shops and restaurants we love, corners we've kissed on, crosswalks we've held hands at. Is this the end of us? If it is, I deserve it, I guess.

"I'm sorry." He exhales. "I'm probably overreacting. It just felt like a punch to the gut when you said you knew he lived here and didn't tell me. I hate that I found out like this."

"I know." My voice is soft. I place my hand gently on his thigh as a peace offering. "I'm sorry too. I honestly was trying to avoid the thought of him entirely. I didn't think about how it would make you feel, and I should have."

"It's okay. I shouldn't have gotten so angry." He picks my hand up and intertwines his fingers with mine. "I love you, you know that, right?"

"I love you too."

I finally say it, and I don't think it's a lie. The thought of losing him makes me realize that maybe I am falling in love with him. I squeeze his hand, and then he kisses my forehead.

Three words can change so much. Three words can make you completely forgive someone and forget why you were upset with them in the first place. Three words can make you feel like the most important person in the world, and to Reese, I was. I knew that.

25

Sloane

February 2018

I've always found peace in traveling alone. I love getting to the airport a little early, even though I breeze through security with PreCheck. My typical routine has been to find a bar and order a glass of sauvignon blanc and a side of fries while I people-watch and catch up on work. I feel inspired watching the planes take off and land, wondering who's in them, where they're going, or where they'd rather be.

I pay my bill and make my way through the terminal to find my gate. Somehow, in a sea of people waiting to go to Boston, I manage to snag a seat. I'm scrolling on my phone, waiting for boarding to start, when I see the post—Graham proposed to Emily.

Their story is a sweet one. They met at the Clark family's company party, where her dad is the head of marketing. The next morning, Graham sent me a text saying he'd met his wife. In the moment I laughed it off, but now I know he was serious. I can't believe some people just know that easily. I wonder if that was the feeling that jolted through my body the moment that I met Ethan or if that was just my body's way of telling me to stay far away from him. I'm so happy for them, but I can't help but feel a little nostalgic and sad. I pictured Graham's wedding day going so much differently.

Ethan and I would be sharing a hotel room. I'd be putting on my dress while he was just getting in the shower. He'd blast Frank Sinatra and sing at an unreasonable volume because it always made me laugh. He'd try to dance with me, and I'd playfully push him off, careful that he didn't mess up my hair or makeup. I'd still let him kiss me though. I always let him kiss me. Well, until last weekend that is.

"Now boarding group five," the gate agent's voice echoes over the speaker.

I'm thrown back into reality, grab my bag, and head for the line. I scan my boarding pass and find my way to seat 13A. I always choose a window seat, and I used to wonder if that would have to change if I traveled with Ethan. Would I get comfortable in the middle seat? Or would we be that couple that sits across the aisle from each other? Now I'll never know. How is it that he's still such a prominent part of memories that I'm not even making with him?

Halfway through the flight, I get bored enough to start clearing out my camera roll, so I click to the top of the album. It shoots me up to my first-ever iCloud photos, which happen to be senior year move-in day. I usually try to avoid looking back at photos of Ethan and me, but sometimes late at night after I've had a few glasses of wine, the heartbreak convinces me to scroll through the pictures that I can't get myself to delete. Today it decides to strike midafternoon.

Swiping through the memories stored on my phone, I watch our story unfold. A blurry shot of the boys sitting on our couch the first night we hung out, playing cards. A selfie of Lauren and Graham while Ethan photobombed in the background. The first picture we ever took of just the two of us on my twenty-second birthday. It's all here. It's so easy to look back and romanticize the good. The laughs, the kisses, the dates, the road trips. But what about the fights? The screaming, the crying, the nights he stormed out of the room and retreated to his own bed. Never documented, hardly discussed. It's like they never existed. It's easy to remember the good moments when they're all we want to see.

On this plane, in the weeds of pictures I wish never existed, something in me finally breaks. This wasn't how we were supposed to be. I was supposed to be flying home to him while we were figuring out long distance. Instead, I am consuming him through old memories. I hate that I have to disturb my seat neighbors as I excuse myself to go to the bathroom, and I try not to grip the headrests of other people's seats as I make my way to the front of the airplane. I lock myself in the bathroom and lay my head in my hands. Good thing it's a short flight.

• • •

My alarm goes off earlier than usual, and I lie there for a few minutes before the day starts. I look around the cold modern hotel room and try to remember when I used to dream about having a job like mine and traveling on my own. That thought and the craving for a vanilla latte gets me out of bed and into the shower. I'm still surprised that Annie chose me to present for her at this year's Boston Writers Workshop, but I'm sure it was because my open letter still holds *The Gist* title for most read this year.

There's a Starbucks in the hotel lobby, so I stop there before I head to the conference. If I weren't running late, I would find a local coffee spot, but this will have to do. Boston in February is even worse than New York, which I didn't know was possible. I can barely feel my hands even with gloves on while holding my hot coffee. Luckily the conference center is only a block away, so I don't have to go too far. I feel my phone ringing in the pocket of my trench coat, and I reach for it.

"Hello?" I answer.

"Morning, baby," Reese says on the other line. "I wasn't sure if I'd catch you. How are you feeling today?"

"I'm good. Pretty nervous, but I'm excited. I've been reciting everything basically since the moment I left the city. I'm running late though, and I'm just walking up, so I might have to go," I explain, the words tumbling out in a frantic stream.

"I know," he says, his voice a calm contrast to mine.

"What do you mean, you know?" I adjust the bag on my shoulder and look up to make sure I'm about to enter the right building.

"I'm here," Reese reveals over the phone, and as my eyes lift to verify his claim, there he is, standing in the lobby right in front of me.

"What are you doing here?" The question comes out in a startled gasp, while his arms wrap around me in a grounding embrace.

"I got on the first flight out this morning. I told my boss I'd work from our Boston office tomorrow and meet some clients for him if he gave me the morning to travel. I have some calls, but I blocked my calendar during your session so I could sit in. Think of it as an early birthday gift."

"You didn't have to do that," I say, touched by his thoughtfulness and feeling even more guilty for not admitting the full truth about Ethan.

"I wanted to. I feel bad about the way I handled things over the weekend, and I know how much this means to you, so I wanted to come and cheer you on. Plus, picturing you giving a presentation onstage turned me on a bit." His words are playful.

"Oh, stop it." I blush. "I have to go check in and prepare. Will you be okay on your own until I'm done?"

"Yeah, I'll work from the coffee shop across the street and make my way back over around ten thirty. Your portion will be about an hour, right? Do you have to stay for the others, or will you have time to get lunch after? I haven't been to Boston in years, but I have some spots I want to show you."

"I'm yours for lunch and dinner," I promise before kissing him on the cheek and heading toward the front desk.

You know those little moments you long for in relationships? This was one of those. I always wanted someone to surprise me. Whether it was knocking on my door unannounced, sending flowers to my office just because, or showing up at a special event I wasn't expecting them at. Reese showing up makes me feel important.

A few hours later, I present Annie's slides on the importance of storytelling, which I helped her create, and make sure to put my own personality into them. In college, I never understood a lot of what was taught to me in class, so I made sure to make the presentation relatable and easy to understand. I used my article "An Open Letter to the Guy Who Didn't Want to Date Me" as an example. The reason it gained so much momentum almost overnight wasn't just that it's a topic that was often written or talked about, but because I was vulnerable. I told my story and left the rest up to fate.

I walk back into the lobby to find Reese on a bench right outside of the doors.

"Baby, you crushed it." He grabs my face and kisses me. "Seriously, what a boss."

I'm surprised he's so supportive of a piece of content that's about someone he despises.

"Okay, okay. Calm down," I say in a giggly tone, even though I don't want him to stop.

"Just saying, I'm proud of you. It's cool to see how passionate you are about work." He nudges me. "Now, let's explore. And celebrate of course."

"What about your meetings?"

"I pushed them. We're here; let's take advantage of it." He grins.

I don't consider myself a spontaneous person. I'm a planner, and I like to be able to prepare for whatever lies ahead, but something comes over me. Before we find a place for lunch, we drop off his suitcase in my hotel room. I chose to stay in Seaport because that's where the panel is being held, but I knew Reese would want to show me around downtown and take me to his favorite spots. I'm not as much of a foodie as he is, so I usually just follow along and trust that whatever reservations he makes are good.

We get to the door of my hotel room, and a wave of spontaneity washes over me. I unlock the door as Reese follows me in and sets his things near the closet. I come up from behind him and wrap my arms around his stomach.

"Someone's in a good mood." He turns around, and I stare up at him with a look in my eye that I hope says, *Kiss me.*

He towers over me, and in this moment, I realize that I love how tall he is. His lips come down over mine, and I completely lose my train of thought.

Reese gently pushes me up against the wardrobe doors and continues to kiss me but with more force this time. I push against him, and my mouth follows his motions until he pulls away and leads me toward the bed.

We simultaneously undress, and I motion for Reese to lie on the bed as I make my way on top of him. At this moment, I need to feel in control.

After, I kiss him, and then we lie next to each other, breathing heavily in silence.

I pick up my pants off the floor and fold them as I try to remember what other clothes I packed for this trip so I don't have to wear slacks for the rest of day. I sort through my suitcase and pull out my favorite pair of jeans and a chunky neutral turtleneck—the perfect cold-weather outfit.

"Your phone's been going off." Reese hands it to me as he slides his belt through a loop on the waistband of his dark blue slacks. I swipe it from him to see I have four missed calls from Lauren.

"What the fuck!" she shouts into the phone.

Reese looks at me with an *Are you okay?* expression on his face, and I nod as I brace myself for the conversation that I know is about to unfold.

"You saw the post?" I assume.

"You knew? Why didn't you call me? Or even text?" Lauren's slightly angrier than I would've expected.

"I saw it when I was turning my phone on airplane mode and then had two glasses of wine on the flight, so by the time I landed, I think I forgot it happened. I'm so sorry, Laur."

"It's fine. I mean, it's not fine but I get it. I can't believe this! They've been dating, what, a little over a year? We're only twenty-three; what's the rush in getting engaged?" she spirals. "Oh my god, do you think she's pregnant?"

"I doubt she's pregnant. I think he's just ready to settle down. Plus, you know his family. They're so by the book that if they can't live together until marriage, this was probably the next step."

"Did you know it was happening?"

"No, I had no idea."

"That makes me feel better." I hear her sigh. I can't imagine how she feels, and I hope I never have to. "How'd today go? When are you coming home? I miss you."

"It was great! I just got back to the room, and I'm about to go grab something to eat, but I'll be back tomorrow. Let's go out?" I suggest.

I hold off on mentioning Reese surprising me in Boston because it doesn't seem like the right time to bring it up.

"A bestie date? I'm in. I'll make us a dinner res, and then we can hit the bars. Love you. Hopefully, tonight isn't too miserable. Try somewhere besides the hotel restaurant!"

Lauren knows I hate going out to eat by myself; it just makes me feel so alone. I look across the room at Reese, who's patiently waiting for me with no complaints.

"I will. Love you too." I hang up and let out a sigh I hadn't realized I'd been holding in.

"Time for lunch now?" Reese asks, heading for the door.

As I follow him down the hall, I can't help but wonder what Ethan thinks about Graham getting engaged. Is he thinking about me, the same way that I'm thinking about him?

• • •

I get back to the city the next day still not knowing what it's like to travel with a significant other, since Reese stayed in Boston for work. In a way, I'm kind of glad. The Uber driver pulls my suitcase out of the trunk, and I thank him for the ride before greeting Phillip at our door.

"You've got some out-of-town guests this week, I hear?" he says.

"Do we?" I wonder if Lauren invited the girls from her nanny group out with us. Guess I'll find out soon enough.

"Have a good night, Sloane." He nods, leaving my question hanging in the air.

I continue through the lobby and up the elevator. As the doors open and I step out onto the third floor, I hear loud music and laughter coming from our side of the hallway. At least Lauren's in a better mood than when I last talked to her. I unlock our front door and see a pair of shoes under our entryway table that I don't recognize.

"I'm home!" I announce myself.

"Is that Sloane?" a familiar female voice says from around the corner. It takes me a second to recognize who it is.

"Jordan!" I drop my bags and run into the kitchen. "Holy shit, what are you doing here?"

"Someone had to come to pick up the pieces, am I right?" She motions over toward Lauren as we all laugh. "But also, I'm here for your early birthday celebration!"

"It's a roomie reunion!" Lauren chimes in, grinning from ear to ear.

I take off down the hall to get ready and catch up to their level of drunk. In my bedroom, I throw open the suitcase and pull out my favorite pair of jeans, which probably need a wash, but I decide they can make it one more night without one. I stare into the small abyss that is my closet and try to decide on a top to wear before I settle on a black bodysuit. Another go-to. I pull the outfit together with a pair of black ankle boots and touch up my makeup before heading back to the kitchen to pregame.

A weekend with Lauren and Jordan brings me a cocktail of emotions—mostly excitement and anxiety. I've been trying so hard to move on from the person I was in college. I want to make new memories, fall in love, and stop comparing everything to Ethan. With Jordan here, that feels impossible.

"Are you okay?" Jordan whispers to me.

"Just exhausted from traveling," I lie. "I'm so excited you're here though!"

"I've missed you guys so much. Wilmington isn't the same without you," she replies.

"Move to the city, J! Haven't you seen those people who fit like five roommates into a two-bedroom apartment using flex walls? We could totally do that." I can't tell if Lauren's being serious or not.

"Maybe I'll consider it next year. I'd rather not have a flex wall for a bedroom and hear both of you having sex all the time. Speaking of which, Lauren sort of filled me in. Ethan? Living in this building? So bizarre." Jordan turns to me.

I run them both through the awkward elevator encounter between Reese and Ethan, how mad Reese was after, and then his surprising me on my work trip. When I say it out loud, my life doesn't really sound that bad. I'll admit, it isn't. Bad, I mean. If only they knew what I am actually feeling. Usually I'd tell them, but tonight doesn't seem like the right time. Tonight is about Lauren.

"Second date says that him and some friends will meet us out!" Lauren announces. The look on Jordan's face says she's more than confused. "Anywhere in particular you want to try, J? If not, the early-birthday girl can choose."

"*Second date* is his nickname," I explain, while shaking my head no to her question. "He's the only guy in the city who's made it to a second date. What's his real name again?"

"Miles, but let's not get ahead of ourselves."

Jordan and I shoot each other wide eyes and a smile. I have a feeling this is more than a second date to Lauren, and I think Jordan does too.

• • •

The line at Flying Cock isn't long, so we breeze through. Miles orders a round of tequila shots with orange slices, and I can tell why Lauren likes him so much. Not only is he tall, built, and good looking, but he takes care of her and her friends. To Lauren, that is nonnegotiable.

"Let's get another shot." Jordan links her arm with mine and pulls me towards the bar. "What's the deal with Miles's friend?"

"Which one? I don't really know any of them, but I can try to find out," I reply.

"The shorter one," she says. "You don't know them? Haven't you all been out together?"

Now I'm in my head. Have I been a shitty friend to Lauren? I don't know Miles, I wasn't there for her when Graham announced his proposal, and I can't even name any of the people she's been spending time with the last few weeks.

I've been so caught up in the Ethan and Reese saga that I've been putting everyone else on the back burner. I told myself that once I got into a relationship this was something I'd never do.

Yet here I am, doing just that.

"Honestly, I haven't spent much time with them. Let's go mingle! We can introduce ourselves, and I'm sure Lauren will set you up." Jordan follows as I walk through the crowd.

Three hours, two drinks, and one more shot later, I find myself in line for the bathroom checking my phone for any new messages. None. I walk back to the corner where we've been stationed all night and notice the group has dwindled.

"We're gonna head back to his," Lauren whispers. "I think J is hitting it off with Miles's friend, so we'll offer to take them back with us. Do you want to come?"

"I think I'm good. I'm getting tired, so I'll get a ride home and save myself for tomorrow. Brunch?"

"Definitely brunch."

Soon enough, I'm the last person from our group at the bar. I head to the bathroom one last time before walking home. I pull out the pair of gloves I always keep in my coat pocket and shove my hands into them. As I walk down 3rd Avenue, I can't help but think about the time Ethan came to visit. He was so overwhelmed by the city, I thought he hated it. Now he lives here. How is that possible? I know I shouldn't, but I dial his number.

"Yes, Hart?" He answers quicker than I expect him to.

"Will you come get me? I'm trying to walk home from Flying Cock, and I think I'm going the wrong way. I can never follow the walking directions Apple Maps gives." My voice wavers, wondering if I should hang up.

"Where are you? What do you see?" His questions come rapid-fire.

"I'm near a laundromat and a Duane Reade." I clutch the phone a little tighter.

"That's less than helpful. Drop a pin?" His tone is practical, grounding.

"Alright." I unlock my phone and follow his directions. "Done."

"Stay there, I'll meet you," he assures me.

Within minutes, I'm face-to-face with Ethan Brady, unsure what to feel and how to act. My entire body lights up when I see him. How is anyone supposed to compete with this feeling? It's impossible.

"You shouldn't be walking home alone. Where's Lauren?" he asks.

"They all left before me." I continue walking, and he follows.

I pray that he doesn't bring up Reese, because I already know what I'm doing is wrong. I don't want to think about hurting him. In this moment, all I want to think about is Ethan. I want to pretend that we're back where we were the night before he got on a flight back to Wilmington. I want to pick up where we left off like we never ended, because in my mind, we never really did.

"So where's Reese?"

There it is.

"He's away for work." I bite my tongue, wishing we were talking about anything or anyone else.

"How'd that get rekindled anyway?" His question is gentle, yet it unearths a feeling I don't want to face.

"Do we really have to do this?" I plead, not just for a change in conversation but for a break from my own conscience.

He pauses. "No, I guess we don't."

As we approach our building, a knot of anxiety tightens in my stomach. I can't shake the feeling of Phillip's silent judgment, even though he's nowhere to be seen. The anxious feeling disappears as we call for the elevator and the doors open instantly. Saved by the bell.

Ethan and I step inside a space that seems far too intimate for comfort. My heart rate increases as the doors slide shut, sealing us inside. I reach out to press the button for the fourth floor, and Ethan does the same, aiming for the sixth. In a moment that almost feels choreographed, our hands touch.

Then, without warning, Ethan's hand moves from the button to my wrist, his grip firm but comfortable. In one swift motion, he steps closer, pinning me gently against the cold metal wall of the elevator. Our faces are inches apart, our breath mingling, his eyes searching mine for a sign, any sign to tell him it's okay. Is it okay? I can't breathe, let alone think, with him this close.

"Yours or mine, Hart?"

Suddenly, we're twenty-one again in the parking lot of Ascent, and Ethan is asking me the same question right before we go home together for the first time. I would give anything to go back and tell us how it all plays out. I'm just not sure that would change anything.

The elevator dings, announcing my floor, and I muster up the courage to say exactly what I'm thinking.

"Mine."

It's a bold move, fueled by a mix of fear and desire. I pull him with me, my fingers laced with his, leading him out of the elevator and down the hallway to my apartment.

Anticipation runs through me as I fumble with my keys, my hands betraying the casual demeanor I'm trying to maintain. I remind myself that this is my doing, things are on my terms, and I'm in control of this moment—sort of. Ethan Brady still has me wrapped around his finger, and I know that he knows it too.

"This layout is different than ours. You guys have a lot more space," he comments as soon as we step into the apartment.

"I bet they're both the same size. You probably just got screwed on living space since you have that third bedroom," I point out. "Do you want a drink?"

"Not really," he responds.

"Let's go to my room," I suggest. We both know this is wrong, yet he follows me and stands in the doorway surveying the bedroom.

"Going somewhere?" he asks, pointing at the suitcase on the floor, which looks like it's been ransacked.

"No, I got back today," I say, brushing off the question.

Settling back on the bed somehow feels too intimate and yet not intimate enough. I invite him to join me with a pat on the comforter.

"Can I ask you something?"

"Is that why you invited me over? To interrogate me?" He laughs. "Ask away."

"Why could you never get there with me?" The question hangs in the air, waiting for an answer.

He sighs.

I'm sure this isn't what he expected when my name popped up on his caller ID after midnight. He probably thought I was booty-calling him. While he wasn't necessarily wrong, this booty call comes with stipulations. I need closure before I'm ever going to move on.

"I don't know, Sloane." His use of my first name, instead of Hart, tells me that we're not treading in shallow waters anymore. "I can't put it into words. It isn't about you. It's about me. I just can't get there with anyone. If I could, it would be you," he admits, and in that admission, there's a raw honesty that comforts me.

That's all I need to hear. I turn towards him, my hand reaching out to rest on his leg, silently telling him what I want. He understands the language of our bodies better than our words and finally kisses me.

"I've missed this," he mutters against my mouth, and my heart feels like it might explode out of my chest.

"Me too," I say.

I used to wonder if I'd ever kiss Ethan again. I can't believe I'm kissing him now.

The next thing I know, we're both down to just our underwear. I get goose bumps as his fingers run up and down my stomach.

"Do you want me to touch you?"

I have a brief flash of honesty—I know what I'm doing to Reese is wrong, but this moment with Ethan feels so right. Is it bad if I say

I don't feel even the slightest bit of guilt? This is what Ethan does to me, he makes me toss my morals to the side like a bra I've been waiting to take off all day.

Tension rises inside of me, and instead of answering with words, I take his hand and put it exactly where I want it. He brings his mouth up to my ear; he knows it's a weakness of mine. My back arches and body trembles. I lose myself in him.

"I want you," I beg.

"I was hoping you'd say that." His voice is thick.

My hand finds its way to his underwear, and I can feel how much he's grown. I pull them off of him and then reach for a condom.

He presses into me with a sense of familiarity and relief washes over me. The past few months without him, I've felt homesick, and in this moment with him, I am home.

Afterward, we lie so still. His breaths are heavy and mine are short. I turn my back to him and pull the sheets over my naked body.

"Ethan?" The name is a whisper on my lips.

"Yeah?" His voice is low.

"I think that maybe I would always let you come back," I confess. "Not that I would sit around waiting for you, but if you told me that you were ready and wanted me back, I'm not sure there's anything that I wouldn't drop for you."

He doesn't say anything, but he pulls me in closer and molds himself to me, my back curved to his chest. I've missed being held by him. I've missed the way he smells. I've missed the way he feels. I've missed him.

We fall asleep like that, and it's like a dream I never want to wake up from.

• • •

The next morning, I open my eyes to find my cheek pressed against Ethan's bare chest, and I lift my head to make sure I didn't drool on him. His light snoring calms me for a second until I remember where we are and that he's not supposed to be here. I shoot up out of bed to put on clothes, throwing his onto the bed in the process.

"Good morning to you too," he groans.

"Oh, shut it. We both know you need to go," I demand. "Well, first I need to make sure no one's home yet. Jordan might have slept here. I'll be right back."

"Jordan's here?" He yawns.

I throw on a T-shirt before I head out of my room and scope out the situation. I see no purses on the counter or shoes tossed by the front door except Ethan's. That would've been a dead giveaway if they came back here last night.

"Okay, you're good," I yell to him.

"It's just barely eight a.m., and you thought those two would be home already?" He grabs his shoes but doesn't bother putting them on. "Don't you remember what they were like in college?"

"I didn't know if Jordan slept out or not; that's why I was worried," I explain.

"Don't worry so much." He pulls me in for a hug and kisses my forehead. "Bye, Hart."

"Bye," I reply and close the door behind him.

I feel my entire face break out into a smile. I can't help but feel excited and hopeful for another future with Ethan, even after what I just did to Reese.

Oh god, Reese.

I find my phone and to my surprise have no missed calls or texts from him. I decide to take a shower and think about how I'm going to handle this. I turn on the water and wait for it to get hot to the touch before I step in. I stand there for a minute and let the scorching water hit my skin before turning down the temperature a bit. A hot shower usually rights all my wrongs. Not this one though.

I don't know what it is about Ethan that makes me forget everything and everyone else. We've always had this bond that doesn't quite make sense. I think I've always known, deep down, that we probably won't work out in the end. I still can't help but hope that we do.

26

Ethan

February 2018

It's harsh to say, but I know exactly what I'm doing to Sloane. I know I shouldn't be here—in New York City, in her apartment, in her life. I should leave her alone, but I can't. Well, I can, but I don't know that I want to.

I watch her move through the kitchen as she gets a glass of water, offering me a drink, which I decline. She's lost weight since last summer, not that she had much to lose, but her face is slimmer, and her legs are bonier. I wonder if I have anything to do with that.

I can tell by the way she stumbles into the living room that she drank more than she's let on. I'm not sure exactly how I feel about being around her while she's drunk and vulnerable, but my temptation gives in, and I decide to follow her down the hall and into her bedroom anyway.

Without much pause, she starts hammering me with questions. This is always how it goes when she's drinking.

"Why could you never get there with me?" Her hazel eyes are sad.

I sit in silence for a second and think about how to answer her. I want to be honest, but I don't know how. What is the right place or time to tell her my parents were arrested when I was young and by default I grew up with Graham's family? How am I supposed to tell her my family didn't love me enough to stick around? How am I supposed to tell her that I worry I'll leave her one day, just like my parents left me?

I wonder what love is like for other people. Is it easy? I know it's not supposed to be this hard. But all of that feels too personal to say out loud. Instead, I feed her a bunch of bullshit that I know she wants to hear.

"It isn't about you. It's about me. I just can't get there with anyone. If I could, it would be you." I sugarcoat the truth.

And just like that, she's mine again.

27

Sloane

April 2018

t's been over a month since I slept with Ethan, and I still can't get that night out of my head. I haven't told Reese or Lauren. It's not that I haven't wanted to—I've even tried to a few times—it's just a lot harder than I expected. The thought of disappointing either of them crushes me. I also haven't heard from Ethan, unless you count the two-word text he sent me on my birthday. Am I wrong for expecting more?

"Sloane?" Lauren calls out. "Can you and Reese go to dinner tonight?"

"With you and Miles?" I inquire, emerging from my room.

"Duh. Miles snagged us a res at Dante at nine. Can you be there? I thought it was about time we went on a double date with our boyfriends."

"Boyfriend, huh?" I raise an eyebrow.

"Finally! Right? I was afraid I would have to follow the three-month rule, but he asked before then. Thank god!"

"Three-month rule?"

"You haven't heard of that?" she explains. "A few podcasts I listen to have covered it. Technically there are two three-month rules. One is that if someone has been pursuing you for three months, that usually means they want to date you. The other three-month rule is that once you're exclusively seeing a guy, you give them three months max to make it official. If they don't, you're out of there."

"Interesting. I like that." The wheels in my mind start turning.

"Sorry, I didn't mean. Well, you know." I know that she's referring to Ethan.

"No, I know you didn't. I like the three-month rule. I think the problem with it is that sometimes when you're three months in, you look at it like, *Well I'm already three months in.* You know? That's what I would have said if someone told me that back in college. I would have waited, and that's where I fucked up. I waited for him to come around. I waited to see if things would get better. So much waiting. Before I knew it, almost a year had passed, and I was still waiting."

"I know, and that's why this is such a great rule. Hopefully, it keeps people like you from wasting more of their time on someone who isn't meant to be in their life for more than three months."

"Yeah, hopefully," I reply, knowing that if someone told twenty-one-year-old me how things with Ethan would've played out, I still would've done everything the same.

I'll never regret him.

• • •

We arrive at the restaurant, and it's exactly like I've been imagining. Checkered tiles line the floors, and sage green accents carry through the entire space. Tables of friends and lovers laugh over cocktails and appetizers. It might be the only restaurant here that captures the aura of the city and the feeling of living here so perfectly.

The host leads us to a table near the window, and the couples opt to sit next to each other instead of across. As I browse the cocktail menu, Reese puts his hand on my leg and kisses me on the cheek.

I look up to see if Lauren or Miles are paying attention, but they're too enthralled in each other's company, pointing and giggling at the drink menu while they decide what to try first. Reese has been traveling a lot for work this month, so we haven't spent a lot of time together. Honestly, I've been using it as an excuse to figure out how to tell him about what happened with Ethan. I know I need to tell him; we just need to make it through this dinner first.

After we clear our plates, Reese puts his card down to pay the check, and I wish I could stop him without making a scene. Not only do I feel guilty about sleeping with Ethan, but now I'm lying to his face and letting him foot the bill for an expensive tab. I've never felt worse. We part ways from Lauren and Miles on the sidewalk as Reese and I walk towards his place, since it's not far from the restaurant.

"You alright?" he asks as he reaches for my hand and locks his fingers in mine. "You were quiet at dinner."

"Yeah, I'm fine. Just tired," I reply, mustering a half-hearted smile.

"Miles is cool, and seems like Lauren is happy. What do you think of him?" he asks.

I pause, considering. "I think he's nice and seems to really like her. I just worry they're moving too fast." The words spill out, echoing my own doubts about rushing into things with Reese.

"Too fast?" Reese gives me a questioning look, his brow furrowed in mild surprise. "Haven't they been seeing each other for a few months?"

"Yeah, I don't know, it just feels fast." I shrug, trying to dismiss the topic.

"You do remember we started dating after two weeks, right?" he laughs.

I don't reply.

We walk the next few blocks hand in hand until we get to Reese's. I don't even want to step foot inside his building, let alone spend the night here. But I also don't want to have this conversation with him. I don't know which is worse.

"Do you want wine or anything? We could finish that episode of *The Walking Dead* we were watching," Reese suggests as we approach his front door.

"Can we just go to bed? I'm exhausted," I say.

"Yeah, of course. You're sure you're feeling okay?" His eyes search mine.

I nod. He follows me into his room and hands me one of his T-shirts to sleep in. I strip out of my jeans, turtleneck, and bra so that I'm only wearing his shirt and my underwear. I slide into his bed and wonder if this is the last time I'll ever be in it. I feel bad that this is how it's ending, but no matter how much I've tried to love Reese, it'll never live up to the way that I feel about Ethan.

Reese climbs into bed after me and tries to touch me; we haven't had sex since Boston. I can't bear the thought of being with him after what I did with Ethan. I know I have to tell him.

"Something's up. Please just tell me what's wrong?" he pleads.

"I had sex with Ethan."

The words leave my mouth before I even realize what I'm saying. My back is turned, and somehow, I find the courage to sit up and make eye contact with him. He stands at the foot of his bed with a blank stare.

"Fuck. I knew it." I can hear the disappointment in his tone of voice. "I'm not blind, Sloane. I knew this was going to happen; I was just hoping it wouldn't. I was hoping I meant more to you than that."

"It's not that you don't mean anything to me—"

"But I'm not him. No one can compete with a ghost, Sloane. You chase after a guy who's never certain about you, while I stand here seeing you, wanting you, choosing you, and you don't even care."

His words sting.

"You just don't understand," I whisper.

"What don't I get, Sloane? That you would do anything for someone who couldn't give two shits about you?" His question is rhetorical. "What was all of this with me then? Did you even love me? Was I just something to keep you distracted until you found your way back to him?"

I feel a tear roll down my cheek, and for once, Reese doesn't bat an eye.

"It's not like that. I loved you; I really did. But now that he's around, it's just...different. I can't be in a relationship with all of these unresolved feelings. It's not fair to either of us," I say, trying to keep my composure.

I stand up and bring my clothes into the bathroom to change back into, because the thought of being naked around him ever again makes my skin crawl. I fold the T-shirt, place it on his dresser, and feel him watching my every move.

"I hope you realize it someday," he says. "He's never going to change. I know you think he will, but he won't. He's going to hurt you again."

My throat tightens as he continues.

"He'll hurt you again, and next time, I'm not going to be there to put you back together."

The next thing I know, I'm sitting on the front steps of his walk-up in the middle of the West Village wondering what to do next. I order an Uber because taking the subway this late alone was one thing I promised my parents I'd never do. I charge the ride to my mom's credit card as I wait for the car to pull up.

As I stare through the window of the black Toyota Camry that smells like cigarettes, I wonder if I'm making the right decision. On paper, Reese is husband material. He's kind, attentive, reliable, and listens to me—he pays attention and understands what I want and need. That feels like a rare quality to find in a guy these days. I just don't think I'd ever be able to shake the feeling that he isn't the one.

Maybe Ethan isn't either, but I sure as hell have to give myself another chance to find out.

I hesitate to get out of the car as it pulls up to my building. I'm alone. Is this a good thing? Or did I just give up the kind of person most women long to spend their lives with? What did I just do?

The lobby is completely empty; even Phillip isn't around. I wait for the elevator and hit the button to take me to the sixth floor. I pause at the door of Ethan's apartment. Why did I think this was a good idea? He's probably not even home.

I debate going back downstairs but knock on the door anyway. Seconds later, he opens it.

"This is a surprise," Ethan greets me. "Everything okay?"

I cut right to it. "I broke up with Reese. Can I sleep here tonight?"

"Why'd you do that?" he asks, opening the door so that I can come in.

"What do you mean, why did I do that? We had sex, Ethan. I cheated on my boyfriend. How was I supposed to be in a relationship with someone that I was lying to?"

"I don't know. I'm sorry, Hart."

"Why didn't you text me after we slept together?" I ask.

"Well, up until now I thought you had a boyfriend. I already felt shitty enough about what happened. I really didn't want to make it worse."

I don't say anything.

"Did you break up with him because of me?" Ethan asks.

"No." I don't hesitate. "I just knew he wasn't it for me. But if I'm being honest, I don't know that my feelings for anyone else will be able to compete with the way I feel about you."

"Don't say that. Don't put me on some kind of pedestal. I don't deserve it."

"I can't help it. Even before I ran into you again, I kept thinking of how much I missed you. I'm attached to you in this weird way—like our paths were meant to cross and they'll continue side by side until it's time for them to cross again."

"I get that," he says under his breath, as if he doesn't want to admit he feels the same.

Neither of us says anything for a few minutes until Ethan goes to the kitchen to get me a glass of water. When he returns to the couch, he sits so close to me that our legs are almost touching.

Even after years of knowing him, his body near mine makes me extremely nervous. I swing my legs up so that they're over his thighs, and he rests a hand on my knee. We talk about work and life lately. For a second, it feels like we picked up right where we left off. He leads me into his room. I get under his navy bedsheets, and he pulls me toward him.

We don't have sex. Instead we fall asleep with our legs intertwined, my head on his chest and his arms around me. I wish I could fall asleep like this every single night.

• • •

I sneak back into our apartment the next morning without waking Lauren and Miles. I put on sweatpants and a T-shirt and crawl into bed. Instead of trying to go back to sleep, I scroll my feed. Graham and Emily were working on their wedding website, Jordan went to sushi with some of her coworkers, and Reese didn't post anything—which isn't out of the ordinary, especially considering last night's chain of events, but I type his name into the search bar anyway.

No user found.

He blocked me. I toss my phone and pull the covers over me. Maybe I do need a few more hours of sleep before I can face today. After all, I know Lauren isn't going to be ecstatic when I tell her what happened.

• • •

"You did what?" Her eyes widen in disbelief. "Why would you break up with him?"

Miles pauses, a hint of discomfort flickering across his face before he plants a kiss on Lauren's cheek.

"I'm gonna…go. I'll text you." With that, he turns on his heel and makes a beeline for the door, leaving as if the apartment itself is caving in.

"Start from the beginning," she demands.

I take a deep breath. "The weekend Jordan came to visit and you guys left the bar, I called Ethan. I was drunk. We slept together, and then I didn't talk to him again after that."

"Bullshit." A skeptical look crosses her face.

"Swear. I wanted to tell Reese right after it happened, but then he was traveling almost every week for work, and the longer I waited, the harder it got. After dinner, I just couldn't keep it in. So I told him."

Lauren takes a sip of her coffee, steam rising from the mug as she processes my words.

"How did he react?" she asks.

"He said he knew it was going to happen. I mean, he was still pissed, but he wasn't surprised. I don't know if that was necessarily helpful, but I think the fact that it wasn't completely out of nowhere might make it an easier pill to swallow." The memory stings as I recount it.

A pause hangs between us.

"You guys just seemed so...good. Before you knew Ethan was here anyway."

"Maybe that's how I made it seem, but my relationship with Reese was so one-sided. I knew he loved me, and I strung him along because it felt good to be someone's everything. He was never my everything though," I explain.

Lauren takes in my words before asking, "So what's going on with Ethan?"

"I don't know. I've been more open with him this time around. It hasn't scared him off yet, so I think that's a good sign," I confess.

"Has he changed at all? What would be different this time around?" She leans forward, her frustration obvious.

"I don't know yet," I say again. The weight of her question is unusually heavy. "It hasn't even been twenty-four hours since I broke up with Reese. I need time to process things before I think about the future."

"Why are you still doing this after all these years?" She shakes her head. "What is it about him? It's like he has some hold on you or something."

I sigh before trying to rationalize the irrational. "Sometimes it feels that way. This might sound crazy, but it feels like something is telling me to wait a little more. That one day soon something is going to happen. I know he still thinks about me and has feelings for me; I'm just waiting for him to be ready to act on them."

"That's exactly it. He probably does still have feelings for you, but that isn't what matters. What matters is what he's doing about it, which is nothing. If he's doing nothing, you should most certainly be doing the same. Not breaking up with your damn near perfect boyfriend for him. You deserve someone who goes out of their way to make it obvious that they want you in their life." The truth in her words is undeniable.

"If I didn't break up with Reese, I would've been doing the same thing to him that Ethan did to me. It wasn't fair."

Her gaze softens. "I just hope you know what you're doing."

I make my way down the hall, shut my bedroom door, and dial Graham's number. After talking to Lauren, I need reassurance that I didn't just make a huge mistake and I feel like Graham is the only person who understands my relationship with Ethan. Probably because he's the only person in the world who understands Ethan. I'm jealous of him for that.

"Hey!" he answers.

"Hi, sorry to call so randomly. How's wedding planning going?" I try to ease into the conversation.

"It's going. What's up? Usually when you call it's with an agenda," he teases.

"You make me sound like such a bad friend," I say. "You know how I've been seeing Reese for like a year? Well, I hooked up with Ethan recently and finally told him last night."

"God, Sloane…" His voice trails off.

Trying to ignore his clear disappointment, I continue. "I broke up with him. I mean, it's what I wanted to do all along, I think. I liked the comfort of him, but I never liked him the same way I like Ethan."

"Can I say something?" he interrupts. "You're never going to like anyone in the way you like Ethan. Honestly, it would be unhealthy if you did. You guys are each other's first loves. No one ever wants to experience that twice because it's usually so toxic."

I can't help but defend my feelings, though a part of me wonders if he's right. "We're not toxic," I argue, more to myself than to him.

"You're missing the point. Did you talk to Ethan? Is he ready for a relationship?" His question is pointed.

"Well, no." I admit.

"Exactly. So, you're right back at square one. I'm not saying that you shouldn't have broken up with Reese, because clearly you didn't want to be with him. But you don't have to go back to Ethan. You can be alone or meet someone else too. You know that, right?"

I let out a breath I didn't realize I was holding. "I know. But do you think it ever could work out with him?"

There's a heavy sigh on the other end of the phone.

"I don't know. Ethan's a hard person to love." He softens his tone. "He's been through a lot of shit in his life. I don't know if settling down or getting married is something he'll ever want. And you can't wait around forever to find out."

The truth of his words sink in. He's right.

"Thanks, Graham."

"That's what I'm here for, right?" He laughs, trying to lift the mood. "Save-the-dates are coming to a mailbox near you. Oh, and Emily and I are planning a trip to the city in the next few months. We'd love to grab dinner or something."

"Sounds great! Just let me know when, and I'll book us a reservation."

After an exchange of goodbyes, I hang up the phone and feel more confused than I did before talking to either of them. I know Graham and Lauren are right. If I start hanging out with Ethan again, I need to lay down some ground rules. He needs to be all in. I just don't know that I'm strong enough to give him an ultimatum.

28

Sloane

June 2018

I've missed having sex with Ethan.

The chemistry between us is unlike anything else I've ever experienced, and the sex is even better. Maybe I like having sex with him so much because that's the only time he really lets his walls down. It's the only time I truly feel like we're on a level playing field.

"Will you get a towel?" I ask.

"Yep, got it," Ethan mumbles.

After I broke up with Reese, Ethan and I picked up where we left off practically one year ago. I never found the courage to talk to him about what we are. I let it continue the way it always has because it means he's back in my life, and right now that's enough for me. He hands me a towel and makes his way back under the sheets before turning on my TV.

Bzzz. Bzzz. Bzzz. His phone lies face down on his stomach as he lets it ring.

"Aren't you going to see who it is?" I ask.

He shows me the screen so I can see it's an unknown number with a Wilmington area code. He turns the phone back over and keeps flipping through Netflix to find something for us to watch.

"You don't want to answer?" I ask again.

"It's probably just spam." he replies, unfazed.

I let it go and lay my head on his chest. He decides on our favorite season of *Breaking Bad* and turns off the lamp beside him so that the only thing lighting up the room is the glow from my thirty-two-inch flat screen. I tilt my head up to look at him because sometimes small moments like these don't feel real. I used to lie in this bed longing for him, and now he's back like he never left. He smiles and strokes my hair as I fall asleep on him.

• • •

"Alright, so Graham gets into town around noon. I'm going to meet them at their hotel after lunch with the guys from work," Ethan recites with a mouth full of toothpaste.

"Did he say which one? We probably need a res. It's a Friday," I suggest as I hurry to pack my bag for work and find a pair of shoes that will go from day to night.

"Not sure. That's why they're going to try and get there at three o'clock. What time do your Summer Fridays usually kick in?"

"Around two. I wanted to come back here to change, but maybe I'll just throw an extra outfit into my bag."

"Why change? You look great." His compliment sends shivers down my spine.

Ethan comes up behind me as I'm looking at myself in my mirrored closet doors. I chose a light blue minidress with tiny embroidered flowers, paired with an oversized white blazer because the office is always freezing. I just had to decide between white ankle boots or sneakers.

"Go with the sneakers." He whispers in my ear and proceeds to grab me by the waist and kiss my neck.

"Okay, fine, they're easier to travel in anyway." I turn around and kiss him back. "I'm about to be late."

"It'll be worth it." I can feel him as he presses up against me.

"Seriously, Ethan," I plead. "It's not the morning for this."

Something about Ethan in a button-down and slacks turns me on. I kiss him goodbye and leave him to finish getting ready in my apartment. I got him a copy of our key about a month after we started consistently seeing each other again. Lauren wasn't a huge fan of the idea, but she didn't say no either. She's been spending so much time at Miles's, it's like she lives there now.

I get to work early in hopes that I'm able to leave early. The office is deserted, the usual hustle of the day yet to begin. My cube has become a collage of sticky notes, a mosaic of deadlines and reminders. Today feels like a good day to declutter, so I start by removing a few outdated ones and diving into crafting new articles.

"Gem tonight?" Mila's voice breaks the silence as she settles into her cube opposite mine.

"Our college friends are coming into town today, and they're wanting to find a rooftop, but I'm definitely going to try and convince them to hit Gem after," I reply, still typing away.

• • •

"Sloane? Do you have a sec?" Annie summons me, and a familiar knot of anticipation tightens in my stomach. Usually we only meet in her office for our weekly one-on-ones, so I'm a little nervous not knowing what this conversation entails. I enter her office, my laptop a shield of sorts, and stand in the doorway.

"Sit."

Her expression is unreadable.

"So," she starts, clasping her hands on the desk, "you've single-handedly driven our website's traffic to fifteen million views in under a year. The whole team is impressed, so I talked to HR... We're giving you a raise."

"A raise?!" I say, completely surprised.

"Yes," Annie confirms with a nod. "It's a recognition of your work and the impact you've had on *The Gist*. Your salary needs to reflect the growing importance of your contributions."

"I don't know what to say," I manage. "Thank you so much!"

"You've earned it all." Her smile is warm, genuine. "Now go on. Kick off your weekend early and celebrate."

I head back to my desk, my heart lighter, and quickly wrap up the rest of my tasks. Glancing at the clock, I decide it's time to leave. As I walk to the subway, I shoot a text to Ethan, mulling over whether to call my parents about the good news. Just as I'm about to dial, my phone vibrates with a new text.

12:45 p.m.

Ethan Brady: Leaving lunch now. Graham and Emily are insisting on Mr. Purple. Meet us when you get off?

12:45 p.m.

Me: 🙂 You know how I feel about Mr. Purple...

12:46 p.m.

Me: Kidding (sort of). Wrapped up early so I'll see you soon!

I hit send as I head down the steps into the subway to take the next train to the Lower East Side. According to every New Yorker I've ever met, Mr. Purple was only decent the first few months after it opened. No one really goes there anymore, mostly because of all the tourists. But as a former tourist, I see why she wants to go.

"Sloane!" Emily waves me down from across the roof.

"Hi, guys!" I say as I approach the table.

"It's so nice to finally meet you!" She immediately embraces me in a hug.

Emily is a breath of fresh air, much more Graham's speed than Lauren was. *No offense, Laur.* She has beautiful long brown hair and a smile that seems like it never leaves her face. From what I've heard from Graham, Emily is kind, genuine, and always makes him laugh. Even though I've only known her for a few minutes, I can tell right away they're meant for each other.

"Whatcha want to drink?" Ethan asks me.

"Get the blackberry mojito! They're so good!" Emily chimes in.

"I'll have that." I smile and watch him walk to the bar. "So how've you guys been?"

"Oh my gosh, you wouldn't believe how intense wedding planning is. It's like one thing after another. Don't even get me started on how expensive flowers are. Who knew?" Emily laughs.

"What about you?" Graham interrupts before we get in so deep with the wedding talk that we can't get out.

"Actually"—I pause until Ethan reaches the table with my drink—"I got a raise today! It was a surprise, and my boss says it was based on merit, so I'd say things are great."

"I'm so proud of you," Ethan whispers and then kisses my cheek. Success feels great, but his affirmation makes me feel better. Ethan puts his arm around me as the table echoes congratulations and Graham orders us a round of celebratory shots.

"Lauren's calling me," I murmur, looking down at my phone.

I excuse myself and move to a quieter spot before answering. "Hey!"

"Hey, where are you?" Lauren's voice comes through.

Shit. Guilt pinches at me. I never got the chance to tell her that Graham was coming to town this weekend.

"Are you working late? I wanna go out!" she asks again.

"Don't hate me…" I start. "I totally forgot to mention Graham is here this weekend. I'm out with him and Ethan."

"Is Emily there? Would it be weird if I came? I'm not trying to stay in tonight." She sounds eager to join.

"She's here, but I think it would be fine. Is Miles around? Not sure if that would make things more awkward or less," I suggest, trying to navigate the situation.

"I'm sure I can convince him. Where are you?" Her voice is upbeat now.

"Mr. Purple." I laugh.

"You're shitting me," she replies. "Okay, we can be there in thirty."

Walking back to the table, I think through the best way to tell everyone Lauren and her boyfriend are on the way. After we moved to the city, Graham stopped mentioning her, as did she, until he got engaged anyway. Now that she has Miles, I think she's feeling less jealous.

I glance up from my phone, hesitantly breaking the news to the group. "Lauren's coming with her boyfriend; is that okay?"

"Yeah, all good. I'm happy for her. Is he a good guy?" Graham asks.

I nod, a smile touching my lips. "He is."

"That's all I need to hear."

After a few awkward introductions and another round of drinks, we decide to get dinner before going to Gem.

Two blocks away is one of the best Mexican restaurants in the city, according to Miles who dubs himself a foodie. We order a round of margaritas, tequila shots, queso, and guac before putting in our entrees. By the time we're ready to leave, I'm more than tipsy, but the night is young, so I try and pull myself together.

"Fuck this line," Lauren complains.

"It's not that bad," Graham counters, trying to keep the peace. Ethan and I exchange a loaded glance, an entire conversation in a single look. I peer through the window, watching everyone inside dancing and mingling. Suddenly, my pulse quickens as my eyes land on Reese.

"We could always try Flying Cock?" Desperation seeps into my voice as I try to find any excuse to avoid going inside.

"It's too low-key. Let's go there after this," Ethan says.

"Are you sure? They hardly ever have a line, and this is taking forever," I say, pleading for anyone to agree with me.

"We've already been waiting this long." Graham shoots down the idea.

I turn to Ethan before whispering, "Reese is inside."

He offers some reassurance. "It'll be fine, I'm sure we won't even see him."

Inside the bar, the crowd swallows us. Ethan's hand in mine is an anchor in the sea of people. He leads us to the bar, orders a round of drinks with a confidence that makes me forget how uneasy I feel. But as we navigate back through the crowd, Ethan's shoulder bumps into someone. I freeze. It's Reese.

His voice is rough, edged with anger. "So what is it? You guys dating now, or still just fucking?"

Ethan's response is immediate and slightly surprising.

"Don't talk to her like that, Reese," he warns.

"Or what, Brady? You're gonna fuck her behind my back again?" he slurs, clearly more intoxicated than the rest of us.

"I'm serious, man, just let it go. You're wasted." Ethan's tone is steady and sure.

In a flash of motion, Reese's hand sends Ethan's drink flying, shattering the glass against the floor. My heart pounds in my chest as I jump between them.

"Stop it, both of you!" I demand.

Within seconds, our friends rally to us. Graham encourages Reese to find his group, while the rest of us decide it's time for us to finish our drinks and head home for the night.

. . .

I slide under the covers, feeling the contrast of the cool sheets against my skin, still warm from the night out. Ethan is already in bed, staring at the ceiling, lost in thought.

"Sorry about the Reese situation," I say before changing the subject. "Graham and Emily looked so happy."

"Yeah, they did. Can't believe Graham's getting married." Ethan turns to me.

The knot in my chest tightens, and I gather my courage. "Ethan, do you think we'll go to Graham's wedding together?"

He pauses, his eyes searching mine.

"I don't know, Sloane; that's like a year away."

"So? What are we doing then? We can't keep avoiding the inevitable. It's just like college all over again."

"It's been a month since you broke up with Reese, and clearly from tonight's sequence of events, it's still all pretty fresh. Not to mention I've barely lived in the city for six months. Things are working right now, Sloane. Can you just focus on the good instead of the bad?" Ethan sighs, a hint of frustration in his voice.

"What do you mean?"

"It just reminds me of college. You'd pick a fight or find a way to turn a good night into a bad one. I answer one question the way you weren't expecting, and it's like the rest of the night just goes out the window," he says.

I feel a rush of anger and hurt. "I'm so glad to know you think that."

Ethan doesn't respond, just turns his back to me and tries to sleep.

The saying about never going to bed upset crosses my mind, but I'm not letting this one go. Once I'm sure he's asleep, I grab my pillow and a blanket and head to the couch. Lauren's not home, and I want Ethan to notice my absence when he wakes up.

Morning comes with the smell of coffee.

I open my eyes, still on the couch, to see that Ethan is in the kitchen looking regretful.

He hands me a cup, his eyes meeting mine. "I'm sorry about last night. Of course, we're gonna go to the wedding together. I just wasn't thinking that far into the future."

I want to believe him, to trust in his words, but a little bit of doubt still lingers. With a small nod, I accept his apology, letting the warmth of the coffee seep into my hands, wondering where our relationship will be a year from now.

29

Ethan

July 2018

Living in New York City is exhausting. Ten-hour days in the office, followed by happy hours, followed by sleepovers with Sloane don't leave a lot of time for myself. I used to go to the gym every day; now I'm lucky if I get there once a week. I can see and feel a difference, and I don't like it, if I'm being honest.

Ever since our last fight, things with Sloane have felt off on my end. I didn't expect to jump back into things so quickly, but I guess that's what happens when you sleep with your ex who was in another relationship. She gave up someone else for me, so I feel like I owe it to her to try. Sloane's been questioning me about our relationship more than ever. Every time she has more than two glasses of wine, she begins the hypotheticals. I get where she's coming from, but I don't know how much longer I can take it.

The gym is packed, and I wonder why I pay almost two hundred dollars a month to not even find a machine. Coming here is supposed to clear my head, not make me more stressed. After an hour of hitting weights, I sit in the sauna and lean my head back against the wood planks. I forgot how much I missed this uninterrupted time. No phone, no people, no thoughts. I close my eyes and stay in there until I feel like I'm going to pass out, grab my backpack from the locker, and take the subway home.

"Hey!" Sloane greets me from the kitchen before I can even close the door behind me. "Noah let me in. Lauren and Miles are cooking at my place, so I figured I'd bring food over here so you didn't have to worry about cooking. I know it's been a long day."

Not only am I slightly annoyed that she invited herself over but also that she's here in general. I just got done sweating my ass off at the gym and in an air-conditioning-less subway; I was looking forward to a quiet apartment and an ice-cold shower. I force a smile as I walk into the kitchen.

"Thanks, you didn't have to do this," I say. "I'm all sweaty, so I'm gonna shower before I eat. You can start though."

I continue to the bathroom without turning back to look at Sloane because I know I'll see the disappointment in her face. She means well, and I appreciate the effort, but sometimes it's just too much. I take an extra-long shower to try and bring my mood back up, but I still feel just as shitty afterwards. I throw on a pair of boxers and basketball shorts before making my way back into the common area where Sloane is waiting for me.

"Do you want me to leave?" she asks. "I'm sorry. I should've texted before coming."

"No, no, it's fine. I'm sorry. I'm just tired," I lie, trying to reassure her. I pull her into a hug and rest my chin on the top of her head. Sometimes I forget how short she is.

"Okay…if you're sure. Want me to heat up your food?"

"That'd be great. I'll find something for us to watch." I kiss her and then get comfortable on the couch. I feel bad for being standoffish.

Minutes later she hands me a microwaved bowl of hibachi chicken and rice, then sits on the side of the couch opposite from me. I can tell she's upset by my attitude earlier, but I try not to think too much about it. We watch a new movie that's in Netflix's top ten. By the time it's over, I notice Sloane's drank more than half a bottle of wine by herself. With wine usually comes a fight or a game of twenty questions, but before she has the chance to start either, I start kissing her. I pick her up off the couch and kiss her the entire way to my bedroom, where I take off her clothes and stare at her in the glow of the streetlights. Sloane falls back on her elbows, and even though I can't see it, I know she's blushing.

She's lying on her back as I'm on top of her, and in between breaths and moans, she says it—the words I've been dreading to hear.

"I love—" She stops once she realizes what she's about to say. "Fucking you."

I immediately bring her mouth to mine to avoid any further conversation until I've finished. We remain quietly in our positions for a few seconds before I get up to go to the bathroom.

When I come back, she's lying in one of my T-shirts on the far side of the bed with her back facing me. I climb into bed and bring my body closer to hers. I can tell she's upset with me, but instead of addressing it, I lie behind her until she falls asleep. Then I turn over and scroll on my phone for a while until my eyes start to get heavy.

What have I gotten myself into?

30

Sloane

September 2018

Suddenly, the seasons have changed. Fall in New York is a different kind of serotonin rush. The crisp air, burnt orange leaves, rainy days, and cooler temperatures bring out a different side of New Yorkers. I swear, people only smile at me on the subway between the months of September through December. The city never loses its magic, but especially not in the fall.

I decide to make my way down to SoHo after work to treat myself to a little shopping spree in honor of the cooler weather. I weave in and out of stores until I have a new pair of jeans, a few sweaters, and a jacket. After spending what feels like half a paycheck, I call Lauren to see if she wants to meet for dinner.

She picks up almost immediately. "Where are you? I've been home for like two hours, and I'm starving."

"Wanna meet me in SoHo? Annie was out today, so I wrapped up an hour early and did a little shopping."

"Without me? You're the worst!" Lauren jokes. "Yeah, sure, see you soonish."

It's early and the restaurant is nearly empty, so I snag us seats at the bar and order two extra-dirty martinis, Lauren's favorite.

"Martinis on a Wednesday?" She sneaks up behind me, her voice playful. "What's the occasion?"

I smile at her, feeling the warmth of our friendship. "Just some light roommate bonding. I feel like we haven't spent a lot of time together lately," I say with a soft sigh. "I hate it."

"I know, me too. The boys are getting in our way!" Her laughter is infectious. We clink glasses and take a sip.

"So how are things with Miles?" I ask.

"He's great, Sloane. Really like the best person I've ever met— besides you, of course," she quickly adds, a hint of blush touching her cheeks. "I see a future with him."

"I'm so happy for you!" I say, raising my glass again in silent toast.

"How about Ethan? How's that going? You seem to be spending a lot of time together, so that's good! Right?" Her brows arch with a hint of concern.

"Things are good!" I lie. "Same old, same old."

As time slips by, our easy chatter fills the space around us. The buzz from the martinis makes us more talkative, more laughable.

Lauren's phone goes off, the buzz breaking our bubble. With a gentle nod, I urge her to take the call because I can see that it's Miles.

"Hey!" she answers. "I'm with Sloane getting drinks. Yeah, we'll probably get checks soon; we've had three already. Okay that works. I'll meet you outside of our building. Love you too."

They say *I love you* already? I mentally count the months they've been together in my head. Well, I guess it's been about six. Do six short months warrant *I love you*s?

When we get home, Miles is already waiting outside for Lauren. They come upstairs for a few minutes so she can pack a bag with a change of clothes. I say goodbye and go into my room to call Ethan, hoping he'll want to hang out tonight.

"Hey," he answers. "Everything okay?"

"Yes, does something have to be wrong for me to call?" I ask, more defensively than I intended.

"I didn't mean it like that. What's up?"

"Do you want to hang out tonight?" My tone is hopeful.

The conversation that follows leaves me with a hollow feeling, one that's becoming all too familiar.

"Not tonight," he replies as I sigh into the phone. "Tomorrow? There's a game on. We can watch it together and order in. I'll even bring wine."

"Fine," I groan, unexcited to spend another night apart.

"Get some sleep, drunkie. Good night." His laughter is supposed to be comforting, but it echoes the distance between us.

"Night," I whisper before hanging up.

Sometimes loving him feels like I'm lingering in the doorway of his bedroom, waiting for him to let me in. Will he ever let me in?

• • •

The following night Ethan shows up at my apartment with a large pizza and a bottle of cab. Something about him feels off, distant even, but I can't quite put my finger on it.

"Your phone is going off," I say and gesture toward the coffee table. I watch as Ethan picks it up and immediately sets it back down again.

He writes it off. "Spam."

For the past few months, I've noticed that he's been getting phone calls from the same number. I'm not sure if he knows that I've picked up on it, but I have. He passes it off as spam or a wrong caller any time I address it, but I can't tell if it's the truth. The logical part of my brain says that he's lying, and the emotional part says maybe there's more to the story than I want to know.

Could there be someone else?

I can't shake the feeling that it's a possibility, but I'll continue to ignore it for a little while longer if it means not losing Ethan. In the same moment, midthought, my phone rings.

I answer and walk into my bedroom. "Hey, Mom. What's up?"

"Do you have Thanksgiving plans yet? We're thinking of going to London for a few weeks, and well, it overlaps with Thanksgiving. I don't want to leave you, but..." she rambles on.

"You should totally go! I haven't thought about Thanksgiving yet, but worst case I can go see Dad. I've always wanted to go to London."

"Me too," she says. "You're sure, honey?"

"I'm sure. Love you, Mom."

"Love you too." She hangs up.

I sit back on the couch, closer to Ethan this time. He puts his arm around me and lays my head on his shoulder. I wish I could stay in this moment forever.

"What're you doing for Thanksgiving?" I ask, partially afraid of the answer.

"Not sure," Ethan says. "Why?"

"My mom's going to London. I guess I can call my dad, but I don't know..." I ramble.

"I'm sure I'll be in the city, so we could just do this?" he casually offers. "Order takeout and watch something."

"That'd be nice."

Maybe all of the feelings of uncertainty are in my head. Maybe he does care. Maybe he is trying. It's hard to know when he won't tell me, and even if he did reassure me, would I truly believe it? He broke my trust when he came to New York, lied straight to my face about long distance, and then broke up with me in a text. How does someone get over that?

. . .

I arrive to work the next morning early because I have a deadline today on an assignment that I've been putting off all week: Do half of all marriages really end in divorce?

I interviewed six people, some married, some divorced; some had parents who stayed together until they passed, and some had parents who split before they were even born. The interviews were harder on me than I expected, so I took a weeklong break from writing, and now I only have nine hours to finish it. I open my laptop, pull up the document. and read what I have written so far:

Being married to the love of your life must really be something. Waking up and falling asleep next to your soulmate sounds like the perfect start and end to each day. I imagine your conflicts seem less earth-shattering when you have someone to overcome them with. I hope everyone gets to experience that kind of love one day. Including me.

"My wife and I have been together for ten years, married for six, and I still get excited to see her every single day when I get home from work. She makes even the worst days bearable, just by existing."

I shut my laptop and place my head in my hands. Why did I pitch this topic? Not only does it break my heart all over again thinking about how one day my parents' seemingly perfect marriage disappeared into thin air, but it makes me question a future between Ethan and me.

One day, five years from now, if he were stopped on the street and asked to talk about the love of his life, what would he say? Presuming he was thinking about me, of course. Would he say that he's never met anyone like me? That I make him feel like a different, better version of himself? That he feels safe when he's with me? I wonder if he'll ever love me the way I love him. I wonder if he's even capable of a love that deep.

The clock on my phone reads 7:18 p.m. when I finally submit the piece for final review and pack up my things. The office is dead, cubes are empty, and I can hear a vacuum humming down the hall. I hope I'm never the last one to leave again. It's nothing like TV shows make it out to be. I feel less like a girl boss and more like a potential murder victim.

As I hurry out of the building, my phone vibrates in my bag. I dig through it to find it, and when I do, I see Lauren's name on the screen.

"Hey, sorry just getting out of work," I answer.

"I figured. I just got home with sushi and wine. See you in twenty?"

"See you in twenty," I assure her.

• • •

"You're home!" Lauren's voice echoes from the kitchen.

"Finally." My laughter rings out as I leave the long day and my shoes at the door.

I enter the kitchen to find it transformed into a cozy nook. Lauren's lit a candle, poured two glasses of red wine, and arranged four sushi rolls on the board we typically use for charcuterie.

"What's the occasion?" I ask because I know she doesn't put in this level of effort for a random weekday dinner.

"Oh, just sit," she insists.

I obey and take a sip of my wine, afraid of what is about to come.

"Are you leaving New York?" The words just come out.

Lauren's response comes quickly. "No, oh my god. Just the apartment. Miles wants me to move in with him. I know it's soon, but I really want to. I spend almost every night there anyway, so it makes sense, but that's not the only reason why I want to. I love him, Sloane. Like really, really love him. I think he's it for me."

I pause, letting her words settle in the space between us as I take another sip.

My voice is steady, because I want to let her know I mean what I'm about to say. "I'm happy for you. Seriously."

"Oh, fuck off," she teases, dismissing the weight of the moment.

I laugh along, but my heart is both full and heavy.

"No, really, I'm happy for you! I'm just going to miss you. The past two years have flown by so fast, and I think, thanks to *New Girl* and *Friends*, I had this preconceived notion that we'd be living together until our thirties."

"I get that. I did too. I didn't think I'd meet someone this fast. Or at all, really." She nods.

I'm happy for her, I really am. I just can't help but compare her relationship with Miles to mine with Ethan. Will we ever be more than an almost?

31

Ethan

October 2018

I stare at my phone as it rings in my hand, even though it's an unknown number. I know exactly who it is on the other side of the call. I just can't bring myself to answer. I take a seat on the edge of my bed and stare at the screen until the call gets sent to voicemail. I've accumulated over eleven new messages that I'll never listen to over the past few months, and I constantly wonder when it'll end.

In June, Mrs. Clark called to let me know my dad was being released from prison. She and Mr. Clark seemed to think he'd show up at their front door asking to speak to me, but after what my mom did, or didn't do rather, I highly doubted that. A month later they called to say he was at their house, and I let them give him my number, never expecting him to call and not knowing if I would answer if he did.

Noah and Alex are traveling for work this week, and Sloane is getting drinks with Lauren, so I have the night to myself, which is a nice change of pace. I find the bong and put on Thursday night football. Every few minutes I glance over at my phone, which sits face down next to me on the leather couch, and after a few bong rips, I finally pick it up. I hesitate before clicking the first voicemail I received and bring the phone to my ear.

"Ethan it's your, um, dad—if I can even call myself that. I've been trying to get ahold of you, and I know you've been ignoring my calls, but I'd really like to talk to you. The Clarks said you're in New York now. I never pictured you as a city boy, but then again, I don't know the adult you. Anyway, I hope you're taking care of yourself. Call me back if you can. Okay, well, bye." His voice sounds different than I expected. Older, raspier. It makes me wonder what he looks like now.

Instead of chucking the phone across the room like I expected to, I listen to the next voicemail. Then the next, and the next until I reach the one he left tonight. I pace around our living room and debate what to do next. Do I call him? What could he possibly have to say?

I'm sorry I fucked up your life?

I'm sorry I stopped calling?

I'm sorry your mom never came back for you?

I hold my head in my hands and close my eyes before making my decision. I scroll through my call log until I find Graham's name, and I hit it.

"Hey, Brady, surprised you're not out tonight," he answers.

"Needed a night in. Do you have a few minutes to talk?" I ask, my voice lower than usual.

"Yeah, of course, what's up? Sounds serious."

I hesitate because the topic is one I hate to touch on. "My dad's been calling."

"Fuck. What about?" His response is sharp, the opposite of his usually relaxed tone.

"That's just it, I don't know. He says he really needs to talk to me, and I just can't decide if I should call him back. Have your parents mentioned anything to you?"

The line goes quiet for a moment before he speaks, "They told me that he was getting out of jail a few months ago. What are you gonna do?"

"I don't know, man." I can feel myself start to tense up.

"If you're asking me, I think you should call him back. I know they both really fucked you over, and it's okay to never forgive them, but maybe talking to him will help. Maybe hearing exactly what happened or why he stopped calling will allow you to understand the situation from his side." His advice is surprisingly insightful.

"Yeah, maybe." I sigh.

"How are things with Sloane?" he asks.

"They're good, I guess," I reply.

"Uh-huh." Graham doesn't believe it. "Just know if you keep this shit up for much longer, you're gonna lose her for good, and from what I can tell, you really do like and care about her. A girl like Sloane won't wait around forever."

"Alright, alright. Talk to you soon man." I hang up the phone and set it on the coffee table before taking another hit.

Am I ready to unearth something that happened over ten years ago? I just want to forget it ever happened, and it feels like a phone call with my dad would do the exact opposite of that. I decide to sleep on it—I don't need to decide right this second, so why am I acting like I do?

I text Sloane and tell her the door's unlocked because I don't want to sleep alone tonight, and less than fifteen minutes later, she's curled up next to me. Sometimes I don't realize how much I need her.

32

Sloane

November 2018

Lauren moves about the room with a practiced efficiency, the sound of her suitcase's zipper cutting through the quiet. She pauses to glance at me, sprawled on her bed, concern crossing her face.

"Just take the train in and out tomorrow. I don't want you to be alone for Thanksgiving! Miles's mom invited you. They have more than enough food," she urges.

Last week, exactly ten days before Thanksgiving, Ethan told me that he made plans to go to Wilmington. He didn't ask if I wanted to come, and I guess I didn't expect him to, but that didn't make it hurt any less. It was official: I'd be spending Thanksgiving alone.

"It's fine, really! It'll be nice to have a day to myself. I thought about trying to go to the parade but some of my coworkers said they get there before five a.m., which is a huge no from me." My laughter is genuine, if a bit forced, trying to hide the disappointment.

"Next year, you should have one of your parents come, and maybe mine will, and we can all do the parade!" she offers. "I've always wanted to go!"

Lauren's heading to Connecticut to meet Miles's parents for the first time, and as nice as it was for them to extend an invitation, that sounded like the last plan I wanted to crash. The good part about being in the city for Thanksgiving is that nothing really closes, so my takeout options are endless.

"So what do you think you'll do tomorrow then?" Lauren asks.

"*Sex and the City* reruns and an entire bottle of wine probably," I respond, the plan sounding more appealing as I say it out loud.

Lauren settles next to me on the bed, the mattress dipping slightly under our weight. She looks at me, her expression softening.

"This reminds me of college," she says, a hint of nostalgia in her tone. "Remember when we'd lie in each other's beds for hours without saying anything? Scrolling Instagram and playing *Candy Crush*?"

"I'm gonna miss living together," I admit.

"Me too," she echoes.

This is probably the most intimate moment we've ever had. Our friendship is deep, but it's never been too emotional. That's the beauty of Lauren; she keeps life so lighthearted. This moment was different. I could feel our friendship start to shift. It made me scared for the future and made me wonder if I needed to take my relationship with Ethan more seriously. While I hate the thought of having that conversation with him, I hate the thought of being single while all my friends are in love, getting married, and having kids.

With Ethan I know there will be more than just one Thanksgiving alone. There will be weddings with no plus one and office holiday parties where I'll get asked where my boyfriend is or if I'm single. I remember the days I used to love being single. I think I could get there again. It's not the thought of being alone that scares me, it's the thought of losing him.

Loving him is hard, but leaving would be harder.

Why can't it just be easy?

• • •

The TV asks if I'm still watching as I grab the remote to start the fourth *Sex and the City* episode of the night. Before I hit yes, I pick up my phone to see if Graham or Ethan have posted anything. Odds are they're either downtown or at the beach bars. It's Thanksgiving Eve in their hometown after all. My anxiety gets the best of me, so I go to the kitchen to pour myself another glass of wine. I empty the rest of the bottle into my glass and toss the remnants into the trash can.

I sit back on my favorite side of the couch and decide to turn on the movie instead of the show. Every time I watch the scene where Mr. Big leaves Carrie at the altar, I cry. And right now, I'm feeling a good cry.

I curl up under a blanket as I watch a fictional character go through something I'm so afraid of. If I'm terrified of it, why does a small part of me still imagine it happening between Ethan and me? Why do I want to be with someone who I think would leave me at the altar? Even the smallest inkling of that feeling should tell someone that's not who they're meant to end up with. So why am I still with him?

"Some love stories aren't epic novels. Some are short stories, but that doesn't make them any less filled with love," Carrie says.

For once she makes sense.

Tears stream down my face. Is Ethan my Mr. Big? I've always hated Big, but this scene just highlighted what I've been contemplating for the past few weeks. I'm so afraid to leave Ethan, even though I know it's the right thing to do. I can't keep waiting around for someone to love me who doesn't. Maybe he does love me. It's not enough though.

Usually I hate pity parties, but I can't help but feel a little sorry for myself tonight. I'm spending Thanksgiving alone in my small New York City apartment while two of my favorite people are in our college town without me. Ethan probably doesn't even realize how fucked up it is that he left me here. But it is. It's really fucked up. He might not know what it's like to have someone who wants to love him, someone who doesn't want to leave him, but that doesn't give him an excuse to treat me as if I don't exist.

I wake up the next morning with a pounding headache (*thanks, wine*) and no missed calls or texts. What a way to kick off Thanksgiving Day.

Groaning at the fact that I don't have a TV in my room, I slowly make my way into the living room to put on the parade and make a cup of coffee. While I wait for the Keurig to finish brewing, I call my mom.

"Hi, honey, happy Thanksgiving!" The warmth in her voice reminds me of how much I miss her.

"Hey, Mom. Happy Thanksgiving to you too! How's London?" I reply.

"Oh, it's amazing, sweetie. How are you? Are you at the parade?" she asks, hopeful.

"No, I just woke up." A yawn stretches through my response.

"Well, your doorman should have some champagne waiting for you downstairs. I'm sorry again we're not together today, but I'll see you in just a few weeks for Christmas. I ordered us new matching pajamas. Your favorite tradition!"

"I think you mean *your* favorite tradition," I tease her.

"Whatever you say. Well, look, honey, I have to get going, but I hope you have a great day. Love you!"

I end the call with a soft "Love you too, Mom."

At least that killed about four minutes of my day. As I pick up the phone to call my dad, it buzzes in my hand. Expecting it to be a group chat, I'm pleasantly surprised when I see Ethan's name pop up.

10:11 a.m.

Ethan Brady: Happy Thanksgiving, turkey. Can't wait to get home and gobble you up 😋

10:12 a.m.

Me: Omfg, you're so cheesy

10:13 a.m.

Me: Happy Thanksgiving, tell Graham I say hi!

10:15 a.m.

Ethan Brady: You ain't seen nothin' yet

For the next few seconds, I uncontrollably smile at the message and forget that he's the reason why I'm spending a holiday all alone.

33

Ethan

November 2018

hate airports and I hate flying. I don't get how people can possibly enjoy it. Everyone's in a rush, my flight almost always gets delayed for no reason, and I usually end up sitting in front of a kid who kicks my seat the entire trip. This flight was no different. I wait for the passengers around me to make their way up the aisle, throw my duffle bag over my shoulder, and follow them. Luckily, Graham's picking me up, which means we'll get a drink before going to his house. God knows I need a few.

"Where's your suit?" he calls out.

Graham is waiting for me in his topless Jeep Wrangler. It's an unusually warm day for late November, but that's North Carolina for you, always unpredictable.

"I thought city boys only wore suits everywhere. At least that's what they make it seem like in the movies," he continues.

I shoot down his poor excuse of a joke. "Who in their right mind would wear a suit on a flight that cost eighty dollars round trip?"

"True. Wanna hit Dockside? I figured we could sit outside and get a bucket of beers before seeing the 'rents."

"Thought you'd never ask." I turn up the volume, and we listen to "Stir Fry" by Migos followed by a few other songs from that album until we pull into the restaurant parking lot.

"Does it feel good to be back?"

I shrug. "I haven't been gone that long."

"Dude, it's almost been a year," Graham points out.

Shit, he's right. January marks one year since I packed up, left Wilmington, and moved to a city I thought I hated.

"It's gone by so fast." I follow him to the outdoor bar, where we take a seat and order a bucket of Corona.

The air smells salty and nostalgic. On one hand, I miss the beach. I miss packing up our surfboards and catching waves to avoid our problems. I miss finding sand in every crevice of my car. I miss having a car. But I don't miss the memories this place brings up for me.

"So how are things? Where's Sloane going for Thanksgiving?" he inquires.

I could've called it. It didn't even take Graham a full hour to bring her up. This happens whenever I go somewhere without her. It's like we're a package deal. What's the point of not being in a relationship if everyone just assumes we are anyway? I'm getting tired of people caring about us more than they care about me. Is that selfish? Maybe. Do I care? No.

"Can we talk about something else? Sometimes it feels like every conversation I have these days seems to revolve around Sloane." I sip my beer. "How are you?"

"Sorry, dude, didn't mean anything by it," Graham promises. "I'm good. Living at home is getting old though. I wish I could speed up the wedding so Emily and I could live together already. Her parents are so traditional, it hurts."

"Have you looked at new places?"

"We have a two-bedroom apartment over in Mayfaire, but it's just her living there until the wedding. I stay overnight a lot though—crazy, I know. We'll probably live there a year or two and then look at houses." There's a hint of excitement in his tone.

"Congrats, man."

We finish the bucket of beers and then head to his house. I already know this is going to be a long weekend, one that I'm not sure I'm even remotely ready for.

• • •

"You're sure that you don't want to come out with us?" Graham asks one last time before getting out of the car.

"Maybe later. I'll let you know. Thanks again for letting me borrow your car," I reply.

"Anytime. Just meet or pick us up later. Good luck." He slams the passenger door, and I watch as he and Emily walk into the bar hand in hand.

I type the address to a motel twenty minutes outside of Wilmington into my maps app. I turn up the volume on the radio so that I don't have to hear my own thoughts, but they creep in anyway.

What am I doing? It's been ten years. Ten years and he hasn't tried to call or write. So why now? Am I just helping him clear a guilty conscience? Should I just turn around? Spend the night with Graham, the guy who's been with me through it all? Or should I just suck it up and hear him out, so I don't spend the rest of my life wondering what he wanted to say?

As I pull into the parking lot of the Motel 6, my palms start to sweat. I sit in the car for another few minutes before finally turning off the engine and getting out. I scan the numbers on the doors until I see the number 105. I hesitate before knocking.

When the door opens, I'm shocked. I don't know what I expected my dad to look like after ten years in prison, but for some reason I thought he'd be the same guy I remembered. In some ways he is, but he's older and smaller than before.

"Look at you," he says, smiling slightly.

I stand in the doorway, still taking in the sight of him. I manage a half smile before he brings me in for a hug. I pat his back and awkwardly wait for him to pull away. This is so much worse than I expected.

I can tell that he's been drinking, but I reluctantly agree to go to dinner with him anyway. Growing up, I never thought of my parents as alcoholics. They owned a bar, so I thought drinking was a part of their job, or at least my dad's anyway. It wasn't until I was older that I understood he had an issue.

He gets into Graham's car, and I drive us to a restaurant a few minutes away from the motel. The car ride is mostly silent, but my brain won't shut off. I can't believe the guy in the passenger seat is the same guy that raised me. The guy who I called Dad, who taught me how to throw a football and ride a bike. He's a sliver of the guy I remember and is now an ex-con with gray hair, a sunken face full of wrinkles.

We sit across the table from each other, and he orders us two Miller Lites. His fingers drum the neck of the bottle before he asks me the question I've been dreading.

"Have you talked to her? Your mom, I mean."

"Not since she got out. Have you?" I take a big swig of beer.

"Her number has been disconnected for years. I was hoping you had a new one," he continues before processing the words that just came out of my mouth. "Did you say you haven't talked to her since she was released?"

"That's exactly what I said," I confirm.

He looks away, his disappointment evident. "She was supposed to go back for you. That was our agreement."

"Well, she didn't. According to Facebook she moved to Texas, got remarried, and has a daughter now," I reply, my tone bitter.

"Fuck." He rubs his temple before taking another sip of beer. "Fuck her. So you were living with the Clarks this entire time?"

"Yep." My reply is short.

Relief washes over him. "They're good people. Real good people."

"So what was so important that you needed to talk to me after years of not calling?" I finally ask.

He looks at me, a seriousness in his gaze that wasn't there before. "Son, I stopped calling because that's what your mom wanted. She wanted a clean slate and a life that didn't include me because she hated me for the mess that I got us into. She hated me because we lost you."

"Clearly she didn't care too much about losing me if she never came back," I huff, finishing off my beer.

He leans forward. "I know it doesn't mean much, but I'm here now. I'd like to start over. Get to know you."

"Do you have a job?" I ask skeptically.

"At the marina. I've been picking up every shift, trying to hit overtime, so I can rent a place and get out of that motel," he assures me.

The server brings us another round, and I consider his offer. Is he being genuine? It would be nice to have a parent of my own again.

34

Sloane

December 2018

Ethan hasn't returned any of my calls or texts since Thanksgiving. Which, despite his lack of communication skills, is very unusual for him.

Everything I've been feeling over the past few weeks wasn't just my own insecurities; they were alarm bells going off. My gut has been telling me exactly what I've been trying to avoid: *You're losing him. You're losing him again, and there's nothing you can do about it.*

You can't beg someone to love you, as much as I wish you can, you can't. You shouldn't have to convince someone that you're good enough or you're worth it. That's something I'm still learning.

I insert my key into the lock and turn it, the familiar click signaling my homecoming. The door swings open, and I'm greeted by the smell of fresh basil, a hint of garlic, and the new vanilla candle I bought last week.

"Are you cooking?" I yell, hoping my voice carries through the apartment.

"Homemade pizzas!" Lauren returns the same energy.

"Four?" I ask, gesturing to the spread in front of us. "Who's eating all of these?"

"I figured Miles and Ethan. One for each of us! We can do our own toppings."

"Oh, um," I stutter, trying to wrack my brain for an excuse to come up with for Ethan. I don't want to tell her the truth—that he's been ghosting me. "Ethan's tied up at work, so we won't need one for him."

"More for us!" Lauren shrugs. A weight is lifted from my shoulders knowing that she doesn't suspect anything. I hate hiding things from Lauren, but I know what she'll say. She'll say exactly what I'm thinking.

He's pulling away again. This time though, I'm completely aware.

After dinner, I do the dishes for Lauren and then escape to my room. I sit on the edge of my bed and stare at the lock screen on my phone.

Six days. It's been almost a week of being left on delivered, not even on read. Which is even more frustrating considering I know he's seen the notification. I hate how he has so much control over me. He knows my daily routine, when I leave for work and when I get home, so I know he's been leaving early and staying late to avoid running into me.

I launch my phone across the bed, and it falls into the sliver of space between the mattress and the wall. Silent tears fall down my face and soak the pillow that Ethan usually sleeps on.

Why did I have to fall in love with someone that couldn't love me back? In the beginning, I was convinced he was my "right person, wrong time." Now, I'm starting to think that may just be a phrase people use when they love someone so deeply and know that person doesn't, and never can, love them back the same way. So instead, they'll make up excuses about timing and places to avoid the inevitable ending.

Knock, knock.

Before I have the chance to wipe away my tears, Lauren is standing in the doorway—a scene I'm all too familiar with.

"What's wrong?" There's concern in her voice.

"Nothing, I'm fine. It's nothing." I sniffle.

"Clearly it's something."

"Ethan's been ignoring me for almost a week now." I hug my arms around myself.

"A week? Why didn't you say something sooner?" she replies, surprised.

The confession spills out of me, "Because I'm embarrassed. It's happening again—I'm losing him, and I have absolutely no control over it. How am I back here? Why didn't I learn? I've been so convinced that the reason I never fully moved on was that we were supposed to try again. We were supposed to work out this time. So why haven't we? This might sound insane, and I don't even know if I believe in God, but sometimes I think that he wouldn't keep putting Ethan back into my life if we weren't meant to work out one day."

"Oh, Sloane." Lauren's touch is gentle on my shoulder. "Or he's trying to teach you a lesson. You're not going to want to hear this, but you need to let him go. Look at what he's been doing to you for the past two years. You can't keep living like this, at his every beck and call. This is your life; he doesn't call the shots. You do."

Her words, though tough, are laced with love and a desire to see me free from this never-ending cycle.

I can't manage a reply.

After a few minutes of silence and more sobbing, Lauren turns off the lamp on my nightstand and leaves the room. I fall asleep on top of my comforter, fully dressed, dried tears on both cheeks.

The next morning, I get in the shower and turn the water as hot as it will go in hopes that I can burn off any trace of Ethan. I dry myself off and stare at my naked body in the mirror, thinking about all the times he touched me. Why can't I remember the last time that he kissed me? What if the last time was the last time? I make myself sick over the thought and kneel in front of the toilet bowl.

I finish up in the bathroom and retrieve my phone from underneath my bed, where I left it last night. I power it on, grab my work bag, and head out the door. As I get out of the elevator, I stare at the only text message I received.

7:42 a.m.

Ethan Brady: Hey. I'm sorry for not replying sooner. I needed some space.

That's it? That's all he has to say? I shove the phone back into my bag and, for once, read the advertisements plastered all over the subway car.

• • •

My voice is a mix of frustration and hurt as I confront him. "You can't just ignore me for a week and expect me to forget about it, Ethan."

"I know, and I said I'm sorry," he says, the apology lacking conviction. "What more do you want from me?"

"I want you to stop avoiding me. Stop avoiding us."

"I'm not. I needed to be alone." His defense is weak, and he's avoiding eye contact.

"You can communicate that then, before ghosting me," I remind him.

He looks up. "I didn't ghost you, Sloane. I'm here now, aren't I?"

Sitting on the barstool, I watch as Ethan paces the kitchen.

"Yeah, but for how long?" I question.

"I don't know," he replies. "If I could answer that, we'd be dating."

I stare blankly at him and feel a tear roll down my cheek. Two years ago, any time I'd been around Ethan, I was worried I would say the wrong thing and scare him away. Now, in the middle of my tiny New York City apartment, I'm being the most vulnerable I've ever been with anyone.

"I didn't mean that in a bad way." He takes a seat next to me and puts his hand on my leg. "I just don't know what I can say that can make you understand how I'm feeling."

"I can't keep doing this one-foot-in, one-foot-out thing with you. We're not in college anymore, Ethan. I want a relationship. No more of whatever this is," I say, fighting back tears.

He ignores me for a moment and puts his head in his hands. This is it—this is the moment it all ends. I brace myself for his delivery. I know that's what he's thinking.

How do I tell her I can't give her what she wants?

"I've told you this before, Sloane. I need to do this at my own pace and on my own time." His tone is certain.

I nod; the gesture is small but accepting, and my heart sinks with the familiarity of that sentence.

"Can you promise me something?" I ask, locking eyes with him.

He swallows, visibly uneasy. "Depends."

"Please just don't leave me in the dark like that again. I want to be here for you. I'm on your side, but I can't do that if you ignore me for weeks on end."

"It was less than a week." he replies, trying to downplay the situation.

"I'm serious. It hurts." I'm firm.

Ethan looks at me, finally seeing the pain he's caused.

"I'll try," he says.

Ethan never makes promises he can't keep, which is why he doesn't make promises.

I empty the dishwasher and pour myself a glass of wine, knowing he's probably rolling his eyes behind my back. He plops himself onto the couch and plays on his phone. Is this what our life would be like—that future I've been dreaming of—would it be bad communication, half-assed promises, and awkward silences? I'd like to think our relationship would be different once he's ready to put in the effort and fully commit.

"Should we watch *Breaking Bad*? I can pour you a glass," I offer, holding up the bottle of red.

"I'm not in the mood to drink tonight," he says as he turns on the episode.

Ethan's body molds to mine as we lie on the couch. I drink my wine too quickly and refill the glass three more times during the two episodes we get through. No matter how much I try, I can't get our last conversation out of my head. One of his arms is wrapped around my waist, while my head rests on the other.

"Let's go to bed." His mouth finds its way to my ear.

I turn around so that I'm facing him, even though his head is still a few inches above mine. My hand grips the back of his neck, I pull him into me, and we start kissing.

Our mouths become one for what feels like hours. I can't remember the last time we kissed for this long. Maybe the first time we ever kissed in my bedroom at Ascent. I remember the first time we kissed like it happened hours ago. I'm afraid it's something I'll never be able to forget.

"My room?" I ask.

"I want to fuck you here," he whispers. "On the couch."

So I let him. I let him fuck me on the sectional couch we got from Facebook Marketplace, and the entire time I try not to cry.

Somehow, it feels different than all the other times we've had sex. It feels less intimate, like I'm just an object to him. I try not to let it show, but something tells me he knows. Once we're done, we both lie there. Naked and completely still.

Even though he was just inside of me, he feels so distant. How can I miss him when he's right here?

"Is it okay if I sleep at home tonight?" he asks, as if my opinion holds any weight.

"Okay," is all I can manage.

He gets dressed, washes out my wineglass, and puts his shoes on all while I lie naked on the couch. He kisses my forehead and leaves the apartment. I expect myself to cry, but I don't.

I get off the couch and make my way into my room, where I change into my favorite pajamas and get into bed. Even though it feels like something between us is about to break, something within me feels somewhat at peace.

I don't want to spend the rest of my life thinking, *Is this my great love story?*, because I want more. I deserve more.

I don't want calls that go unanswered or texts that are never read. I don't want to spend holidays, or any day, begging someone to choose me. I deserve someone who chooses me without question. Someone who loves me without doubt. I want someone who shows up, and I realize that my relationship with Ethan isn't any of those things. It likely never will be.

Maybe this really is the end.

35

Sloane

December 2018

Phillip hands me a blush-colored envelope. My name is written in calligraphy, and without even opening it, I know it's Graham and Emily's wedding invitation. The wedding isn't until summer, but being early is on-brand for them.

I enter our apartment, which is filled with half-packed moving boxes, and avoid opening the envelope. I place it on the counter and stare at it for what feels like an eternity.

Am I ready to open it?

I carefully break the seal and immediately tear up. This is all I want—someone who loves me enough to commit to forever. Even though I know that marriage doesn't always mean forever, people don't go into it thinking they'll get divorced. They go in wanting to spend the rest of their lives together. Why can't Ethan give this to me?

I grab a magnet from the drawer next to the sink and hang the invitation on the refrigerator. My phone starts buzzing on the counter.

6:38 p.m.

Ethan Brady: Waiting on our food now. Be there in 30.

For a second I forgot about our plans tonight. I hit send on a simple reply and collect myself.

Even though most of our kitchen is packed, we left out a few wineglasses, knowing we'd need them. I reach into the cabinet above the sink for one, pour myself a heavy glass of cab and finish it before he arrives. Something tells me I'm going to need it.

Ethan reaches for two of the ketchup packets and squirts them on his fries. We eat in silence as the TV plays sports coverage from the living room. I pour another glass of wine.

"What should we watch? We need a new show, but I haven't heard of anything good coming out on Netflix lately. Have you?"

He cuts me off. "I can't do this anymore, Sloane. I think this needs to end."

The wineglass in my hand falls to the floor, and I rush to collect the remnants. Tears fill my eyes as I pick up each piece and place it in my other hand.

Here I am again, crying on the kitchen floor.

"Fuck!" Ethan shouts as he rushes to my side. The urgency of the situation begins to sink in, even as my emotions cloud my reality.

I look at my hand and notice there's a large piece of glass wedged into my palm. Why can't I feel it? I can see the glass and the blood, but I can't feel anything. The blood drips down my hand and onto the kitchen rug. I hope Lauren wasn't planning on taking this with her. Ethan pulls out his phone and helps me up.

I watch as he calls an Uber and grabs my hand to inspect it.

"We should leave it in there. I'm worried about pulling it out. I don't want it to bleed more." He's wrapping my hand with a dish towel while I'm still frozen in shock. Not from the blood but from the heartbreak.

• • •

"Sloane, I'm so sorry," he says as he opens the car door. I get into the back seat, and he slides in next to me.

We arrive at the emergency room in what feels like seconds. I still can't manage to form words, so I can't tell him that I want him to leave. He checks us in and sits next to me in the waiting room, holding the dish towel over my hand and applying the slightest pressure around where the glass is to stop the bleeding.

"Sloane Hart?" a doctor says, entering the waiting room.

We follow her through a set of double doors, and she shows me to a bed, where I sit while she draws the curtain. I don't make eye contact with Ethan, because if I do, I think I might be sick.

She examines my hand before reassuring me, "This doesn't look too bad. I'm going to remove it and then clean the wound before wrapping it up. The cleaning will be the worst part."

I nod in place of a reply.

I feel no pain as she gets the glass out and cleans my hand. I'm trying to wrap my head around what Ethan said after dinner. He's had so many chances to end it. I've given him so many outs. And instead this is how it ends.

The car ride home is silent. Not even the radio is playing. All that I hear is *I can't do this anymore, Sloane.*

I hate how he says my name. I hope I never hear him say it again.

We arrive at our building, and we both stand outside for a moment before walking in.

"Should I come to yours so we can finish talking?" he asks hesitantly.

"No, I don't think we need to talk more."

I finally look up and stare at him, pausing before I continue. "I just need you to know that you can't do this to me anymore. There's no going back after tonight. I can't keep doing this to myself. I love you so much that it hurts. It's made me physically ill on more than one occasion. Love shouldn't hurt. Love shouldn't make you sick.

I know that you're not ready, and nothing I can say or do will ever change that. The only person that can change that is you. I would've done anything for you—"

A tear falls down my face.

I wait for him to say something, but he doesn't. We look at each other for a few seconds, and then I break eye contact, turn around, and walk into the building. I never look back.

The elevator ride feels centuries long. As soon as I'm face-to-face with the empty apartment, I break down. Everything is just as we left it. Our empty takeout boxes waiting to be brought to the trash chute, the remnants of my broken wineglass, bloodstained paper towels. I do my best to clean it up without hurting myself again.

I always believed that we'd find our way back to each other every time things ended. Except this time, it feels final—like I'll never see him again. I can feel it in my bones. This time is really it.

It still hurts. Losing him and missing him still hurts, but in a different way than it did the other times. It doesn't feel like an earth-shattering heartbreak, but a more subtle lingering pain.

I stay up most of the night replaying our relationship over in my head from the moment we met all the way up to tonight. Our first kiss, our first date, our last kiss, and our last date. I wish things could have unfolded differently between us. I know that deep down he loves and cares about me, but it still isn't enough.

Some people don't grow up in a house full of love, and even though my parents aren't together anymore, for eighteen years of my life, they had a good run. I hate what I know about Ethan's past, and I wish he felt like he could tell me. In more ways than one, I hate his parents. I hate them for leaving him, but I hate them even more for making him feel like he isn't deserving of being loved.

36

Ethan

December 2018

When I got back into the city, I avoided replying to Sloane's texts. I needed to clear my head, process the weekend's chaos. Now, two days deep into radio silence, I'm still scrambling for the right play. Even though she won't admit it, I know she's upset with me for ditching her on Thanksgiving. So I can only imagine how she feels now.

Why the hell can't I get it right? With her, with anything? I'm stuck in my own head, which is nothing new, I guess.

Laundry day—the epitome of New York. Bag slung over my shoulder, I step into the elevator and finally crack, shooting Sloane a text. Just an *I'm sorry, I just needed space*, straight up, no chaser, knowing that she's gonna corner me for a full explanation later anyway.

I walk into her apartment and notice that there's a half-empty bottle of wine on the counter. Part of me was expecting that—she always drinks when she's nervous. Usually, I don't mind it, but for some reason, today it really bothers me. It makes me wonder if alcohol is a coping mechanism for her. I can't build a life with someone who turns to alcohol when things get tough. Alcohol is the sole reason my life ended up the way that it did, and I really don't want to sign up for a rerun.

"I want you to stop avoiding me. Stop avoiding us." She addresses me.

I choose to defend myself. "I'm not. I just needed to be alone."

"You can communicate that then, before ghosting me."

"I didn't ghost you, Sloane. I'm here now, aren't I?"

"Yeah, but for how long?"

I'm cornered, no solid game plan, and I can tell she sees right through me. "I don't know," I admit. "If I could answer that, we'd be dating."

I can see the heartbreak in her eyes. I've got to tread lighter—she's one step away from a breakdown, and I'm the one with the sledgehammer.

Trying to backpedal, I fumble. "I didn't mean that in a bad way." I drop onto the seat beside her, still unsure of how to fix this. "I just don't know what I can say that can make you understand how I'm feeling."

"I can't keep doing this one-foot-in, one-foot-out thing with you. We're not in college anymore, Ethan. I want a relationship. No more of whatever this is." For once, she's firm in her delivery.

"I'll try," slips out, and I regret those two words as soon as they leave my mouth.

I know I'll never be the person she wants or deserves. I need to just let her go and stop trying to be someone I'm not, for both of our sakes.

• • •

I spend the next few days thinking through everything. Every moment in my childhood, every moment before Sloane, and every moment with Sloane. I try to remember the last time I was truly happy, and it hurts to know that I can't pinpoint it. Can't most people? My entire life has been a series of unfortunate events. One after another. How shitty is that? What's even shittier though is having to explain these things to people—people like Sloane.

It's not that I don't want to tell her, I just can't. I don't know how. I don't want to see that look of pity in her eyes. I don't want anyone to pity me, but especially not her. I'm supposed to be the one she leans on, not the other way around. I'll never depend on someone in the way she wants me to. I'll never depend on someone other than myself because, sooner or later, people let me down. They always have and they always will.

I stand in line waiting to pay for our dinner and can't shake the uneasy feeling inside of me. I know I need to do this.

"Order for Ethan?"

The host hands me a plastic bag with two to-go boxes inside in exchange for my credit card.

The restaurant is six blocks away from our apartment building, which gives me time to run through how I want this to go down. I hate that I'm going to hurt her, which is why I've put this off for so long. I prepare the conversation in my head and go over it what feels like a hundred times.

The elevator doors open, and a lump in my throat starts to form. I don't want to do this, I really don't, but at the same time I know I have no choice. Nothing between us will change if I can't get my shit together first. I just hope she understands that.

I let myself into Sloane's apartment and greet her with a hug.

Sloane unpacks the plastic bag and hands me the to-go container. I squirt some ketchup on my fries before taking a bite out of my wrap. I chew extra slowly so I can delay the inevitable conversation for as long as possible.

"What should we watch? We need a new show, but I haven't heard of anything good coming out on Netflix lately. Have you?"

I cut her off before she can finish her sentence. "I can't do this anymore, Sloane. I think this needs to end."

I watch the color drain from her face as she drops the wineglass she was just about to take a sip from. She immediately bends down to clean it up, as if it's instinct, and that's when I notice the blood. This is going so much worse than I expected.

The hospital visit is short, but it feels so long. Probably because I'm still avoiding the conversation that we inevitably still need to have.

The car ride home is painfully silent, and I try to put myself in her shoes. I wonder what she's thinking and how she's feeling. Does she hate me? Is it selfish to wonder that? The driver pulls up to our building, and I watch as Sloane pauses for a second before opening the car door. Within seconds, we're face-to-face with each other in the middle of the sidewalk.

"Should I come to yours so we can finish talking?" I ask hesitantly.

"No, I don't think we need to talk more."

I don't bother arguing with her because I know she's right. She deserves someone better than me. Someone who can give her everything I'll never be capable of.

Feeling deflated, I watch as she turns and walks into the lobby. I expect her to look back, but she never does. I don't know if I ever pictured things with Sloane actually ending, but this feels final. I hate that I'm hurting her, but even more so, I hate that I can't be honest with her. I hope she knows that there wasn't anything she could've done differently.

The cold air feels comforting as I wait a few minutes, until I think she's gotten inside of her apartment, to make my way upstairs. My roommates are sitting on the couch smoking weed and watching college basketball, so I join them.

"Want a hit?" Noah holds out the bong.

I grab it from him without replying and rip it one, two, three times.

"Woah, dude, bad day?" Alex asks.

"You could say that," I reply.

None of us speak for the rest of the night. Instead, we get high, avoid our problems, and watch sports. Three of the things that I do best.

• • •

The next morning, I roll over in bed and reach for my phone to scroll the feed. It's not until I see a post that I want to send to Sloane that I remember everything that unfolded last night. I miss her more than I thought I would. I know because I feel a little more empty than usual.

What's wrong with me? Why am I so fucked up? I mean, I know why I'm fucked up—my parents did this to me. Why can't I let someone love me when it's all I've wanted my entire life? All I've wanted was to feel loved, and as soon as someone tries, I push them away.

I really thought if I let Sloane love me, eventually I'd get there too. Instead, this is where we are. Three breakups, two years, and one really broken heart.

37

Sloane

December 2018

Today I decide to walk home from work because I can't imagine dealing with an overcrowded subway car right now. The air is crisp and unusually warm for mid-December. I still zip my coat all the way up to my chin to avoid getting sick. The last thing I need is to miss more time at work. I ruminate on the last three, almost four, years as I walk down Park Avenue. I pull my headphones out of my pocket, plug them into my phone, and scroll Spotify to find a solid breakup playlist, filled with just the right amount of Taylor Swift.

I'm reminded of the night when I tried to convince Ethan that we should walk almost seven miles home because I would've done anything for more time with him. It's funny how some things never change. Now here I am years later, in a different city, wishing the same thing.

I walk into the apartment and am greeted by Lauren who, in typical Lauren fashion, already has a drink waiting for me.

"Get ready," she demands firmly. "We're going out."

I smile as I enter my room, observing the few pieces of clothing that I haven't packed yet. I pull my favorite bodysuit off its hanger along with the jeans that used to fit me perfectly, but now gape a little in the back, and get dressed.

Lauren emerges in my doorway. "Do you want to talk about it?" She takes a seat on my bed as if to say I have no choice.

I shake my head. "Not really. There's nothing to talk about."

She presses anyway. "How are you feeling?"

"Oddly enough, not as bad as I expected to," I confess. "I saw it coming. I think I just hoped that I was wrong."

We throw on coats, and Lauren calls us an Uber to Miles's place so she can drop off a few of her boxes on the way to the new bar in Chelsea that she's taking me to. His loft is a New York City dream. It's everything I used to picture we'd live in until I realized most people can't afford it. Exposed brick, high ceilings, and a spiral staircase that takes you up to the lofted bedroom and full bath.

"This is amazing," I say, feeling a ping of envy.

"Isn't it?" Lauren agrees, prideful as she unloads her boxes.

"Where's Miles?" I ask.

Her response comes with a tilt of her head towards the liquor cabinet. "Out with clients. Want a drink before we go? We can sit up on the roof."

"Sure." I shrug.

I make my way around the loft, admiring every detail, hoping I'll live like this one day. I follow her down the hall to the elevator, and we take it up two floors. The doors open to an empty hallway with one door at the end of it. I follow her through it and watch as a gorgeous view of the city emerges.

"Wow," I breathe.

She leads me to two sling chairs, and we both take a seat, wrapping blankets around us even though we're wearing our winter coats. The city stretches out before us, a canvas of endless stories. I can see people partying on other rooftops, couples making dinner through their windows, cars zipping through traffic below.

Lauren breaks the silence. "Are you going to be okay?" I turn to her because I'm unsure if she's joking or not, but the concern in her eyes tells me she's serious. She's worried about me.

"Lauren." I put my hand out to offer reassurance. "I'll be fine."

She exhales, the sound heavy with guilt. "I just feel shitty," she confesses, her eyes dropping. "Like of course this happens as I'm moving out. Timing's a bitch."

"It always is." I can't help but laugh.

We never end up going out. Instead, Lauren brings up a bottle of tequila, a space heater, and an extension cord as we sift through memories, essentially running through the entirety of our friendship.

"I think my favorite memory of you, a story we'll definitely tell our kids when they're heading off to college, is junior year spring break," she recounts.

"Which part?" I pass the bottle back to her.

"When you almost got arrested at that bar in Key West. I'll never forget the look on your face when the bouncer snatched your ID and told you to stand to the side. I've literally never seen you run, ever, except for that day." She nearly chokes on laughter and tequila.

"I can't believe he didn't recognize us when we went back an hour later. All we did was swap sunglasses and T-shirts."

"Wait, remember sophomore year, when we were so excited to use our new fake IDs, and then the bouncer at Jerry's peeled the film off of them and told us to get lost?" Her laugh is infectious.

"That was easily one of the top five most embarrassing moments of my life. Everyone behind us in line looked at us like we were idiots."

"We were idiots," she agrees, taking a hearty swig of tequila, scrunching her face in response to the burn.

I shake my head in disbelief at our current situation. "I can't believe we're taking a bottle of liquor to the face right now."

"Can you not? We used to do this every weekend with Burnett's and Bacardi." Lauren waves off my comment with another laugh.

"Oh god, don't remind me." I playfully gag; the past tastes bittersweet now.

We lose track of time until there are no more stories to tell. The day we met at our dorm hall orientation, the first time we got drunk together, senior year spending hours applying to any job we could find, thinking we'd never land one in a city like this. Yet here we are—sitting on the rooftop of the apartment she now shares with what I'd like to consider her soulmate.

How lucky is she to have found love at the age of twenty-three?

I glance at my phone—it's getting late, even for us.

• • •

Outside, Lauren's grip on my shoulder halts me. "Hey, Sloane?" Her voice is soft but firm.

"Yeah?" I turn to her.

"One day he's going to wake up and realize that he lost the best thing he ever had. He lost the only person who would've loved him through anything. I hope he hurts. I hope he regrets it. But even more importantly, I hope he learns. I hope he learns that love isn't always easy. Love is compromise. It's understanding and accepting. Someone else is going to give you all of that and more one day, and I can't wait to see who he is."

Her speech is a Band-Aid to my broken heart, and as I hug her, the world feels a little less cold.

"I love you," I say, and with that, I step into the Uber.

A few minutes into the ride, a wave of nausea hits me. I'm more drunk than I thought. I wonder if it's from the lack of sleep or the lack of food. Either way I try to close my eyes and stay off my phone to keep me from getting sick and being charged a cleaning fee.

The drive takes unusually long, so I open my eyes and notice we're taking a longer way through the West Village. Usually, I'd be worried about something like this, but my nauseous state won't allow me to. Before I can close my eyes again, I see Reese's building. In the back seat of the Uber, I start crying because I broke up with a guy who loved me for a guy that never could. Why am I the way that I am?

I scroll through my contacts until I see Reese Thompson. My finger wavers over the call button, but eventually I hold the phone up to my ear. It rings and rings. No answer. I lock the phone and close my eyes until we get to my apartment.

When I finally get into bed, I reach for the charger to plug my phone into. Before I set my alarm and go sleep, I pull up Instagram and type Reese's name into the search bar. I'm surprised to see he unblocked me. There it is—a picture of him with what I'm assuming is his new girlfriend at a wedding a few weeks ago. The cliché caption, *Forever wedding date*, confirms it. I stare at the screen and debate my next move. Before I can stop myself, I hit send on a text to Ethan.

12:20 a.m.

Me: Can you sleep here? Just for tonight? I don't want to be alone.

I put my phone on do not disturb even though I continue to check it every few minutes to see if he replies.

I toss and turn all night, unable to turn off my brain. All I can think about is Ethan. What if I never get over him? What if I go to bed and wake up every day for the rest of my life wanting him? What if I keep waiting for a call or a text or a sign that never comes?

Morning comes, and I check my phone once more just to find no new messages.

38

Sloane

January 2019

The West Village on a Sunday morning in January is cold and quiet.

I tip the movers and thank them before making my way back inside. As I step into my new apartment, I'm greeted by the scent of fresh paint, still lingering in the air. It's a cozy little space, just over four hundred square feet, but it's mine. For the first time, it's just me, and the idea of living alone feels both liberating and daunting.

I stand in the middle of the room, since there's only one, shivering from more than just the chill in the air. The echoes of Ethan still resonate in my heart. It's only been about a month; the end of us is a raw wound that hasn't fully healed yet. I wonder if it ever will.

First loves are funny like that. They're the ones that introduce you to everything and teach you how to love, in the same way that they teach you how to hurt and how to heal. No matter how hurt you are though, you'll never hate them, and depending on who you ask, in ways you'll still love them. I'd like to think that I taught him the meaning of unconditional love, while he taught me how to love myself.

The apartment is tiny, but it's a canvas for my new life. I see potential in every corner, a chance to rebuild and redefine myself. It's my haven, my sanctuary, a place to heal, to grow, to rediscover who I am without Ethan. I didn't realize how much of myself I lost in him until the other night when I sat down to read. I couldn't remember the last time I picked up a book, let alone did anything for myself that wasn't Ethan, Lauren, or work related. This is a new chapter in my life, one in which I'm finally the main character.

As I begin to unpack the boxes, I can't help but tear up. The city starts to wake up outside of my window, and I take a deep breath and tell myself that I can do this. I can thrive on my own, and these boxes and this apartment are a reminder that I already am.

EPILOGUE

Sloane

September 2019

It's been nine months since Ethan ended things between us. Nine months can really change a person. Nine months ago, Ethan knew me like the back of his hand. He could predict my every move. Surely he can still recognize my face in a crowded room, but he doesn't know the things that define who I am now.

I haven't seen or heard from him, not even a *happy birthday* text, which I've come to learn is a good thing. My therapist says you never want an ex who tries to *happy birthday* their way back into your life.

I think back to who I was in December—it seems like such a long-lost version of myself, someone I don't know anymore. Losing Ethan made me realize that I wasn't mourning the memories of him. I mourned the idea of him that I created. I mourned the future I built in my head using our best moments. I mourned the potential I saw in him, and the life that I saw for us.

In the spring I adopted a cat and named him Ollie. He's perched on the windowsill, watching as the neighbors begin their early morning commutes. I never thought of myself as a cat person, but I know a dog is too much for the city.

I turn on the coffeepot and reach for a muffin in the pastry case my mom brought me as a housewarming gift. Once it's brewed, I pour myself a cup and sit at the bistro table, where I typically begin each morning.

Right after the breakup, if you could even call it that, I started journaling again. I pour my feelings onto the pages every day, sometimes more than once, and have filled almost two. Annie gave me the idea of starting a blog so that all my professional work didn't revolve around heartbreak. I loved the idea so much that I worked on it all night.

In just three months, I've gained close to twenty-five thousand subscribers. It was scary at first, being so vulnerable online, but I saw how many people my open letter article resonated with last year and knew I had the opportunity to turn my heartbreak into something worthwhile. Now every morning I wake up and write for thirty minutes before I head into the office. I sip my coffee and stare at the blank screen that sits in front of me while I try and figure out today's post:

The most important thing that I've learned over the last six months is that you need to show up for yourself. I know this might sound bleak, but the only person we really have at the end of the day is ourselves. You're the one that gets yourself out of bed every morning and tucks yourself in every night. You're the one that picks yourself up off of the bathroom floor after a few too many. You should always love that person more than someone who broke your heart.

If you feel like you lost yourself in a past (or even present) relationship, spend time getting to know who you are. Find new hobbies or fall back in love with old ones. Mine are reading and therapy. Both have been reminders of how beautiful, sometimes sad but mostly beautiful, life is.

I read the words on the screen and try to convince myself that I believe them. Sure, I'm proud of myself for how far I've come in six months, but it hasn't been easy, and there are days I still cry because I miss him. I remember when I thought I couldn't live without him. I remember when I thought I'd never meet anyone like him when, really, he was just another person who was coming and going from my life. He's someone who taught me things that I could never teach myself. He taught me how to fall in love. He taught me how to be vulnerable, with myself and others. He taught me that I'm too sure of myself to be crying over someone who isn't ready for me. He taught me how to love myself the way he never could.

• • •

Friday rolls around, and I get out of bed later than usual because I took the day off of work. Lauren's due at my apartment in an hour because that's when I scheduled our Uber to pick us up for the airport.

I went back and forth for months about what to do regarding Graham's wedding. In fact, I missed the RSVP date, which is why Graham called me in the middle of a workday last month. I was avoiding his texts; if I'm being honest, I didn't want to think about the wedding. I wanted to avoid it (and Ethan) for as long as possible. Begrudgingly, I stepped into the lobby and answered his call.

"Hey, Graham," I answered wearily.

"Wow, you picked up," Graham teased. "Why have you been dodging me? Well, I think I could probably guess, but I'd rather hear it from you."

"I'm sorry. I know I've missed the RSVP date. I just couldn't think about it," I apologized.

His tone softened. "I don't care about the RSVP date, Sloane. Well, Emily does, but we care more about you. I know this is an awkward situation, which is why I'm calling. Emily and I talked, and we think you should bring Lauren."

"Really?" I remember how shocked I was to hear that.

Besides the one night out in the city last summer, Graham and Lauren haven't spent any time together. They also haven't spoken. I guess they don't really have a reason to speak, but I was surprised to hear he didn't mind her being in attendance at the wedding.

"Yeah, everything with us is water under the bridge. We dated for a few months in college and broke up; it's not like we got divorced. We're both with other people now; everything worked out the way it was supposed to." His explanation was matter-of-fact.

I smiled, though he can't see it. "I love that. Thanks, Graham."

As we were about to end the call, Graham's voice held me back. "Sloane, one other thing."

"Yeah?" My pulse quickened. Was he about to drop a bomb on me? Was Ethan seeing someone? Or worse—bringing her to the wedding?

Graham let out a heavy sigh, and I could almost picture him running a hand through his long wavy hair.

"I realize how ominous I just sounded. Ethan's not bringing a date, but that's not what I was going to say. I've been keeping up with your blog, and I just wanted to apologize," he said.

"What do you mean? Apologize for what?"

"I feel like I played a part in all of it. I encouraged you to wait around for Ethan, to cut him some slack. I should've done the opposite. I just wanted the same thing you did. I wanted it to be you. We all did," he confessed.

I knew he meant well, but hearing those words choked me up. I felt a lump in my throat forming as tears welled up in my eyes.

"There's no one here to blame except for him and me," I assured him.

"So I'll see you next month?"

"I wouldn't miss it."

"You tried," he reminded me.

Thank god for Graham and Lauren. They've both gotten me through some dark times, and if they weren't so mature things would have been a lot different.

• • •

"My stomach is starting to hurt," I whisper to Lauren when we arrive at the venue.

She places a hand on my shoulder before firmly reminding me, "You're gonna be okay! Just remember, no direct eye contact. And no crying."

Two ushers appear, and they lead us past a champagne wall, encouraging us to take a glass before finding our seats. Somehow we manage to snag two spots in the third row. I twirl the glass between my fingers as I anxiously wait for the ceremony to start.

The groomsmen descend the aisle, and I watch one by one until I notice the back of his head. When he gets up to the altar, he stands to the right of the best man, Graham's brother, and I watch him scan the crowd. Is he looking for me? And just like that, he finds me.

A slight smile falls over his face, and my entire body locks up. My heart sinks to my stomach as I realize I'm in the crowd, watching him stand at an altar, and it's not our wedding. It never will be. I used to dream about the day we'd eventually figure out our qualms—he'd ask me to be his girlfriend, we'd move in together after a year or so, and soon after he'd propose to me in a park or on a rooftop when I least expected it. I thought about what it would be like to have the guy who wasn't sure about love or commitment finally get down on one knee because he knew I was the one he wanted to spend the rest of his life with. But this moment isn't that.

Instead, we both exist in the same room and act as though we're strangers now. A polite smile is the only moment we share. No small talk or asking how each other has been, because it hurts too much to know. It hurts too much to go back there again. I know he feels it too.

Countless nights I've tossed and turned, wondering if the end of us affected him as much as it did me. Or even slightly. I watch his eyes dart down to his feet, and I know exactly what he's feeling. The same pain I've felt almost every night since we parted ways on that sidewalk in Murray Hill. The pain of wanting something you can never have. The pain of wondering if it was the right person at the wrong time or just the wrong person. The pain of his first real heartbreak.

I often wondered if he ever loved me, because he was never able to say it. Sometimes I felt it though—in quiet car rides, in the way his heart would beat faster whenever my head rested on his chest, in the smaller moments that I can hardly remember now. I know he loved me, and I'd like to think that a part of him still does. Maybe, like me, a part of him always will.

The pianist strikes the keys to the tune of "Can't Help Falling in Love" by Elvis Presley, and the guests rise to their feet to watch the bride's grand entrance. With a trembling hand, I grab Lauren's, and she reassures me with a gentle squeeze. The entire room is left in awe as Emily glides gracefully down the aisle. She's beautiful.

"We're gathered here today to witness the union of Emily Miller and Graham Clark. Marriage is a journey that will have its ups and downs. It's not always easy, but it's worth it. To make a marriage work, it takes love, patience, understanding, and forgiveness. It's a bond that grows stronger each day."

"Graham, you've shown me nothing but unconditional love since the day I met you. Throughout our relationship, your love for me has never wavered. You've never made me question or doubt how important I am to you, because you show me every day," Emily says.

As I sit in the third row, taking in every word of their vows, tears stream down my face. It isn't that I'm not happy for Graham and Emily; in fact, I'm elated to see them so in love. But as I listen to her speak about unconditional love, I can't help but think about the way I loved Ethan. I had been the only person in his life that wanted to love him through anything. Even after years of being strung along, confused, and hurt, I still loved him through it.

Here's the thing about unconditional love though—it isn't one-sided. It isn't standing in someone's doorway begging to be let in. It isn't taking your heart out of your chest, bloody and beating, and handing it to someone to do whatever they want with it. Unconditional love is someone breaking down the cage of your ribs to get your heart and you trusting they'll protect it just the same.

This isn't one of those beautiful love stories where they get back together in the end. This is one of those stories where the hurt and the confusion consumes them. It's one of those stories where the person who is in pain gets up, brushes themselves off, and realizes their worth.

As much as I've always wanted to end up with Ethan, I think I knew he'd never be it for me. Is it scary to think about falling in love again? Opening my heart up to someone who could potentially damage it even worse than he did? Of course, it is. But that's what love is right? Love is taking risks regardless of the outcome.

Our relationship may not have been conventional. It wasn't a fairy-tale romance that we'd tell our kids and grandkids about one day. It was comfortable silences, familiar laughs, and hugs that felt like home. What we had wasn't something I could ever put into words. It was just us.

Call it what you want, but for me it was love.

A Conversation with the Author

What inspired you to write *Call It What You Want?*

My dating life has been a string of "almost relationships." For so long, I was embarrassed and insecure about it because I never felt good enough for commitment. When these relationships ended, I felt even worse. I couldn't understand why it was never me, and even more so, I felt like people around me couldn't understand why I was so hurt over someone who wasn't my boyfriend. Deep down, I knew I wasn't the only person ever feeling that way, but why wasn't anyone talking about it or writing about it? I decided that if I couldn't have a book that made me feel less alone in my embarrassment and self-doubt, I'd write one. I wanted to write something real, raw, and relatable.

I wrote *Call It What You Want* for anyone who's ever been in an almost relationship but also for a younger version of myself who I still grieve occasionally. I wish I could hug her and tell her she deserves so much more than an almost.

What did you enjoy most about writing this novel?

While this novel is fiction, parts were taken from my real life. I loved turning some of my best friends into characters and sharing them with the world—especially Lauren and Graham. They gave great advice and stuck by me repeatedly when, ultimately, the cycle would start over again. They didn't always understand why I stayed in a relationship that wasn't serving me, but they supported it to a fault. My friends played a pivotal role in mending my broken heart, and I hope they'll also help to heal readers who need it.

What was the most challenging scene for you to write?

There were a handful of challenging scenes to write, but the one that was the toughest was the epilogue. I knew that I wanted readers to understand that just because a relationship doesn't have a label or a title doesn't mean what they experienced wasn't love. I didn't know how that message would unfold until I listened to my friends' vows at their wedding. As I sat in the audience, I couldn't stop crying for two reasons—I was so happy for them, and their love made me realize what I deserved. Like me, Sloane gave Ethan unconditional love; unfortunately, Ethan just couldn't get there with her. We can chalk it up to family trauma or commitment issues, but at the end of the day, love shouldn't be difficult.

I wanted to end the novel on the note that love isn't always our be-all and end-all, especially in our early twenties. A happy and fulfilled life can also mean finding new hobbies, climbing the corporate ladder, and fostering friendships—there's no right or wrong way to experience happiness. It's easy to think we've failed if a relationship didn't work out or we're notoriously single. Your worth shouldn't have to depend on another person, and I think everyone, especially women in their twenties, should be reminded of that.

What do you hope readers take from this novel?

I think this novel has two main themes: one is for the people who have been through an "almost relationship," and the other is for those who haven't. For those who have been through a similar experience, I want them to know that sometimes, the best love stories are the ones that teach you how to let go. For those who haven't, I hope this novel opens up your mind and heart to the complexities of relationships. I want people to understand that heartbreak is just as valid when it happens over someone you weren't dating.

What advice would you give to other debut authors?

Be yourself. No one is you, and that is your talent! Playing the comparison game in any aspect of life is easy, especially a new one. I have so many authors and writers I look up to, and if I'm having a bad day or week, it's easy to feel like I'll never be as good as them, but I try to remember that I'm not them, and they're not me. That's the beauty of our uniqueness.

Acknowledgments

In July of 2022, I had this wild idea to write a book. It came out of nowhere. I'd just gotten my heart broken, and I hopped on a flight hoping to run away from all of my problems. I took a stack of books, dug my toes in the sand, and read. I managed to finish three novels on a five-day-long trip, and the only thing I remember about them is that they didn't heal me. I wanted a book that understood me. I wanted a book that felt like a hug from one of my parents when they were too far away to give me one. Two years later, that book is in your very hands, and I have so many people to thank for it.

To all of you, your support, comments, reviews, posts, and messages made this all possible. You've healed my heart and changed my life. For that, I'm eternally grateful.

My sister, Natalie, is four years younger than me, but I often swear she's the older sibling. I'd fall apart without her. So to Natalie, thank you for picking up every 2 a.m. phone call, bringing me back down to earth, and being a shoulder to cry on when I need it most. More importantly, thank you for thinking I'm cool enough to look up to. Being your sister is my greatest accomplishment, and I hope you always know that.

Without my best friend, Michaela, this book wouldn't exist because, in a way, it wrote itself every time I called her. We talked through every idea, every chapter, every scene. Her candid honesty, kind heart, and belly laughs got me through my first heartbreak. Her unwavering support and endless patience turned this book from a small idea into a big reality. Michaela, I've never known a friendship like ours or a person like you. Thanks for being my platonic soulmate.

My mom is the reason I love books. She always said they're an escape from reality when you need it the most. When I was younger, I would stay up past my bedtime to read in the dark (which now explains the glasses and contacts), but whenever I got caught, she wasn't mad. Mom, you are the strongest person I know. Thanks for being an inspiration, a sounding board, and my toughest critic. You taught me that being able to take constructive criticism will get you far, and it's one of my favorite pieces of advice to date.

My dad is my number-one fan. From gymnastics to field hockey to talent shows to writing books, he was always seated in the front row with the proudest smile (and my mom with the loudest cheer). My dad is the most driven, passionate, hardworking person I'll ever know, and I'd like to think he's given those qualities to me. Dad, thanks for setting the standard for the kind of love I deserve and the kind of man I should wait for. I never imagined I could do half the things I've done, but you did. Thank you for always being proud of me.

To Kristyn and Tia, who changed my life with just one email. You both held my hand throughout this entire process. You went to bat for me and hit a home run every time. Thank you for teaching me patience and persistence. I'm so glad that we found each other.

To Kate, my editor, who took a chance on me. Thank you for encouraging me to dig deeper, think harder, and feel more. You handled this story with such care and love these characters just as much as I do. I couldn't have asked for a better accomplice.

To my grandparents, who let my imagination run wild and saved every letter I wrote to them. Thank you for the sleepovers, trips to Barnes and Noble (where I still use your discount), and movie nights. Thanks for buying that condo in Marco Island all those years ago, because that balcony is where I wrote the first page of this book.

To Jenna, Brie, and Kayla, who have been there since the awkward middle school days. You wanted to be my friend even when I had a perm and a retainer. When I moved five hundred miles away from New Jersey to North Carolina, you texted daily, FaceTimed weekly, and visited quarterly. Fifteen years of encouraging me to shoot for the stars, keeping my secrets safe, and loving me without judgment (most days), you three are the reason I believe in soulmates. You're my soulmates.

To my friends—you know who you are—thank you for showing up for me. Thank you for telling me it hurt you to see me go back repeatedly, but you understood why I did. Thank you for the advice, the laughs, the tears, and the memories (so many of which are baked into these pages). I love you more than you'll ever know.

To Hailey, who created the most beautiful cover I've ever seen. Thank you for listening to dozens of voice memos and deciphering hundreds of text messages until we had this masterpiece. This book would not exist in the same way it does now without you. I know they say, "Don't judge a book by its cover," but in this case, I hope everyone picks it up solely because of its eye-catching beauty.

A younger version of myself would have sobbed for days over this book. She would have had to buy a second copy, maybe even a third, because the pages would have been riddled with endless annotations and tearstains. I never believed I was good enough for commitment. For most of my life, I've believed that love is fleeting. It's taken me years to realize the right people will never leave. So, to a younger Alissa, I'm sorry you spent years doubting yourself. All of those feelings and experiences brought you this book. I'm so proud of us.

About the Author

Alissa DeRogatis is an author based in Charlotte, North Carolina. *Call It What You Want* is her debut novel and a love letter to anyone who has had a hard time getting over someone they never dated.